SHAFT OF TRUTH

CHOCTAW TRIBUNE SERIES, BOOK THREE

SARAH ELISABETH SAWYER

ROCKHAVEN PUBLISHING

SHAFT OF TRUTH

RockHaven Publishing

P.O. Box 1103

Canton, Texas 75103

Scriptures taken from the Authorized King James Version, Holy Bible. Used by permission. All rights reserved.

This is a work of fiction. Names, characters, places, and incidents are fictitious or used fictitiously. Any resemblance to real persons, living or dead, is coincidental and unintentional.

Editors: Lynda Kay Sawyer, Catherine Frappier, Mollie Reeder

Cover Design: MiblArt

Author Photo by R. A. Whiteside. Courtesy of the National Museum of the American Indian, Smithsonian Institution

Print ISBN-13: 978-0-9910259-6-1

LCCN: 2020905856

To Catherine Frappier, Mollie Reeder, and my mama, Lynda Kay Sawyer – y'all were my heart and soul and shining lights for this book.

Nana hosh achukma ka, hattak a, pisachi tuk oke; Chihowa yvt nanta asilhha, amba nana kvt ai vlhpesa yvmohmikma nukhaklo ya i hullo micha hopoyuksa hosh Chihowa iba nowa hinla cho?

He hath shewed thee, O man, what is good; and what doth the LORD require of thee, but to do justly, and to love mercy, and to walk humbly with thy God? Micah 6:8

ndian Territory
April 1894

The rocky path was speckled with sunbeams, but the cold spring wind bit through Matthew Teller's coat. His gelding Little Chief sent another shiver through his body, warming himself. The men riding through the woods around Matthew snugged their hats down. It was a bad day to do what they had to do, but then, any day was a bad one for a shootout.

He kept Little Chief in tight rein, not letting him drive ahead like the other men on horseback. Most of the posse charged recklessly over boulders as they climbed higher in the Sans Bois Mountains. They were still miles from the infamous cave where outlaws like Belle Starr and the James gang once hid, but there was no sense in announcing the posse's presence.

Matthew was at the back of the group, which suited him fine. He hadn't put his boots on that morning to hunt down outlaws. There was other business he had come this far from home for.

But curiosity at the excitement in the street outside his hotel earlier led Matthew to be standing in the wrong place when the Gaines County sheriff pointed out men in the crowd to deputize on the spot. The Abernathy gang had raided the General Store for ammunition, and it was said they were holed up in the caves of the Sans Bois Mountains.

The sheriff planned to arrest the gang and save the town from further abuse. This would also line the sheriff's pockets with the reward money after his feverish posse caught the gang.

Only one kind of fire burned in Matthew, and rounding up an outlaw gang would do nothing to quench it. But he had to fulfill this unexpected duty before moving on, provided he didn't get killed. The Abernathy gang was one of the most deadly in Indian Territory.

Matthew pushed his gelding enough to keep up with the posse but stayed at his own pace. The sounds in the woods changed as the path molded and disappeared among boulders that grew larger the higher they rode. Lack of any creatures scurrying about and the quietness unnerved him. Something was amiss.

Matthew stood in the stirrups and eyed an outcrop ahead. Its sheer wall rose twenty feet, the rock-face hard and taunting, like a gravestone waiting to have his name etched in it. The memory of a rifle bullet ripping through his chest made him jerk Little Chief to a halt.

A horse behind him whinnied. No one from the posse was behind him.

Little Chief answered the call. Matthew dropped low in his saddle.

"Ambush!"

A string of gunshots rang through the woods, striking the rock face ahead. Chips of gray splintered and flew, showering the posse who rode alongside the outcrop. Their horses reared and bolted. Bullets blasted in front of them. They were surrounded.

A chip from the rock face arched through the air and struck

Matthew's hat. But no shots came from his right. He was far enough back to escape through that gap and make it clear.

Ahead, the men in the posse dismounted and took cover the best they could. A youngster no more than fifteen dismounted less gracefully. He landed hard, his yelp reaching Matthew's ears before he scrambled forward on his hands and knees over jagged rocks, an easy target for a marksman in a vicious gang.

Matthew turned Little Chief in a circle, indecision crowding his good sense. When he finished the turn, a bullet found the youth, and he fell with a scream.

Withdrawing his rifle from its leather scabbard, Matthew spurred his gelding forward into the flying bullets, hunched close to the gelding's neck. He almost made it.

He heard the bullet strike Little Chief's flesh. The horse whinnied and tumbled headfirst over the rocky trail. Matthew was barely able to kick free from the stirrups and push away from getting trapped under his horse.

Matthew hit hard but rolled to his feet. He fired in the direction where the rifle flashes came from the overhang above the rock face. A perfect place for an ambush with guns firing from three directions.

He reached the youngster where the boy thrashed and clutched his left shoulder. Blood seeped between his fingers. So close to his heart. Matthew pulled him down and forward at the same time.

"Stay low!"

The youth's eyes were glassy and wide, his thick brown hair soaked with sweat despite the chilly air that gusted around them. Hot lead made the toughest man sweat. This boy's skin was smooth as a baby's, not yet marked with a first shave.

"Don't tell Ma! She wanted me to stay home, but the sheriff—"

"Be quiet and stay low!"

The boy babbled on, blinded by terror. Matthew dragged him from the open space. A bullet whizzed by Matthew's ear. He turned and fired two quick shots in the direction of the bullet. A howl rose above the din, but he felt no satisfaction. He settled the youngster on the ground behind a tree.

The shooting went on for a quarter of an hour. The Abernathy gang had stolen a good supply of ammunition from the General Store and didn't care how much they wasted. The men in the posse buried themselves deep.

Finally, with whoops of cynical laughter, the Abernathy gang pulled out. Matthew heard them on the other side of the cliff face, hollering and firing their guns in victory as they rode off. It was as though they'd taught the posse a lesson and had no fear of reprisal.

Slowly, the posse from Wilburton came out of hiding, assessing wounds and trying to catch their horses. Most faced a long walk back.

Matthew breathed deep, and his chest rattled from the cold. And memories.

He checked on the youngster who had long since passed out. The handkerchief bandage Matthew had applied to the bullet hole was soaked through. The boy had been hit in nearly the same place Matthew had not so long ago.

He called for one of the men from the posse and turned the youngster over to him. He had something he had to do.

Holding his rifle loose at his side, Matthew retraced his steps, navigating between the posse men who scrambled, shouting, and trying to make a plan.

Matthew found Little Chief where his faithful horse lay. The gelding's body trembled, his gut heaving with the effort to breathe. The blood flow from his wound had slowed but seeped out fresh with each gasp for air.

Kneeling by Little Chief, Matthew brushed aside strands of the black forelock from his eyes. He remembered the day his father had given him the stout bay quarter horse on his sixteenth birthday, a gesture he hadn't been able to truly appreciate until after his daddy died.

Matthew took a deep breath, stood, aimed his Winchester, and fired.

How much would this trip cost him before it ended?

It was a long walk back to Wilburton with toting a saddle, saddlebags, and rifle, but Matthew chose to walk alone. He waited until the other men from the posse had collected themselves and headed down the Sans Bois Mountains before taking his own trail down. Matthew had enough thoughts to keep him company without the chatter of men as they built heroic stories around the harrowing encounter. He didn't feel like celebrating survival. The loss of Little Chief cut deep, but still not as deep as the thoughts that kept him up at night.

Ever since the Choctaw woman, Takba, had told him he would find his father's killer in Krebs, Matthew had hardly slept a full night. He tried, tried to rest so he'd be sharp and alert. But every night he tossed and turned, and came to his feet long before daylight to get busy, set things in order for him to leave, chase down the clues in the cryptic message, and to take the journey out there to see justice done for his father and brother.

Yet there was so much work at the newspaper in Dickens and on Uncle Preston's ranch. The Dawes Commission issue was heating up, barreling through the Choctaw Nation, though it was met with a resistant force. The politics among Matthew's people too often turned into deadly confrontations. He had hoped to make the journey over the winter, but he was consumed with getting the real news out from both sides in his newspaper, the *Choctaw Tribune*.

Still, the present was never enough to stop his dreams at night, dreams of his father laughing, kissing his mother, holding his children close. Then the dreams would move forward. Matthew was older, and his father and uncle took him down to their favorite fishing spot on Uncle Preston's ranch and told Matthew how proud they were of him, how the Creator had great plans for his life.

Before long, Matthew would realize he was awake and remembering, not dreaming. And the night went on.

His thoughts inevitably turned to Philip, his only brother, the one who earned the most whippings in their early years. Philip often complained it was because he was the oldest and that Matthew had better turn out good despite the coddling he got. This memory always brought a smile. Philip laughed, teased, complained, and dared more than any of them. He'd say if he couldn't be an example for Matthew, he could at least be a warning.

Philip had died alongside their daddy that day in the Winding Stair Mountains during that fateful trip. Matthew's father and brother had taken work to distribute some payments along with their freight delivery, and died by the hands of selfish, violent men like the Abernathy gang. They hadn't cared about the pain that ripped through an entire family all at once and left nothing for them to hold onto. But the Teller family held on to one another and to their faith and the legacy of their strong ancestors who had survived betrayal and death long before.

When Takba's son, outlaw Cub Wassom, was killed in a shootout with U.S. Marshal Bass Reeves, the memories of his father and brother's deaths were cut open and Matthew bled, but he thought it was over. Then Takba appeared and told him it wasn't. That he would find the answer—an answer that didn't want to be found—in the coal mining town of Krebs. That a man there, Al Percy, knew the ones who had ambushed his father, who had wrecked content lives with a few puffs of gun smoke.

Takba's words and the truth Matthew sensed in them had plagued him for five months. He hadn't told his mother or sister what the woman said. There was no need for them to be tormented. He'd worked at the ranch, taken care of family, the newspaper—all the while plotting how he could leave a few weeks and track down Percy.

The months flew by until he finally let everything go. There was work to do on the ranch in the spring, and political debates would flare up again. He and Ruth Ann discussed ways to expand the newspaper over the next three years including distribution to Washington, D.C., letting the U.S. government know what was really going on in the Choctaw Nation. Matthew took on a load of new advertisers and hired and trained two new workers for the *Choctaw Tribune*.

But it was time. He got the newspaper and his family in the best position he could, then packed his saddlebags and rifle and rode away with minimal answers to his family's questions. He told his sister Ruth Ann and their mother, Della, there was something he needed to do that would require extensive time and travel. He planned to send news stories as often as he could.

Working side by side with him in the print shop most every day, Ruth Ann must have known there was something very personal in his plans, but she never asked outright. Maybe deep down, she sensed it had to do with the murders of their father and brother.

CHAPTER 2

ate that afternoon, Matthew finally made it back to
Wilburton. He'd only arrived in the town the day before,
already lost a dependable ally, and was no closer to the
man he was pursuing.

When he and Little Chief had arrived in Wilburton after
getting off the Frisco train in Talihina, he planned to work his
way west to Krebs, making friends with those who might know
Al Percy and give him information to trap the man for Matthew's
questioning about the ambush six years ago.

His plans had been derailed, like so many false starts even
before he left Dickens, but he was determined to take the next
step. He needed a horse.

On the way to the livery stable, an excited redhead from the
posse leaped in front of Matthew, his emerald eyes glowing like
he'd been to a circus, not a shootout.

"Hey there! Did you see me drop three of those outlaws? One
had a gun aimed right between my eyes, but I split him in two
before he could blink! I can give you a photograph of myself for
your newspaper. My name's Carl Duncan, Carl is spelled C—"

"I got it."

Matthew sidestepped the man. None of the posse had so much as glimpsed the outlaws, much less shot one. How many of the men wanted him to print sensationalized stories about the encounter? If only no one knew who he was. When he'd arrived yesterday and started asking questions, people asked him questions in return. When they learned he was the publisher of the *Choctaw Tribune,* some wanted to hear the latest on the controversy between the two political parties in the tribe—Nationals and Progressives. Still others wanted updates on the Dawes Commission. There was a rumor that Henry Dawes and his commission was coming to McAlester that month.

Matthew thought he'd left the newspaper business behind. How could he get anything accomplished as long as people knew about his life's work?

Carl Duncan dogged Matthew all the way to the livery. He spelled his name and said it would only take a minute to get the photograph from his mother's house, how proud she'd be, and on and on until Matthew flat out told the man the only name going in the story was the sheriff's and the Abernathy gang. The glow went out of Duncan's green eyes, and he quit pestering Matthew.

The blacksmith greeted Matthew as he pulled on the bellows handle to nurture his red hot coals, "Howdy, stranger."

Matthew preferred the smells in the livery over what he'd experienced that morning—fire smoke instead of gun smoke, fresh hay rather than fresh blood. He wondered how that youngster was doing. He was afraid to find out.

"Evening. You're working late."

The blacksmith released the bellows and took up his tools. "What with the posse and all…" He squinted at Matthew in the evening dusk. "You in the posse, were you? Need a new horse, I'm reckoning."

A sudden realization struck Matthew. This man didn't know he was a newspaper reporter. Didn't know he was looking for his father and brother's killers. He didn't know Matthew Teller, a Choctaw citizen from Dickens.

Matthew needed to keep it that way.

"Yeah, a new horse, a rented one to get me to Krebs. I have people to see along the way, so I'm not taking the Katy."

The short branch line of the Missouri, Kansas, and Texas Railway—the Katy—stopped at Krebs, but Matthew had inquiries to make along the way. Though he'd planned to do it with Little Chief.

"Got a nice little mare for the job. Just put her on the east-bound branch line when you get to Krebs. They'll ship her back here. It'll cost you, though."

Indeed. If only the man knew just how much this cost Matthew.

Matthew rode out in the coming darkness, knowing he'd have to make camp along the twenty-five mile stretch to Krebs. He mulled over the adjustment to his plan. From now on, he needed to ask questions without giving away who he really was.

It wouldn't be easy.

No, he wasn't looking for a ranch job or a farmstead. No, he wasn't passing through on his way to Texas. No, he wasn't a land speculator.

Of all the reasons people roamed the Choctaw Nation, none fit him but the truth. Or the profile of an outlaw. That should stop the questioning cold, and let Matthew accomplish his mission. In his investigation before this trip, Matthew learned Al Percy was a former Pennsylvania miner who came hoping for steady work in Choctaw country. The man supposedly stumbled into bad company, other miners who turned to robbery to get the riches they wanted. Charges were never brought against Percy himself, other than he was suspected of helping outlaws hide out.

Several U.S. marshals had tried to find Percy, but he always managed to elude them. The one deputy marshal Matthew spoke with who did find Percy couldn't get him to testify. Percy was too afraid of what the criminals would do to him if they were set free instead of hung.

The only way to get Percy would be to trick him into telling what he knew. Because above all, supposedly Al Percy had helped hide one of the gang members who shot and killed Matthew's father and brother.

Most recently, Percy worked in the Osage Coal and Mine Company mines at Krebs. It might take a while for Matthew to find him. The Osage employed 800 miners throughout their operation in the Choctaw Nation.

Darkness came slowly in the springtime, but it still came. Matthew had followed the rails of the M.K. & T. Railway's short branch line that ran from Wilburton to McAlester and he made camp a short distance from it.

While unsaddling the rented horse, Matthew's arms suddenly felt heavy. He tossed the saddle aside, making the horse shy against the hobbling. He put a hand on the mare's warm flesh.

He wouldn't think about the long journey ahead without Little Chief. The gelding had carried him over more mountains and roads than he could remember in his frequent travels. They'd partnered in dangerous tasks, and fun ones too.

But thinking on all that did no good. Matthew would have enough time to think when he got home, and Ruth Ann grieved. She had a tender heart for horses, especially their own. She'd be brokenhearted.

Matthew dragged the saddle to the spot he picked to bed down. He ate a cold biscuit with slices of pemmican before pulling his tablet and pencil from his saddlebag. The shootout with the Abernathy gang needed to go into the next edition.

Though he had confidence in Ruth Ann to run the *Choctaw Tribune* with their two new workers, he couldn't help feeling responsible for making sure she had front page stories. Their distribution covered half of Indian Territory now. They'd sacrificed much to reach the point where the newspaper had widespread effect. He was gambling by leaving for an extended period, but this must be done. There would never be a good time.

Matthew had written two sentences when he sensed a presence close by. Knowing hesitation could cost him his life, he dropped the tablet and leaped for his Winchester leaning against his saddle. Grabbing the barrel, he spun around and braced against a tree in the shadows. He held the Winchester ready, peering back at his fire and the direction the presence was.

A deep chuckle echoed through the woods around Matthew. He peered into the darkness behind him but detected nothing. When he looked back at his fire, a man stood there.

He was a burly fellow, but not the least bit threatening. Dressed in a gray wool coat, trousers, and heavy boots, it was the cloth cap with its leather brim and metal brackets that marked him as a coal miner. The man's black hair was slicked back under his cap, two days worth of stubby growth on his light brown face. He didn't look Indian, Italian, maybe?

The man leaned back on his heels, thumbs hooked on his pocket seams, and grinned toward where Matthew stayed in the shadows.

"*Salve*, my friend! I guess I should be scared you're an outlaw de way you are so jumpy, but I'm supposing no outlaw would be writing on a clean sheet of paper. Seeing anyone who can read and write in these parts happens *ad ogni morte di papà*. Every time a Pope dies! Ah, how you say it in English—once in a blue moon?"

Matthew eased away from the tree, keeping his Winchester aimed in the man's direction, but the barrel low. He nodded toward the paper. "I'm fond of writing." He stepped closer to the fire. "What about you?"

The man laughed deeply and it echoed through the woods

again. He swayed. *"Una volpe!* Clever like a fox, you are. You're more asking about me than my literacy, yes? Well, I'll tell you. I was on my way back from visiting my cousins in Carbon when I sort of lost my way. Started off too late, you know. We had such a good time."

The man took a well-calculated step forward. In his inebriated state, he wouldn't make it far in the woods alone. Matthew gestured to the ground near the fire.

"You'd better stay with me. It'll be cold tonight."

The man swept off his cap and bowed. "You're a true delight and a true son of this land, aren't you? I thank you for your kindness. I am Raphael Bianchi!"

His bravado carried to the treetops, and Matthew winced. If any outlaws were looking for easy targets tonight, this man was it.

Raphael Bianchi plopped on the ground by the fire. Matthew lowered himself into a squatted position, the Winchester cradled in his arms.

"I'm Matthew..." He paused. "Matt Jameson."

As he said it, Matthew reasoned through the name. He was the son of a man named James. Jim Teller. Matt Jameson. It made sense. "I'm not exactly a native of these parts."

Matthew didn't want to lie, but if miners knew he was Choctaw, they would be on guard. European immigrants were considered intruders by most Choctaws. They were allowed to stay because mine owners hired them and paid their permit fee to work in the Choctaw Nation, even paid for them to bring their families over if it included more workers. But there was plenty of animosity from tribal factions that didn't want whites in the Nation at all.

Raphael Bianchi eyed Matthew critically. Matthew didn't flinch under the man's stare. It would be difficult, in the shadows, to tell he was Choctaw. His dark hair was cut and combed the same as any white man's, and his work shirt and pants looked like what many of the outsiders wore. People usually assumed he was half of whatever they were.

Bianchi nodded in acceptance. He produced a face-splitting yawn, and Matthew hoped he'd fall over asleep. But the man pointed a relatively steady finger at the tablet in the dirt.

"What are you writing there?"

Matthew leaned forward and picked up the tablet with the article. He wasn't a good liar, and never wanted to be. It was best to stick to facts when he could.

"A letter home about the shootout with the Abernathy gang. You hear about that?"

Bianchi nodded vigorously. "Heard a boy got shot and died later. Horrible thing. *La vita e cosi.* That's life."

Surely the rumor wasn't true. Had Matthew sacrificed his horse for nothing?

That's life.

Bianchi stretched big over his head and yawned again. "You seem like a good fellow with no destination. How would you like a job in the Osage mines? I'd vouch for you, Matt Jameson."

Matthew started to decline, then halted. The Osage mines in Krebs? That was where Al Percy had worked.

"I appreciate that, Mr. Bianchi. Thank you."

Should he mention he'd never even been inside a mine before? Bianchi didn't ask, so Matthew let it be. This might be an answer to prayer, though he hadn't heard much from Chihowa about this quest.

Matthew prayed through it every night and tried to discern if the delays in his going were because he needed to push hard through every obstacle, to rely on God for strength and courage. Or was it because God didn't want him to go, that the past should be left behind?

But Takba had kindled a fire in Matthew, a burning desire to know the whole truth and seek justice. He held onto a scripture verse from the book of Micah:

Nana hosh achukma ka, hattak a, pisachi tuk oke; Chihowa yvt nanta asilhha, amba nana kvt ai vlhpesa yvmohmikma nukhaklo ya i hullo micha hopoyuksa hosh Chihowa iba nowa hinla cho?

He hath shewed thee, O man, what is good; and what doth the LORD require of thee, but to do justly, and to love mercy, and to walk humbly with thy God?

After Bianchi was bedded down and snoring loud enough to rival a train, Matthew thought through each line of the verse, working it backward to make sure he'd missed nothing.

Walk humbly with thy God.

"This isn't for me. It's for my family. For You."

Love mercy.

The murderers. Could he show them mercy if given the chance?

Do justly.

Would he?

Laying on his back, Matthew stared through the tree branches with fresh buds of spring shimmering against the night sky. He whispered, "Lord, You know what I mean to do. Bring justice for my father and brother. If anything happens to me, I trust You'll take care of my family. They can always go back to Uncle Preston's ranch, can't they?"

Matthew rolled onto his side, not wanting to look at the stars anymore. He needed to set his mind on going down in the mines, going down as far as he had to find the truth. How far that might be, or what he might lose along the way, or how long it would take, he couldn't say.

Bianchi's snore behind him, the dark woods before him, Matthew sang quietly. When they were boys, Philip teased Matthew about his unsteady singing voice. He only sang when he was alone.

O to grace how great a debtor
daily I'm constrained to be
Let thy goodness, like a fetter,
bind my wandering heart to thee.
Prone to wander, Lord, I feel it,
prone to leave the God I love...

He moistened his dry lips, thinking on the scripture verse. *Do justly, love mercy, walk humbly with thy God.* All that the Lord required. But too much for this season in his life?

Here's my heart, O take and seal it,
seal it for thy courts above.

CHAPTER 3

They started off for Krebs the next morning, Raphael Bianchi jabbering from where he hung on behind Matthew's saddle. It had taken the man awhile to get a move on, but once he did, Raphael Bianchi talked nonstop. Matthew didn't mind the chatter since it might give him useful information.

Bianchi talked about the Krebs Opera House built in 1885 to present Italian opera, then he moved on to area churches—Catholic, Baptist, North and South Methodist and Presbyterian—the company store, drug store, meat market, cotton gin, and dozens of company houses where miners and their families lived.

The woods thickened, and there was an odd silence beyond Bianchi's voice. Matthew rubbed the back of his neck, using it as an excuse to glance around. It felt like someone was watching him. He nudged the mare up to a trot.

The Italian was right. Matthew was jumpy after that encounter with the outlaw gang. That and being shot by Cub Wassom last fall.

At noon, they broke through the woods a short distance from Krebs. A train whistle sounded. Matthew spotted the depot as the Katy train pulled in for a brief stop. A shipment of coal was ready to go out. Coal was used to fuel the train, but also make the railroad their cash and pay royalties to the Choctaw Nation.

The operation had been going since before Matthew was born, but plenty of Choctaws still objected to their natural resources being hauled out of the Nation by the ton. It sparked arguments—which found their way into the *Choctaw Tribune*—about the royalties paid, where the money went, and how it was used. The first mine in the area of what became Krebs, only a few miles outside of the industrial coal city of McAlester, was started by an intermarried white citizen in the Choctaw Nation.

Matthew halted the mare to observe the community of Krebs. He read an article once that listed the countries where these people hailed from. They were Poles, Czechs, Germans, Russians, Irish, British, Mexicans...Matthew no longer regretted missing the Chicago World's Fair last fall. There it was in front of him now.

Bianchi gave Matthew's shoulder a shove and pointed toward rows of wood-frame buildings. "Look at that! It's a Mexican fiesta right now!"

A group of Mexicans danced with streamers and wide-brimmed hats decorated in colorful designs. Bianchi pinched his fingers and kissed the tips before flinging his hand up and back, throwing him off-balance. Matthew twisted and grabbed the man's coat to keep him on board.

"A fiesta?" Matthew chuckled and shook his head. The World's Fair indeed.

"A great big Mexican family works at the mines, you know. They live like this, always a fiesta or a siesta. Come, let's take part. With everyone's allegiance to the traditions of their Mother Country, every day is a holiday!"

Matthew glanced to the right where a slope mine sat not far away; the machinery silent, the gaping black hole abandoned. He clicked to his mount and crossed a stream. Up the rise from the bank and they were on the road to enter the din in the street.

Loud voices greeted Bianchi in Italian. He leaped off the back of Matthew's horse and waved at those gathering around him, his jovial spirit adding to the celebration.

"*Salve!* My friends, gather round and meet Matt Jameson!"

Matthew dismounted, though he'd already been forgotten. Bianchi's fellow Italians dragged Bianchi toward the center of town, straight into the festivities. Matthew observed from a safe distance.

The different nationalities tried to imitate the Mexican songs and dances, laughing and passing around crocks.

Matthew tied the horse to a hitching post in front of the meat market. Before he could turn back to the crowd, a squeal rattled his ear. Someone grabbed him from behind, slender arms thrown around his waist.

"Toby! I did not know you would come for the fiesta! Come, we must dance!"

Jolted, Matthew glanced over his shoulder, down at the breathless young woman.

"Whoa, wait, I'm not..."

She released him and stepped back. He turned around, and her hands covered her mouth, cheeks flushed red. "Oh! Oh, I thought you were..."

Matthew lifted his hat and smoothed his hair back. "I'm sorry, ma'am, but you've mistaken me for someone else."

The young woman's dark eyes intensified, studying him. "From the side, you look just like Toby Nicolas. Are you related?"

Her black hair was straight, pulled tight in a bun, gold hoop earrings swinging as she shook her head, wide eyes showing amazement.

She wasn't Mexican. She was more like...

"Cadenza, *mi bambina!*"

Raphael Bianchi came up behind the young woman and wrapped an arm around her shoulder. "My little niece. You greet the newcomer, I see."

Bianchi's words were cheerful, but he looked at Matthew with curiosity, as though really seeing him for the first time. "Mi bambina, this is Matt Jameson. He's come to work the mines."

Cadenza melted into her uncle's embrace, but her bright eyes never left Matthew. "He does look like Toby, doesn't he? *Buona fortuna.* I thought it was good fortune."

She looked up at Bianchi, who kissed the top of her head. She stood a good foot shorter than him, a petite young woman.

"I wish Toby worked the Krebs mine here instead of McAlester. But he will come visit us soon, *Zio* Raphael?"

"Of course. Of course! He will come soon and you can dance. But you mustn't rust over like an old bucket while you wait. Now go, dance!"

Raphael Bianchi spun her around and sent her trotting through the dirt street toward the crowd with a laugh. She vanished.

Matthew finally settled his hat and dropped his hands to his sides. He looked to Bianchi. "Toby Nicolas?"

Raphael Bianchi shrugged, his lips turned up in a sad smile. "My niece's husband, Antonio, was killed in the great mine tragedy of '92. She has grieved deeply, and then a few months past, she met a man who caught her eye. Toby has been kind to her, and she is finally dancing again. I do not think it is love, but it is good for her to smile. We will see." He cocked his head at Matthew. "I did not realize it before, but you do bear a strong resemblance to Toby Nicolas. A cousin, perhaps?"

Matthew shook his head. "No relatives around here that I know of."

A shotgun blast resounded above the music. Matthew ducked toward his horse. He gripped the stock of his Winchester in the leather scabbard then realized no one else was alarmed. One look at Bianchi's face showed the Italian was simply annoyed. He crossed his burly arms and spat in the direction everyone had turned in the sudden quiet.

Three white men stood in the bed of a wagon near the side of the street. The wagon was parked in front of a two-story building with a sign marking it as the Osage Coal & Mining Company office. One of the men sported a badge and held a shotgun. Another wore a suit, his narrow jacket sleeves short enough to reveal his cuffs. Though the man stood toward the back, Matthew knew he was the one who held the power. It shined in the way he hooked his thumb in his vest pocket near his gold watch chain.

The third man wasn't dressed much differently than the miners, but he had a scowl for those beneath his crooked nose. He propped one foot on the sideboard of the wagon bed and rested an arm across his knee. He shook his head and spoke in a clipped tone.

"You people complain about your empty bellies, but all I see are dossers who want to vacation every time there is a mark on someone's calendar—always a wake or wedding, holy day or holiday."

Matthew had overheard the term *dosser* when he was at college in the States before he had to return home to take care of his family. The term meant a "lazy, ne'er do well," according to a British classmate. Matthew might have learned more sayings if he'd been able to stay in college.

This man wasn't finished with his insults. "If you know what is good for you, you will work while you can. You think hard times are behind; wait until you live what is to come."

The people grumbled, and the Italians whistled loudly in disapproval.

The man straightened and waved his hand dismissively. "You were warned!"

The three men climbed off the end of the wagon while the crowd continued to boo them.

Matthew glanced around, wondering if he should throw in a

catcall to make him one with the miners. But the noise died after the three men left, and the music resumed.

Raphael Bianchi turned to Matthew, his scowl replaced with the now-familiar grin. "You sure you want to stay 'round here, Matt Jameson? We have bosses who think they sit on the throne of God. Does not help that they have the Choctaw government backing them."

While Bianchi spoke, Matthew took inventory of the miners. Was Al Percy among them?

Bianchi didn't pause for a breath. "They promise more work, a bright future, but *tra il dire e il fare c'è di mezzo il mare*, between saying and doing is the ocean, yes?"

Matthew turned his attention to the burly Italian, grateful the man didn't know he was Choctaw. At least for now. "Yes, an ocean between words and actions. But you're a man of action, aren't you? Suppose we see about that job?"

Bianchi waved him off. "Plenty of time for work. The contract will be filled by next week, and we'll have empty bellies soon enough after that money is gone. Today, we celebrate!"

He turned to the colors and sounds of the fiesta and chuckled. "Whatever it is we are celebrating."

Bianchi stomped his foot and clapped in beat with the music. Matthew tilted his head toward him.

"I need to send my horse back on the next train to Wilburton and get settled in. Do you know a place where I can stay?"

Bianchi's hands slowed until they no longer came together while he watched his niece, Cadenza, twirling in the center of the Mexican dancers.

He finally said, "You can board with my brother and his wife, for sure. Rooms are two dollars a month for bachelors around here, and my brother can use the money. Where did you say you were from, Matt Jameson?"

Matthew didn't hesitate. "South."

Hopefully, they would think he was a Southerner whose

family had never recovered after the war, and he'd come looking for opportunity in Indian Territory. And in truth, he was from Dickens, which lay southwest of Krebs.

Whatever he might have suspected, Raphael Bianchi welcomed Matthew into the mining community and began introducing him to Italians, Germans, Russians, Mexicans, and other nationalities Matthew couldn't determine. But no former Pennsylvania miners named Al Percy.

Raphael Bianchi's brother was not among the festival-goers. Matthew didn't meet him until that evening, after shipping the horse back and being hired on by the crooked-nosed Englishman who had given the speech earlier. It turned out "Tea Kettle Thomas" was boss of the Osage mines in the area. Matthew was assigned to work in No. 2, a slope mine.

The shaft Mine No. 11 hadn't reopened since the disastrous accident two years before that had taken the life of Cadenza's husband. It killed nearly one hundred miners and injured twice as many. Matthew remembered an article the *Dickens Herald* published about the incident—barely a mention. Now Matthew stared into the eyes of the disaster. More specifically, the eyes of Ricco Bianchi, Cadenza's father and Raphael's hardened brother who had survived it.

Raphael and Matthew stood at the bottom of the two steps leading into Ricco's home, which was identical to dozens of other company houses. Standing in the open doorway, his stockinged feet planted at the corners, Ricco Bianchi didn't even look at Matthew. He stared at his brother. The two could have been twins, except Ricco did not possess his brother's jovial grin.

Ricco folded his arms. He wore bib overalls, a close-fitting work shirt, and a stiff expression.

"We have no room."

Raphael waved a hand over his head, keeping his mood light. "Come, now, this fine young man needs a place to board. He got me back safely from Carbon. I owe him at least—"

"No room."

Matthew shifted the weight of his gear—saddle, bags, and rifle. If Ricco didn't invite his own brother out of the evening chill, what chance did he stand of boarding there?

But Raphael wasn't deterred. "You know it is a good thing, Ricco. Come now." He pointed at Ricco then put both palms on his own chest. "You owe me..." He pointed to Matthew, "...and I owe him. We even it out, yes?"

Ricco rolled off a few words in Italian and stepped back, clearing the doorway. Light from a lamp inside illuminated the area around Matthew's feet.

Ricco kept his arms folded and jerked his head at Matthew. "Come inside."

Raphael clamped Matthew's shoulder. "You see? It all works out. I will see you in the mines tomorrow. *In bocca al lupo!*"

Matthew's question must have shown. Raphael chuckled.

"It means 'into the mouth of the wolf!' As to say, 'good luck.'"

Matthew nodded. "Yak—" He caught himself before saying the Choctaw word, *yakoke*. "Thank you."

"No, no, you say, *crepi il lupo*! May the wolf croak!"

Matthew nodded. "Crepi il lupo. Tomorrow."

"*A domani!*"

Matthew maneuvered inside with his gear, and the door clicked shut with a snap behind him. He felt trapped in the oppressive atmosphere within the walls. Ricco's face showed his displeasure, but that didn't compare to the infuriated look of the woman standing near the stove, glaring at him.

"Ricco Bianchi! No *bordanti*!"

She continued speaking brusquely in Italian. Matthew had a feeling if there were any children in the home, their ears would be burning.

Matthew knew better than to offer an explanation or try to soothe things. He made himself one with the wall and watched Ricco Bianchi respond to her in kind, their screeches sure to bring a knock on the door.

Matthew took inventory of his new residence. The room was square like the house itself, and just as plain as the outside. A plank board table stood in its center with an oil lamp in the middle. Four chairs sat around the table, but only one work jacket hung beside the door, and there were no children's toys lying around. To the right, two closed doors added to the suffocating feeling in the home.

According to Raphael Bianchi, most of the company houses had one or two rooms. Three-room homes were reserved for larger families, but there was no sign of anyone else, though perhaps Cadenza lived in the house. Matthew recalled how she'd mistakenly flung herself at him earlier.

Hopefully not.

The woman screamed herself hoarse and burst into tears. Ricco folded her into his arms and buried his face in her dark hair. He lifted his head enough to speak, his own voice rough from shouting.

"Your room is on the left."

Matthew felt dismissed like a child sent to bed without supper. He hadn't eaten since morning, other than a tortilla someone gave him at the fiesta.

But he wouldn't ask to be fed. He quietly lifted his gear, went through the door, and closed it softly behind him. He listened a moment to the voices on the other side, then lowered the saddle and dropped his saddlebags. He leaned his rifle against the wall near the door. At least he wouldn't be sleeping outside.

He fumbled in the dark for the matchbox he spotted on a small table by the bed. Moonbeams shining through the dirty window helped little. He struck a match and lit the lamp beside the bed, surprised to find the room had two beds. They were pristinely made with the dark wool blankets tucked in around the edges as though with great care. Otherwise, the room was bare.

Matthew lowered himself onto the cot nearest the window and dragged his saddlebags closer. He ate a can of beans, finished and sealed the letter to his family, then reached deep in the bag and pulled out his Bible. Fanning the pages, he breathed in the familiar scent among the strangeness around him.

Love mercy.

Staying with Ricco Bianchi might give him opportunity to practice that part of the verse.

The light from the main room went out.

CHAPTER 4

The next morning, Matthew realized how ill-equipped he was to start work in a mine. But Raphael Bianchi came for him early with an extra pair of boots and a rough wool coat with work gloves hanging from the pockets.

They met on the steps of Ricco's house. Matthew had exited long before dawn to avoid his hosts.

He accepted the coat Raphael offered. Several holes were burned through the sleeves.

Raphael laughed at the look Matthew gave him. "Don't ask, my friend. Don't ask."

He handed Matthew a leather brimmed-canvas cap with metal brackets for holding a lamp. "You've never a set foot in a mine, have you now?"

Matthew shook his head as he sat on the steps to put on the worn boots.

Raphael pounded him on the back. "Nothing to it but a stout heart! Most of the men here never saw a mine until they immigrated to Indian Territory. Skilled workers come from the British Isles, but us poor fools take any work we can get."

Matthew finished lacing the boots and stood. "I suppose I'll fit in."

Raphael gave him a critical look. "If you mean by looking poor, you are most right."

Matthew donned the cap and coat. He fingered the scars on the sleeves. Exactly how much would this journey cost?

"Now then, we have to swipe you a lamp."

"Where do we…swipe one from?"

"Same place we swipe the Black Jack."

Matthew had no idea what the mining jargon meant. "Of course."

He strode with Raphael as the man called greetings to fellow Italians who were flowing the same direction in the gray light of morning.

"*Buongiorno!*"

"*Come stai?*"

"*Non mi posso lamentare.*"

"*Tutto fa brodo!*"

They rattled on. Matthew didn't understand what they said, but he understood their meanings. Jokes layered with truth. He wondered if the mine bosses understood Italian.

Close to the slope mine entrance, four men were at a building near mining machinery that hadn't started for the day. One man held the door to the building open with his back and glanced around. When he nodded, someone inside handed him a jug. He passed it to the two men on the steps below him. They used the jug to fill their lamps with thick, black oil.

Matthew glanced at Raphael. "Black Jack is the lamp oil?"

Raphael stepped up by one of the men, clicked softly and pointed to Matthew. "A lamp for him, too."

"What is this building?"

"Engine house. It's where we can get cheap supplies. That company store clerk is a thief."

The men chuckled quietly and finished their task. Raphael

handed Matthew a tiny lamp filled with Black Jack. Matthew imitated the other men in hooking the lamp to his cap. He'd have the lamp and oil taken out of his pay later.

Raphael grinned. "Black Jack saves money on haircuts."

Matthew didn't want to think about what that might mean.

Raphael sized him up. "And now you're as ready as we were our first day. We just need to find you a buddy."

"We're friends, aren't we?"

The other men chuckled and moved toward the mine. Raphael shook his head. "You'd make plenty of friends if you smiled more. But that's not the kind of buddy I'm speaking of. We pair up as buddies, mostly with our own kind, sometimes a relative, though that does not always work well."

Raphael glanced toward the row of company houses. Matthew followed his gaze and saw Ricco going toward the mine. Raphael watched his brother but spoke to Matthew. "We'll fix you up, maybe with someone from the south."

A plethora of languages struck Matthew as he joined three hundred miners heading toward the entrance of the slope mine, realizing why it was important for the men to buddy up with their own kind. In this work, they had to be able to communicate in their native tongue. Confusion cost lives in this business.

Matthew had no one to speak his native tongue with, even though the richest coal mines in Indian Territory lay within the Choctaw Nation. But his parents had taught him English at an early age. He had no trouble conversing in either language and other tribal languages like the neighboring nations of the Chickasaws and Cherokees.

So many nationalities, so many stories. It was a treasure trove for the *Choctaw Tribune*. But Matthew wasn't there for that kind of story.

Raphael gave Matthew a push toward two other Italians.

"You go with Torre and his son Fabio today. They speak pretty good English!"

The two men glanced at Matthew, sizing him up and grinning. The son, Fabio, eyed him critically. He stood a head shorter than Matthew, though their skin color was a close match.

"You won't last, *grignollo.*"

Torre jabbed his son with an elbow. "That's a no way to talk to a newcomer, even a soft one."

The pair moved toward the mine entrance and Matthew followed, the closed space making him recoil inside himself. Mine No. 2 was a slope mine, not a shaft like the one that had trapped hundreds of miners in 1892. Still, he'd never liked tight, dark places.

Fabio glanced at Matthew, still grinning. "This is it, grignollo —last stop before the gates of hell!"

Hundreds of miners crowding close rapidly depleted any clean air as they tromped down the tunnel. Matthew could only see the shoulders in front of him until his eyes adjusted. Light from the headlamps made a soft glow rather than a glare in his eyes. He copied the others in lighting the lamp on his cap, keenly aware of the scalded jacket he wore and Raphael's ominous words about not needing a haircut again. He sensed the rapidly heating oil dangerously close to his scalp.

They walked down, down the slope, most stepping to the side of the rails used for transporting pit cars pulled by mules. The crowd thinned as sets of buddies turned off the main slope and into rooms on each side of the tunnel. The mine had a shifting, creaking feel. Black dust sifted through the ceiling.

Nothing to it but a stout heart.

Torre and Fabio turned into a room on the left, Matthew ducked his head just in time. The ceiling was no more than five feet high, the room fifty feet wide. He couldn't see how deep it went.

Torre motioned to a shovel laid on a pile of coal. "Why don't you start shoveling that pile into the pit car? We'll get started back here with the picks. I don't want you swinging one until I see you handle a shovel!"

Matthew nodded. The less he spoke, the better. He would watch and listen for the opportunities he needed, the chance to locate Al Percy and befriend him. He'd be patient, build trust, become one of the miners. It was the best way. Or maybe not.

Black dust floated through the air around him, and Matthew coughed into his jacket. He held the sleeve there, using it to filter enough air for a decent breath. But black grit already coated the sleeve.

Gloves on and shovel in hand, Matthew set to work on the coal pile. One shovelful at a time, he loaded it into the pit car nearest their room.

During the mindless work, his thoughts drifted to home. How was the newspaper faring? He didn't doubt Ruth Ann's abilities, but even together, they struggled to keep the *Choctaw Tribune* healthy. She had Peter to help, and the two new employees he'd hired, Bill Dodd and Caleb Gentry, but was it enough? What threatening force might come against the newspaper in his absence?

And what of his mother? She was strong, but was she happy? The losses of his father and Philip weighed heavily on her even after six years. Would what he was doing help or hurt her in the end? Would the justice he sought bring her peace or pain?

"Whoa there, grignollo!"

Young Fabio came over to Matthew, his pick settled over his shoulder with a grin on his face already blackened from the short time in the mine. "You have a personal grudge against the coal, *si?*"

Matthew straightened and tried to relax as he turned to the young man. "How long have you worked in the mines?"

Fabio shrugged. *"Per cent'anni.* For a hundred years, it seems. But not as long as most men my age. I didn't start until I was fifteen, after my parents immigrated from New York. We came to

America because we heard the streets were paved with gold. When we got here, we found out three things: first, the streets weren't paved with gold, second, they weren't paved at all, and third, we were expected to pave them!"

Fabio boomed a laugh to rival Raphael's. "We are immigrants to America. Now we are immigrants in the Choctaw Nation. Here, there are trees and stars to look at in the night, but men are the same everywhere. We working men have to band together and fight, or our rights will be trampled."

His father, Torre, harrumphed from behind them. "I don't see work getting done, and last I checked, our wages depended on fulfilling the contract. *Capisci?*"

Matthew thought he'd have the pile shoveled quickly and start on something else, but Torre and Fabio kept him busy by adding to it. He wondered when the miners ate and where. Surely they'd take a break in the sunshine.

A few hours into the work, Torre came to him and held out a canteen. "Thirsty, newcomer?"

Matthew took it gratefully. He hadn't brought his own canteen. He'd be better prepared tomorrow.

He took a long drink, but the water tasted terrible. At first, he thought it was because of the coal dust in his mouth. But there was enough of the liquid on his lips to get a good whiff. He choked and spewed the rest out, coughing.

Torre laughed and pounded his back while he took the canteen in the other hand. "Have you never had a swallow of Choc beer? Water around here isn't fit to drink."

Matthew spat on the pile of coal. Alcohol was illegal in Indian Territory, and he'd never had a drop in his life. His people had witnessed the destructive power of liquor enough in the past century.

Torre, still chuckling, pointed to the spilled drink. "Don't be doing that now, there are enough flammables around here!"

His gaze shifted to the room across the tunnel, fifteen feet away. His expression darkened, and he muttered, "Speaking of fools and flammables…"

He shouted, "Paolo! You fool, don't be sweeping out gas with a naked lamp right there—"

A boom rattled the tunnel. The force of the explosion threw Matthew into the wall where he slammed hard. He blinked and saw hellfire all around him. He slowly slid down the wall and onto the pile of coal.

Lord, help me…

His eyes closed as all thoughts left him.

CHAPTER 5

*R*uth Ann Teller tried to catch her breath between giggles. "Stop it!"

Her cousin, Peter Frazier, pulled another pin from her carefully woven bun and tickled her neck with the pin. "Not until you promise."

Ruth Ann jumped from the chair behind Matthew's desk and swatted at Peter. Missing, she backed against the wall of the *Choctaw Tribune* newspaper office, holding her hands up in surrender.

"All right, I promise! I'll make you *walakshi* tonight."

Peter stepped back, a crooked grin on his baby face. At seventeen, he'd had another growth spurt, and stood a head taller than Ruth Ann. But she could still outmuscle him if she needed to. A stiff wind would knock him over if he wasn't braced for it.

He crossed his arms. "You promised before, then stayed here half the night."

Ruth Ann slowed her breathing. It was a dusky morning, too early for the employees at the *Choctaw Tribune* to be at work yet, nor the Levitts who shared the building. Ruth Ann had hoped for quiet time to edit articles for Thursday's edition. It was the first edition she would publish in her brother Matthew's absence, and she wanted it to be a standout so he'd be proud. Peter hadn't helped by following her to the office first thing and badgering her about the coming evening. She grabbed the pins from him and redid her hair. "If you don't stop being a nuisance, I'll fire you."

Peter mocked her by raising the pitch of his tone. "I can do whatever I please, Peter Abraham Frazier. Matthew left me in charge and—"

The bell over the door saved Peter from the kick Ruth Ann was about to land on his shin. She tucked the last pin in place and turned toward the door, prepared to greet whoever had arrived.

Blane Johnson, the young manager for the brand new Enterprise Hotel, strode in. He was a stylish young man, sporting a mustache and close-cropped hair. Hat in hand, he nodded curtly at her and Peter. "Good morning, Miss Teller. Is your brother about?"

Ruth Ann hoped she had smoothed any ridiculous strands of hair back into place. She was self-conscious and shy when men came around, losing her sense of being a professional newspaperwoman. Matthew said her dove-shaped brown eyes made her fetching. But if she was going to fill his role, she needed to keep her posture—especially concerning the Enterprise Hotel, their largest advertising client that Matthew had won before its grand opening last week.

Their town had continued growing steadily. The *Choctaw Tribune* sat on the first crossroad from Main Street, but since then, more crossroads had been added, along with 50 more families, dozens of individuals, and businesses to accommodate them: boarding houses, two hotels, a second general store. Dickens was almost large enough now to justify its two competing newspapers. Almost.

Ruth Ann focused on the man who stepped over to Matthew's

desk on the right side of the large building. The Levitt Repair Shop took up the other half of the building.

"Good morning, Mr. Johnson. My brother is away on business. What may I do for you?"

Blane Johnson pinched his lips together and hummed. "I see. Well, I had a visit yesterday evening from Christopher Maxwell of the *Dickens Herald*, and he offered a much more generous rate for the hotel's advertising."

Ruth Ann struggled not to clamp a hand over her lurching stomach. She had expected Christopher Maxwell, publisher of the *Dickens Herald* and part-time enemy of the Tellers, to try and take advantage of Matthew's absence, but she hadn't thought it would come so soon. Nor so hard. The Enterprise Hotel account was the final advertiser they had needed to secure their expansion.

Johnson continued. "I had thought to give Mr. Teller the opportunity to counter the offer, but as he is away, please inform him on his return that we will not hold an advertising account with the *Tribune* after all."

Ruth Ann kept her back straight, postured despite her despair. "Mr. Johnson, in my brother's absence, I am fully authorized to make decisions on behalf of the newspaper. May I ask what Mr. Maxwell's offer was?"

Blane Johnson eyed her. "Miss Teller, I haven't the time to go over the intricacies of business with you. We are opening the hotel restaurant this morning. My supervisor will make an inspection any day, and I intend to see the restaurant is filled whenever he does."

Ruth Ann felt the account slipping through her fingers. He didn't want to discuss business with a woman, but she had to try. "I will, that is, we can—"

Peter folded his skinny arms over his chest and interrupted, "How about a friendly competition that you win no matter what, Mr. Johnson?"

"I beg your pardon?"

"You want the hotel booming with business for your boss. Both the *Herald* and *Tribune* want you as an advertiser. Say both papers run identical ads with a special for the restaurant, like a free slice of pie if folks bring in the ad. The only difference in the two will be that one says, 'courtesy of the *Choctaw Tribune*,' and the other 'courtesy of the *Dickens Herald*.' Whichever ad brings in the most at the end of three weeks gets your business."

Ruth Ann stared at her cousin, trying to comprehend his stroke of genius, then chanced a look at Blane Johnson. He glanced around the newspaper office, and she couldn't help fearing he doubted they could get even one edition out after whatever nonsense Mr. Maxwell told him.

She raised her chin to what she hoped was a professional, not arrogant, level. "You really have nothing to lose, Mr. Johnson, and you will gain free advertising in two newspapers to fill your restaurant."

Johnson looked around once more and shrugged. "Very well, though I don't mind saying I was relieved to receive Mr. Maxwell's offer. I've been hesitant about using the *Choctaw Tribune* since it's a specialty newspaper."

Ruth Ann resisted bristling at the insult and offered to shake Mr. Johnson's hand. "We look forward to earning your business."

Johnson looked at her hand a moment and finally gave it a polite shake. "We will see in a few weeks, won't we?"

After he left, Peter swung around and sat on the edge of Matthew's desk, taking a bow.

"What did you think of that?"

"I think we just took on a challenge we might not be able to make if Matthew doesn't come home right away."

"Aw, come on, Annie. We can do it. Our newspaper comes out before the *Herald* each week. Everyone will use our advertisement first."

"If we lose this account…"

"We won't."

Ruth Ann sighed and sat down hard in Matthew's chair, her mind going over the possibilities and problems with the challenge. The two papers had relatively equal distribution. The *Tribune* needed an edge to win.

Her thoughts scattered, she tried to return to the article she'd been working on. There were three more she could include in this edition, but there simply wasn't room in the weekly.

Something tickled her neck, and she shrieked.

Peter snorted. "Keep a smile on your face so we don't have bitter walakshi tonight."

Della Teller kept the buggy horse at an even pace, resisting the urge to put him into a run. The early spring morning might have been pleasant, with the freshness of the air, mother birds darting about and building nests, and sprigs of green grass making bright shoots along the road.

But the air and Della's thoughts on the renewal that came after winter were filled with Mrs. Warren's chatter. Susan Warren hadn't stopped talking since she opened her door when Della stopped to pick her up. Her clothing askew as usual, Mrs. Warren had jerked the buggy frame mightily while lifting her hefty self into it with barely enough gasps of breath between her words to make it.

"Just imagine the reports coming out of Washington. We're on the brink of another civil war! And don't think Indian Territory will be spared. An economic crisis affects everyone, and there's no escaping. Why, it's the end of all comfort and security..."

Della hid her smile. It was a mix of amusement and simple joy she experienced at having the woman beside her for a visit to the Jessop place. Anyone who saw them—a Choctaw woman with her deep sable hair folded up in the old way, and a city dressed woman with a blooming hat—would think them an odd pair.

If they looked closer—most people didn't—they would see how the spring weather brought some color to Mrs. Warren's pallid skin. But since her husband's abandonment, she had aged considerably. Thaddeus Warren, the former mayor of Dickens, had driven her to attempt suicide six months ago. Susan Warren was still lonely inside. At least she had her nephew, Lance Fuller, and their cook, Mabel, looking after her. But she needed something to live for beyond her habit of gossiping.

"Did you see those two audacious teens last Sunday?" Mrs. Warren prattled on. "Holding hands indeed! Scandalous behavior, right in church, no less. They've hardly been courting more than…well, I don't know how long it's been, but it's scandalous!"

The road bent and straightened, bringing the Jessop shanty into view. A thin line of smoke from the chimney matched everything about the place—thin window, thin road, thin children.

Since the buggy was now familiar to the Jessops, Della didn't need to worry about being shot at as Ruth Ann and her friends had the first time they'd visited the Jessop place. But this was Mrs. Warren's introductory visit.

The woman stopped talking to take in the sight. She clenched a fist to her heart."Oh, dear. Dear me! Mrs. Teller, it's a pig's sty."

Though the shanty was poorly built, the Jessops did what they could to make it presentable. The young woman of the house, Amarillo Jessop, had planted flowers to line a walkway to the gaping front door. The flowers bloomed now, unhindered by the cold nights they still experienced in mid-April. Former craters in the front area were filled to make a safer road up to the shanty. Della halted the buggy near the door.

Mrs. Warren gathered her bountiful skirts and attempted to make a hasty exit from the buggy as though she couldn't wait to give her full assessment to what ears were around to hear.

Della laid a firm hand on her arm. "This is their home."

Mrs. Warren froze, then her face melted into a soft smile. "Of course. Not everyone has been so fortunate as we."

Her tone was of pity, which was more tolerable than criticism, though Della knew the Jessops wouldn't be bothered much by either. That was why she decided to bring Mrs. Warren on the visit today. The woman needed to meet people to help her heal.

Before the women alighted from the buggy, the yard filled up with children and laughter. That was the marked difference Della noted since she and Ruth Ann began regular visits to the Jessops. Laughter. Smiles on faces streaked with the dirt from a day's work and play.

Della greeted them as she disembarked. They swarmed her like a brood of chicks. "Neches, you have grown an inch since I saw you last. Glenrose, spring is on your cheeks, blooming bright like the young flower you are. Belle—Belle, keep your sweet smile and say hello to Mrs. Warren."

Della untangled the five-year-old child from her skirts and pulled her out from behind her. She put a gentle arm around the girl's tiny shoulders.

"Children, this is Mrs. Warren, Mr. Fuller's aunt that I said might call sometime."

Mrs. Warren stood with lips slightly apart, her eyes filled with tears.

"Oh, you poor, precious children. Look at you. So pretty and full of life. Thank you for having me to..." She cast a glance at the shanty. "...to your home."

The scampering began as the children climbed all over the buggy until Neches succeeded in loosening the basket from the back. He hefted it with his slender arms. Just shy of his teens, he had the experienced expression of a boy who stared adulthood in the eye every day and learned not to fear it. His blonde hair matched Glenrose's, the eleven-year-old flower who maintained a sweet presence no matter her circumstances. Little Belle, on the other hand, liked to skip along with them until she felt the eyes of a stranger on her. Then she hid behind her siblings, her bouncing golden blonde curls never failing to bring a smile.

"You young'uns mind your manners!"

A voice too squeaky to be taken seriously made the three children giggle and dart into the house. Stephen Austin, the oldest boy, came around the corner of the house, an axe laid across his boney shoulder. Just past fourteen years old, he tried to project the air of manhood. It was growing on him, since he was the man of the house. Della thought how good it was for him to greet them with an axe rather than a rifle.

He nodded formally. "'Morning, Mrs. Teller. Pardon the young'uns, they're rambunctious, what with school letting out for plowing."

Della introduced Mrs. Warren, who stared wide-eyed at the boy in his tattered work shirt, bare feet, and shaggy blonde hair. Mrs. Warren had no doubt seen him on occasion when the family made it to church, but she'd never *seen* him. Stephen Austin bore a hard and unbending look.

What would the boy become without godly influences, especially men who would show him the way, Christ's way? Della had raised two sons. She knew the great challenges facing a boy growing into manhood. By grace, her boys had strong influences in their raising. Who would fill that role for this one?

Stephen Austin swung the axe down and leaned it against the gray board wall of the shanty. "Y'all come on inside. Sis will have somethin' on the stove since she seen you come up."

Della slipped her arm through Mrs. Warren's and guided the woman over the bumpy path that led to the front door. On a good day, the woman was unsteady on her feet, not having fully recovered her health, and now she looked as though a feather could tip her over. Still plump, she'd lost muscle from lack of moving about.

Mrs. Warren walked alongside Della without a word, and

Della sensed the pity turning to compassion. Her eyes were opened to a world beyond her own pain.

Inside the dim shanty lit only by the morning sun through the window, Della paused to let Mrs. Warren adjust. There wasn't much to see from a material perspective. The small room was crowded with a table and a few mismatched chairs, a long bench pulled up to one side, two cots that lined the back wall, and a wood-burning stove in the corner. A blanket door blocked off the only other room the shanty had.

But when someone looked about the room through the eyes of love for family and God's children, they could see the joy-filled faces of young ones who gathered around the table, rummaging through the basket Della brought. They could hardly contain themselves as they reverently laid aside the head of cheese wrapped in a cloth, smoked brisket, freshly baked rolls. Then squeals exploded.

"Cookies!"

From the blanket closed room, a soft but authoritative feminine voice rose over the din. "Save those for later."

Neches quickly put the cookies in the bottom of the basket. Little Belle tried to reach for them, one finger stuck between her lips as she whined. She was too small to reach the top of the basket.

"None of that." Glenrose took the finger from her crying sister's mouth and hefted her onto her slim waist.

"Sorry, ma'am," she mumbled to Mrs. Warren as she left through the open back door with Belle, who was wailing.

The soft voice in the other room belonged to Amarillo Jessop —mother, father, and oldest sibling of the Jessops. She came through the blanket door with a baby in her arms, not quite a toddler yet, and nodded in greeting. The baby began crying, joining the wail still resounding through the back door.

Amarillo raised her voice over the ruckus. "Howdy, Mrs.

Teller. Good of you to come out today. I have a bundle of fresh herbs for y'all."

Della released Mrs. Warren's arm. She took the crying baby from Amarillo, carefully disentangling his precious fingers from the young woman's blonde hair held in a loose braid. "Mrs. Warren, this is Amarillo, and this is the youngest of the Jessop clan, Charles Goodnight Jessop. We call him Goodnight."

Mrs. Warren seemed spellbound by the crying child. She reached out a trembling hand, almost touching the curls that were darker than any in the family. "Oh my. He's…beautiful."

Della held the baby to where the woman could view him better. Mrs. Warren never had children. Della could not imagine the burning desire she must feel now. Della felt her own longing for children again, grandchildren she had yet to have. She thought they would come from her oldest son first. But he had long since passed.

Perhaps it was more than charity that brought her often to the Jessop place.

When Mrs. Warren beckoned to take the wiggling baby, Della allowed her, though watching closely. But there was no need to worry. Mrs. Warren held the baby naturally and within seconds, Goodnight calmed and snuggled against the woman's ample shoulder and closed his eyes. Mrs. Warren closed hers as well, humming.

Amarillo watched with one cocked eyebrow, then moved to the stove. She was a slender young woman, a bit underfed looking, but even in her worn calico dress and bare feet, she was a natural beauty. "I have a bit of coffee, and dandelion for tea. The young'uns haven't seen many people except each other since school let out. What is Mr. Fuller doing in his time off?"

Though Amarillo spoke casually while she added wood to the stove and put the kettle on, Della detected the change in her tone. Della thought of Lance Fuller, the schoolteacher for white children, and the adjustment he had made in Dickens, Indian Territory. He visited the Jessops frequently to help the children with schoolwork on weekends.

The young man had done well and was honorable. He could use a wife, though.

Della smiled to herself and sat at the table. Neches sat across from her, stealing cautious glances at the new woman who bounced the baby gently as she paced the room.

Della answered Amarillo. "He is still helping Pastor Rand make repairs to the church. They added a storeroom in the back and the bell is in place—"

"You must come live with me!"

Mrs. Warren's outburst silenced everyone. Della stared at her. Few things surprised her, but this woman proved an exception.

Mrs. Warren stopped pacing and stared at Amarillo, who halted in pouring hot water over the dandelion leaves.

"I beg your pardon, ma'am?"

"This…this…" Mrs. Warren waved her free hand around the room. "Your home…there's no sense in living in such a tiny place with so many little ones when I have a big house that needs…it needs…" Mrs. Warren stroked the sleeping child's curls. "It needs a family like yours."

Della glanced at Amarillo, the young woman casting a desperate look at her. But Della had nothing to say yet. There was much to consider.

Amarillo took a slow breath. "That's a generous offer, ma'am, but we're fine right here."

Mrs. Warren burst into tears. Della stood and took the baby from her arms. She put her other arm around the shaking woman and guided her toward the table. Neches jumped up, pulled out a chair, and helped lower Mrs. Warren into it.

Amarillo came over with a tin cup of tea and set it in front of the sobbing woman.

"I didn't mean to upset you, ma'am. Here, drink some of this, it'll help."

Mrs. Warren sniffed loud and coughed. Neches offered her his dirty handkerchief, and she nodded. "Thank you, young man. And it's all right. It's all right."

Mrs. Warren looked up at Della where she stood with a hand on her shoulder. Della smiled.

Belle ran in through the back door, her tears forgotten, a handful of blooming weeds in hand. "Teacher coming, teacher coming!"

Glenrose came in behind her, and she and Neches went to the front window. Della glanced out to see Lance Fuller navigating the rough dirt road on a bicycle, dodging the ruts like he knew them well. A bicycle was impractical with the lack of good roads in Indian Territory, but Lance Fuller did well with his in getting around. He said he preferred it to riding a horse—which he'd rarely done—or driving the Warren buggy.

"Move on away from the window, now," Amarillo said, a notable change in her tone. It went up another octave. "Glenrose, go harvest me a basket of herbs for Mr. Fuller."

"Lance? Here?" Mrs. Warren stayed at the table, looking around, confusion on her face.

Amarillo pulled her braid over her shoulder and answered with what Della thought was considerable effort to sound indifferent. "He comes every now and then. Helped me till and plant the garden earlier this spring. Hasn't been around since school let out, what with working on the church and all."

Mrs. Warren smiled. "Lance is such a good boy, isn't he? Always helping neighbors."

Amarillo blushed right as Neches opened the door to admit the schoolteacher.

Lance Fuller came in with a bashful smile, a book tucked under his arm. He was dressed in work clothes, wood shavings coating his pants. He removed his hat as he greeted Della and kissed his aunt on the forehead.

"I missed you ladies leaving. I meant to have you bring this book for Miss Amarillo."

He finally looked at Amarillo Jessop, who was pouring him a cup of tea. "Thank you, Mr. Fuller. I—we have a basket of herbs for you."

Della suppressed her smile at his feeble excuse for a visit, but she couldn't blame the handsome blonde-haired, blue-eyed young man for wanting to come out and see the pretty girl at the shanty. They came from worlds apart, but the way they looked at one another now, Della knew they didn't mind. Perhaps the circumstances of their lives did away with that, at least where their hearts were concerned.

Before the cup of tea and book could be exchanged, Mrs. Warren stood abruptly. "Well, I'm glad to have met all of you. I will see you in church next Sunday."

She kissed her surprised nephew on the cheek, and headed out, oblivious to her impolite exit after such a short visit. Lance waved awkwardly at the Jessops and followed after his aunt.

Della handed the baby to Amarillo, took the offered bundle of herbs, and bid them all goodbye. They made her promise to come again soon, and that Mrs. Warren was welcome anytime.

Della knew they meant it.

CHAPTER 6

*R*uth Ann toted a heavy picnic basket to the church on the knoll across the grassy field from the back of the *Choctaw Tribune* building. She may as well be off to feed a starving army with how much food her mother packed. But then, two hardworking men could eat an army's portion at the noon meal.

Families in the church had taken turns helping work on the chapel and providing food during the week of repairs that turned into two weeks. The chapel also served as a school for white children in the area. Since the opening of the school, the number of students had doubled as families flocked around the rare opportunity of education for their children in Indian Territory.

After the visit from hotel manager Blane Johnson and Peter's bold challenge that morning, Ruth Ann had been busy at the newspaper office in a nervous jitter when her mother, Della, brought the noon meal.

She was amazed by her mother, who not only ran her own sewing business but also their household and kept them supplied with meals in addition to her charity work and visiting Mrs. Warren.

Ruth Ann felt guilty about what little she did around the house these days. When Peter moved into their new lean-to with Matthew, he took over her old chores of caring for the animals. It helped to have her cousin at home and also manning the telegraph wire. But instead of doing more for her mother, Ruth Ann found herself busier than ever. No wonder Peter pestered her about making the grape dumplings instead of bothering Della.

When her mother arrived at the newspaper office, Ruth Ann volunteered to deliver the food Della prepared for Pastor Rand and Lance Fuller. Ruth Ann needed a break away from the constant clatter in the shop.

It wasn't a long walk from the back door of the *Choctaw Tribune* building to the First Baptist Church of Dickens, still situated alone in its own meadow of spring flowers and fresh sprigs of new grass. There was a chill in the air, and Ruth Ann tightened her shawl closer while adjusting the basket on her arm.

The sound of a hammer resonated from the church roof. Ruth Ann squinted against the sun as she stopped by a ladder leaned against the building.

"Halito! Come down and eat while the food is warm. My mother won't take kindly to even a bite being wasted!"

A hammer tumbled over the edge of the roof, and Ruth Ann jumped out of its path. She laughed when Pastor Rand's red face appeared over the edge.

"Sorry down there. You know I would never offend your mother, though her food, hot or cold or a day old, is the most savory in the territory."

As he chatted, Pastor Rand hoisted his slender frame around the ladder and down. He hopped off the last few rungs. Though in his late forties, he was every bit as healthy and robust as a twenty-year-old. He was a hearty soul, always evident when he took off on a Sunday morning sermon that could well last a day.

Pastor Rand took the basket from her. "I hope this has been blessed already..."

He crammed a biscuit into his mouth and sighed in contentment. "It has indeed. Thank you."

Holding the basket protectively, he called up the ladder, "Come down here, Lance Fuller, before you offend Mrs. Teller's cooking efforts!"

He headed for the front entrance of the church, searching the basket as he went.

"Halito, Ruth Ann." This time, Lance Fuller peered over the edge of the roof. "Would you toss that hammer back up? I need to secure a few shingles first. Wind's picking up."

Ruth Ann checked the short grass and located the hammer. She gathered the light skirt on her black and white gingham day dress to one side and ascended the ladder. Her comfortable work boots made climbing easy. Though her knees trembled, she wasn't nearly as terrified of ladders as she had been before riding elevators and Ferris Wheels at the Chicago World's Fair.

Lance laughed above her. "You don't need to climb up. Just throw it."

Ruth Ann muttered, "If you only knew what happened the last time."

"What did you say?"

She arrived at the top and handed the hammer to Lance, who was squatted on the sloping roof. He kept a secure grip on the ladder for her. Ruth Ann climbed onto the roof with a deep breath.

"When Matthew and Peter were finishing the lean-to, Peter told me to toss up a hammer, and Matthew thought he was talking to him. Peter got hit by both hammers."

Lance chuckled and stood, leaning with the slant of the roof. "Sounds about right."

The slope wasn't steep, and Ruth Ann took in the handiwork of the day. Heavy storms that winter had done their share of damage and spring was sure to bring plenty of rain. But the shingling was almost finished. "Seems things are going well in your world."

Lance sighed. "Mostly."

When Ruth Ann turned a questioning look on him, Lance went to hammering a shingle in place. Though close cut, his ash blonde hair pasted to his forehead from sweat. He seemed to have lost his breath, face reddening from the mild exertion.

"Do you think the building won't be ready for school next week?"

"Oh, the building's just fine. It's me that's not well."

"You're ill?"

Lance knelt on one knee and took great care in lining up the next shingle. "I might as well tell you. You're the only person who won't outright laugh at me."

Ruth Ann gathered her skirt close as a gust of wind kicked up. "What do you mean?"

"I'm in love."

It wasn't easy, but Ruth Ann restrained her giggle, though she did smile. She wasn't the least bit surprised, but Lance spoke in such a deadly earnest way she didn't want to embarrass him. "I see."

"I can't stop thinking about her. When school starts again, it'll be worse."

He pounded the nail, though it was already flush. "I'll see her brothers and sisters every day. I'll wonder if she's walking them to school that time, or I'll try to come up with an excuse to go to their place. It's driving me crazy."

"I won't tell anyone if you don't want me to."

Lance scoffed. "She's probably the only one who doesn't know."

"Why don't you tell her?"

Lance fumbled the hammer. Jaw-dropped, he stared at Ruth Ann. "I can't. I…she's a good woman. When I see how she loves and cares for her siblings like she was their mother, giving them the best life they can have, the way she never complains no matter how hard her circumstances, and how beautiful she is…" He flushed. "Of course, you're beautiful, too. Wait, no, you're not. No! I mean…" He smacked his forehead with an open palm.

Ruth Ann laughed. "After all we've been through together, Lance Fuller, including a ride on the monstrous Ferris Wheel, I believe it is perfectly proper for us to have the understanding we do."

Lance sighed. "You are a good friend, Ruth Ann Teller." He looked toward the east, toward the Jessop home place. "I wish I could take Amarillo to a World's Fair. Or something. But I'm just a fraud trying to mend my ways."

Ruth Ann knelt on the sun-warmed shingles, hands clasped in her lap. She recalled the kind of person Lance Fuller was when he arrived in Indian Territory. If ever there was a changed man, it was this one.

"Lance, you know you didn't earn grace or mercy. It was through Jesus Christ and His sacrifice that you are forgiven. Our Creator's Son paid for our sins."

Lance was on both knees, rubbing his hands up and down his legs. "I want to follow the Lord." He closed his eyes. "Still…"

"You're in love."

He winced and his eyes squeezed tighter. "What should I do?"

"Have you asked Him?"

Lance shook his head. "It's too selfish to pray about."

"Lance Fuller, the Creator already knows your thoughts! Just ask Him, and then listen with your heart. Do you understand what I'm saying?"

Lance opened his eyes, their color matching the hazy blue sky. "I've heard that kind of talk all my life. I never understood any of it until I came here."

"Good. Now come on down and eat my mama's food. If Pastor Rand left any."

~

"So, he finally admitted it."

Beulah Levitt folded her arms in triumph. She was seated across from Ruth Ann in the back storeroom of the newspaper and repair shop, the only place the young women could have a private conversation in a shop full of men.

"Now remember, Beulah, he's very shy about this. He only told me because he knew I wouldn't tease him."

"I have no intention of teasing him. We simply must work to get them together."

Ruth Ann shook her head. From the moment they met a year and a half ago, Ruth Ann had admired the young woman who immigrated from Russia with her father to escape the persecution their people had faced.

Though Jewish, the Levitts were most definitely Russian with blonde hair and blue eyes. Beulah was a tall, confident, and often too determined friend who Ruth Ann loved dearly. But sometimes her friend meddled where she didn't belong. "It's not our business. I advised him to pray about it."

Beulah huffed. "Of course, but I am sure Lance Fuller has already been given an answer. He lacks the courage to act, so we must help him. The next time you speak with him, invite him on a picnic. We will invite Amarillo and—"

"No."

Ruth Ann was as surprised as Beulah at her own stern tone. But she kept it. "I will not interfere. Lance needs to make his own decisions, and if he lacks the courage to do the right thing, that is between him and God."

Beulah's expression softened. Perhaps she remembered what her interfering had done in the past. "I know. But sometimes God works through friends, who give one another courage."

"If He wants to use either of us, He will. If not, we won't butt in. At least, I won't."

Beulah sighed. "I will heed your wisdom."

Relieved, Ruth Ann wanted to ask her friend about starting the children's choir again when school resumed, but the door to the storeroom banged open. Peter stuck his head in. "Annie, you need—"

"Peter Frazier, if you're going to behave like you weren't raised among civilized people, I'll send you home for training."

Peter rapped on the already open door. "Pardon me, ladies, but if I may interrupt, I'd like to inform Miss Teller that her type-setter up and left. Quit."

Ruth Ann jumped to her feet. "Mr. Dodd? Why?"

"Said he had a job offer up in McAlester. He just walked out."

"But he has to get the type set tomorrow so we can print Thursday's edition."

"You better get busy then." Peter disappeared.

Beulah stood and frowned. "This is not right. Your brother hired Mr. Dodd only a short while ago. He said he has an ill mother to support. Why would he move further from her?"

"Higher pay, I suppose." Ruth Ann moved to the door. They offered the two new employees fair wages, but since the recent establishment of a federal court in McAlester, there was plenty of big news to cover in the coal mining town.

Ruth Ann entered the newspaper office to chaos. Peter was in a heated verbal battle with Caleb Gentry, the other employee hired to work at the newspaper. Mr. Levitt stood between the two trying to calm them, but threats flew.

"You're just a boy, and Ruth Ann Teller isn't much more than a kid. I hired on to work for a man, and I don't blame Dodd for walking out. You—"

Peter shouted over Caleb Gentry. "If you're so keen on following Dodd north, go on ahead!"

Ruth Ann hurried up to them, heart in her throat. "Peter, I will handle this. Mr. Gentry, what seems to be the problem?"

Caleb Gentry glared at her. Mid-thirties, he had a tough build and was taller than her by a good head—a former U.S. Cavalryman with no patience. "Just tell your wet-nosed cousin here not to barge in and order me to get busy setting type. I know my work, and I'll good and well do what I get paid to. Nothing less. And sure nothing more."

Ruth Ann put a hand on Peter's shoulder to silence whatever he had opened his mouth to say. Gentry hadn't been a likable man from the beginning, but he had worked for newspapers since leaving the cavalry. They desperately needed him if they stood any chance at winning the challenge for the Enterprise Hotel account. Why did her cousin have to pick this fight?

"That is what we agreed to, Mr. Gentry. However, we may offer you additional hours until we can hire on another typesetter."

"I'm not interested in extra hours—"

The newspaper office door flew open, violently disturbing the bell over the door. Mrs. Warren floated in with the spring breeze.

"Yoo-hoo, my dear! Ruth Ann! I need you at my home straight away as I'm preparing for new residents. That is, once you convince the Jessop family to move in with me!"

Ruth Ann stared at the excited woman, unable to comprehend what she was talking about. Beulah quickly moved to intercept Mrs. Warren, taking her by the arm and guiding her to a seat at the front table. "Do tell me all about it…"

Caleb Gentry yanked off his work apron. "Nothing but a circus around here."

Mr. Levitt tapped Peter on the arm and nodded to his back workbench. Reluctantly, Peter skulked to it and picked up a wooden table leg to carve some of his pride into.

Ruth Ann set a steady gaze on Caleb Gentry. "We appreciate your work. If you have problems with anything, come to me. My brother and I are both publishers of the *Choctaw Tribune*. Please remember that."

It was risky to stress the issue of him calling her a child. But not standing up for herself would cause a man like Caleb Gentry to lose respect for her.

Thankfully, she'd judged his character right. The man put his apron back on and turned to the printing press. "I'll stay on for now. I need the work, and you folks need all the help you can get."

Ruth Ann bit her lower lip to keep from voicing her agreement. The walakshi might be bitter tonight, after all.

A thump sounded at the shop door. She stared through the picture windows at a young boy disappearing from sight on a bicycle. It was the boy Maxwell hired to deliver papers by throwing them at the subscriber's door.

The trouble, though, was that the *Dickens Herald* wasn't due out for three more days.

Ruth Ann hurried to retrieve the paper, the gush of fresh air doing nothing to relieve her anxiety as she unfurled the paper in the open doorway. It was a truncated version of the newspaper. They must have started setting type and running copies as soon as Mr. Johnson visited that morning, because there, next to a mediocre headline story, was an advertisement for a special at the hotel restaurant on its opening day.

CHAPTER 7

A swarm of light flowed around Matthew. Fire burned his skin. He flicked his right hand, wanting to put the fire out, to stop the pain. Instead, he encountered soft flesh. A kind laugh filled the space around him.

"Zio! Zia! He's awake, come and see."

Matthew scrunched his eyes open. They'd never been this sore, even after all night writing.

He tried to lift his head, but the young Italian widow, Cadenza, held up a hand to stop him. "Lie still, there's nowhere you need to go."

Matthew started to rub his eyes, but his shoulder caught, and he winced. "Where am I?"

A man stood over the cot now, face blackened by coal dust. Matthew didn't recognize him at first, then realized it was Raphael Bianchi. His burly frame shaded Matthew from the sunset coming through a far window. This wasn't the room Matthew had boarded in the night before.

"Well, my friend, I see you're still alive."

Coal dust rose up his throat, and Matthew coughed hard. He instinctively held his chest and wondered why it still gave him a sensation of pain six months after a bullet ripped through it.

"Were you hit in the front, my friend? Torre said you took a hard bounce against the wall. Of course, it'll be a few days before Torre sees straight, either. Doc Robinson says you'll be all right, though. Oh, but I don't think you've met my wife, Mrs. Bianchi."

An older woman entered and stood beside Cadenza. Matthew focused on Mrs. Bianchi's face, her expression much softer than Ricco's wife. She wore a bright scarf over her black hair and looked more matronly than threatening.

Matthew nodded to her in greeting. "The others, they all right? Fabio?" He tried to remember. "Paolo?"

The older woman wiped a cloth over his face. It felt good on his hot skin, and his eyes fluttered. But he opened them to see sorrowful looks exchanged. "What happened?"

Raphael's smile was one of pity. "Let's just say you were one of the lucky ones. Paolo and Torre are alive, though. Fabio caught some heat pulling his father out. But he'll be all right."

"Who got me out?"

"A friend."

Matthew knew he owed a debt to Raphael, a man who had left his home country filled with hope, and found a black hole in a land unlike what he hoped for.

Matthew held back on more questions. His throat was raw, but when Mrs. Bianchi offered him a drink from a mug, he politely refused. He suspected it wasn't mere water.

Raphael shooed the fussing women from the room, and it wasn't long before Matthew drifted to sleep.

Soft humming woke Matthew to the gray light of morning. It took great effort to open his eyes and find where the sound came from. He turned his head and saw Cadenza seated in a chair near his bed. She held his coat in her arms and inhaled its scent while she hummed and rubbed rosary beads between her fingers. Her black hair was piled atop her head, almost as though she'd slept that way. Her simple red dress looked a size too large. She was thin, her face pale despite her Italian blood. Matthew wondered what she'd been like before the mine disaster that claimed her husband.

He wanted to study her longer, discern her story without asking questions. But she raised her face from the coat. "Oh, buona fortuna. You were so still. But you are alive."

Matthew licked his dry lips and wondered where he could find fresh water. "So I've been told. Where's your uncle?"

Cadenza smoothed the coat across her lap and folded her hands over it. "At work. But my zia and I will look after you."

"I don't want to put you out."

Why wasn't he at Ricco Bianchi's house? This room was like the one he had at Ricco's, except there was only a single bed here, and the window was on the west side.

The door opened, and Mrs. Bianchi clucked her tongue. "Cadenza, didn't I tell you to leave the poor man alone? Now, go on to the store and get the supper things."

Cadenza laid the tattered coat across the chair and stroked it, her eyes filled with sadness. She left, and Mrs. Bianchi swiped Matthew's face with a wet cloth.

He asked, "The other men? What happened?"

She shook her head with the same look of pity as her husband had. "You had the easiest time with a bump on the head and bruises. Torre's laid up and won't get the rest of his wages for this contract. But at least he's alive. Fabio and Paolo, too. Doc Robinson doesn't expect Paolo's mine buddy to pull through."

Mrs. Bianchi turned to leave. Matthew stretched out his hand toward his coat that Cadenza left on the chair. Mrs. Bianchi followed his gaze and read the question in his eyes.

She gathered the coat and held it close. "It belonged to her husband. Raphael couldn't throw it out, but he didn't realize she would know it was dear Antonio's when he got it out for you." Mrs. Bianchi shook her head and left.

Matthew needed to get up. Do something. It took several tries to detangle himself from the blanket without igniting extreme pain. He swung his legs over the bed, and his feet landed on the work boots Raphael had loaned him. Were they her husband's, too? Matthew would get his own soon. Meanwhile, these would have to do.

He found his shirt at the end of the bed. It showed little damage from the fire. The coat had protected him.

Matthew slipped out into an empty living room identical to Ricco's, only smaller. He exited out the back door in the kitchen.

There was little happening around the company housing neighborhood, and Matthew went unnoticed. His shoulder ached where he'd hit the wall in the mine, but moving around actually felt better than laying.

When traveling to Krebs, he and Raphael crossed a stream not far away. Behind the row of company houses, Matthew followed the sloping terrain to it, pausing by an old oak to catch his breath. Once on the pebbly shore, he took off the boots and waded in.

Generations before Europeans came to the Mississippi home-lands, Choctaws had gone to the water every morning to wash. They valued cleanliness, something they didn't find among the new arrivals to their land. But they did learn of a new cleanliness, a cleanliness of the soul, of washing and purifying that felt right to his people. For pain to be taken away. It was right to be clean, inside and outside.

It was the good way to live.

With the freezing water flowing around him, Matthew gradu-ally grew clean inside. And numb outside. The pain was gone.

CHAPTER 8

The *Choctaw Tribune* was late for the first time in a year. Ruth Ann pushed and eased off and pulled, but nothing came together as it should. Matthew's boots were huge to fill.

When the last delivery went out Thursday evening, two full days after the *Dickens Herald* special edition, Ruth Ann pretended she was preparing to leave the print shop for home. Caleb Gentry had departed at his scheduled time even though they weren't finished. The Levitts went home after tidying up from the rush. Peter lingered near the door, waiting for Ruth Ann.

She shooed him out, saying she wanted to write a few notes. Peter reluctantly complied, but he warned her to get home soon. His aunt Della would have supper warm for them, maybe even the walakshi Ruth Ann had failed to make. But Ruth Ann was too anxious to go home.

Alone in the building that echoed her every move, she straightened bits of paper in the telegraph office, set as a lean-to on the shop. With the *Herald* getting a jump on the Enterprise Hotel advertisement, they were already behind in the challenge.

Back in the print shop, she stared at the desk. It was as messy as Matthew always kept it. There was irony in that, but she was too discouraged to smile at the thought.

Ruth Ann stacked papers together, several news stories that wouldn't fit in the current edition. She caught her breath. An unopened letter lay buried at the bottom of the pile. How could she have forgotten its arrival this morning?

In the frantic pace of getting the newspaper out after their typesetter suddenly quit, there'd been no time to cut open the envelope with Matthew's handwriting on it. They hadn't heard from him since he'd left last Saturday, and were anxious to learn where he was, what he was doing. But it was the thought of his focused ways that had made Ruth Ann lay it aside until they met the deadline—though they hadn't.

She tore into the envelope postmarked two days ago in Krebs. There was an article he'd penned about a shootout with the Abernathy gang near Wilburton. She'd gotten scanty reports on it, but this was detailed. How close had Matthew been to the action? His letter should tell.

Dear Mama and Ruth Ann,

I trust you are both well. I am currently engaged in questioning people in Krebs, but please tell no one. It could compromise my work. I am using an assumed name: Matt Jameson. Contact me only if there is an emergency.

There is disgruntlement among the miners. I will find out what I can, but if any news comes over the telegraph wire, do not hesitate to break it. Don't let the Herald *get ahead. And keep a sharp eye on Maxwell, he may try to take advantage in my absence.*

We have a full staff and a competent publisher at the helm. Steer steady and true until I return.

Matthew

. . .

It was shorter than Ruth Ann had hoped, and not nearly enough specifics about his investigation—whatever it was—to satisfy her. Was he afraid the wrong eyes might land on this letter? Why was he using an assumed name?

He was right about Maxwell trying to take advantage, attempting to steal their new advertiser. And who knew if he wasn't connected to Mr. Dodd suddenly leaving?

But it was Matthew's closing words that choked Ruth Ann with the heavy guilt she'd denied all day.

Steer straight and true...

She had shipwrecked the *Choctaw Tribune* that week. The newspaper should have gone out first thing in the morning, just as it did every Thursday. In the past, Ruth Ann witnessed how quickly advertisers lost faith. She could only hope the newspaper's reputation wasn't too damaged, and that they regained the Enterprise Hotel as a client.

A competent publisher?

Ruth Ann had to keep the newspaper afloat until Matthew returned. He'd straighten everything out, then surge forward with some magnificent story beyond anything the *Dickens Herald* produced.

She tucked Matthew's article about the shootout on a stack already forming for the next edition. There was more news than their weekly paper could handle even though they'd added four pages when they hired help. And now they were shorthanded.

Ruth Ann tucked the letter in her reticule to show her mother and Peter. She went through the front door into the dusky evening light and turned to lock up.

"Miss Teller?"

Ruth Ann jumped at the voice behind her. Blane Johnson halted on the boardwalk near her.

Oh no.

Hoping her voice didn't betray how she'd been startled—

Matthew wouldn't have been—Ruth Ann said, "Good evening, Mr. Johnson. What may I do for you?"

His face was shadowed in the low light of the streetlamp, his tone business-like gruff. "I see the paper finally went out this evening. However, the *Herald's* advertisement brought in quite a few customers this week. As I said before, I doubt the *Tribune's* effect on the general public, and have decided to accept Mr. Maxwell's offer."

The first edition in Matthew's absence couldn't be more disastrous, could it? Ruth Ann didn't want to know. She steadied herself with a fortifying breath. "Mr. Johnson, I assure you our paper—"

"The fact of the matter is, I do not care to turn over the advertisement of one of the grandest hotels in the territory to a..." He folded his arms over his chest. "To be perfectly honest, I believe a woman has no business running a newspaper. It was a grave error on Mr. Teller's part."

Ruth Ann locked the door of the building, giving herself a chance to turn away from the hotel manager to keep from snapping at him. She had to save this account. Somehow.

A sudden idea tickled her thoughts. Oh dear. Surely not! Did she dare?

But when Matthew was up against a challenge, he barreled into it with blinders on. Uncle Preston once summarized Matthew's thought process as, *I'm not sure I can do it, but I will.*

Ruth Ann gave a quick nod, committing herself to the decision that could make the *Choctaw Tribune* the finest newspaper in Indian Territory. Or run it aground.

She faced Blane Johnson, posture in place. "I appreciate your concern, Mr. Johnson, however, you have nothing to lose in continuing the challenge another few weeks. During that time, you will note a marked difference between response from the *Herald* and the *Tribune.*"

"And why would that be?"

"Because the *Choctaw Tribune* is shifting to a daily edition starting Monday."

Johnson raised his eyebrows, his shock genuine. "A daily? Not even the *Dickens Herald*..."

Ruth Ann was lightheaded with a burst of energy. They could enlist Lance to help since school was out, publish articles as soon as they were finished. So many possibilities! But she held herself from showing outward emotion. She had to convince Johnson she was capable of this bold venture.

"In fairness to the *Herald*—" *a concept Maxwell is not familiar with,* "—we will only run the hotel's special once a week. But I'm sure you are aware of the significant difference this will make in the newspaper's impact."

"Perhaps." Johnson's expression was dubious. He shrugged. "As you said, I have nothing to lose. We will keep a tally on the advertisements. The results will speak for themselves."

"Indeed. Good evening, Mr. Johnson." Ruth Ann left him standing on the boardwalk and headed for home, dizzy with what she'd done.

A daily? What was she thinking? But this was what they needed to win the challenge. In order to steer straight and true, one had to have a stiff wind in their sails.

$\mathcal{M}$atthew returned to work in the mines on Friday after moving back to Ricco's. It might not be a peaceful home, but Matthew didn't want to crowd Raphael's family, and it wasn't proper for him to stay in a house with an unmarried young woman.

Even though she was the daughter of Ricco, Cadenza lived with Raphael. Matthew guessed it was because of the trauma they all endured in the mine disaster of '92. And it was obvious Ricco's wife couldn't stand housemates. Matthew avoided the couple when he could.

He'd spent most of Wednesday in bed, worrying about the *Choctaw Tribune* going out the next morning. On Thursday, to calm his anxiety over not distributing the newspaper, and to work out sore muscles, he'd strolled the streets in Krebs, meeting people. What Raphael said was true—the clerk at the company store was a thief worthy of membership in the Abernathy gang. Still, Matthew wrangled a deal to buy his own work clothes and boots on credit against his upcoming wages. If he survived at least one full day in the mine.

Matthew approached the mine entrance and spotted Fabio.

The young man's neck was patched from burns he'd gotten while pulling his unconscious father out of the mine, but he'd recovered quickly. He gave Matthew a smile of respect. No teasing the grignollo this morning.

Matthew silently joined him as jostling to enter the mine began. No one was in a hurry, though the bosses wanted every man working extra to fill the latest order before the company missed their deadline. They warned any penalties would come straight out of wages.

The swirl of languages struck Matthew once again. He paid close attention to the miners today—what tools they carried, how they carried them—all while contemplating how to stay alive in the coal mines of Krebs. But there were no guarantees, even for experienced miners.

The explosion that injured him, Torre, Fabio, Paolo, and killed Paolo's buddy, had been caused by Paolo sweeping gasses from the ceiling and right over a naked lamp—one where the flame was exposed. The gas ignited, triggering an explosion and setting off a chain reaction in the tunnel.

Matthew heard several times how lucky he was, how they all were that it hadn't been worse. He didn't imagine the widow of the man who'd been killed felt lucky.

As the mine closed in around him, Matthew recalled Fabio's words from the first day: last stop before hell.

Well, Matthew had been there and back. Between the shootout that cost him his horse and being blown up in a mine explosion, the worst was surely over. He'd find Al Percy soon and get back to the newspaper before long. Hopefully.

For now, he kept to himself and listened to snippets of conversations—the ones in English—while he shoveled coal into the car outside his tunnel. Matthew probably shouldn't be back to work the way his shoulder scolded him at the first scoop. But he'd learn nothing lying in bed.

Two latecomers passed Matthew, speaking English in a way that said they didn't care who heard them.

"Well, I know what I'll be doing if Hanraty doesn't come out on top at the negotiations in Lehigh and Coalgate."

"Me too. Enough of these conditions and poor wages…"

Matthew kept his head down even after they passed, cursing and complaining. There had been similar talk yesterday in town. A strike? Chief Wilson Jones wouldn't stand for it. The mixed-blood Choctaw chief wanted to keep the mines in operation and royalties flowing into the Nation. Given his past tendencies when it came to dealing with tribal controversies, a strike could hit the chief like gas to fire and explode in a chain reaction through the whole tribe.

Matthew frowned. The last thing his people needed was more killings to bring in the U.S. government, and give Senator Henry Dawes that much more cause to break up the tribal government for good.

If a strike was coming, Matthew needed to get back to the newspaper fast. But then, what better way to get a story than to live it? The mines were the best place to do that, even though it was back-breaking, dreary, dangerous…

"Hey!"

Matthew turned at the sharp sound, preparing to be blown up again. Instead, a baseball flew toward his face. He caught it reflexively, the ball smacking his new work glove. He stared in the direction it had come from. Fabio grinned as he came from deep in the tunnel, teeth startling white next to his dark skin covered in grime.

"Good catch, Matt Jameson. My papà says he'd be proud to have you take his position on third base tomorrow. No one is as sneaky as him at holding a man's belt at third, but you'll do for now, and his uniform will fit you well. Can't let those Lehigh boys win any bragging rights."

Matthew rolled the soiled ball in his hand. Crudely stitched with red thread, it was larger than the balls Indians used in stick-ball games, a sport Matthew preferred to the American game of baseball. He'd played baseball a few times during his short stint in college. But he was used to throwing a ball with two stickball sticks—kapucha—not hitting one with a single stick.

He tossed the ball to Fabio as he joined Matthew near the coal pile.

"Not sure I'll feel up to it." Matthew tapped his shoulder and winced for emphasis.

Fabio laughed. "You'll do, grignollo." He slapped Matthew's shoulder, drawing a genuine wince this time, and turned away. Matthew took a chance.

"Is Percy playing tomorrow?"

"Who?"

"Al Percy. He used to live down where I come from, and I heard he went to work for Osage. Does he play for the Krebs team?"

"Never heard of him. But you keep your eyes on our Iron Man, Joe McGinnity. He's the greatest player that ever lived."

Matthew nodded. "I'll do that."

Fabio cocked his head. "This Percy fellow; he's not Italian, eh? Scotch, maybe?"

"Maybe."

Matthew needed to ease the conversation away from Al Percy. He went back to shoveling coal. "There are a fair number of Germans around, too."

Fabio swung his pickax in a circle and landed it on his shoul-der. He looked more ready to swing a baseball bat than risk his life another day in the mine. "We come from all over. Where did you say you hail from?"

Matthew didn't look up. "South."

"Ah, one of those. I'm thinking you have a murky past, maybe an outlaw?"

Matthew glanced at Fabio from the corner of his eye and tried to sound teasing when he answered, "Something like that."

"Maybe you can teach me tricks of the trade sometime. Anything to get me out of the mines and into fresh air."

Matthew kept shoveling.

The bosses had ordered work on Saturday to catch up from the fiesta and the mine explosion. But the Krebs miners had no intention of canceling their big rivalry game with Lehigh. From the looks of joy and grief of the gathering fans that Saturday morning, Matthew understood this was one way they dealt with tragedy.

Before the game, Fabio gave Matthew a wool baseball uniform. It made him feel trussed up as he walked stiff-legged to the baseball diamond in a field outside of town. When Choctaws got together to play stickball, the men went barefoot, often shirtless, and some tied back long hair with bandanas. A man was free to run, leap, throw, and tackle.

The button-down jersey with its stitched-on letters forming KREBS sported a full collar and front pockets. The Chicago-style cap with pillbox crown had horizontal stripes and a solid red brim. The knickers were even snugger than the shirt, but Fabio insisted Matthew wear them. If all that wasn't enough, the Krebs team wore short black ties tucked into their jersey plackets. How could a man breathe much less play a game wearing this getup?

Nothing to it but a stout heart.

Sobering was the black crepe armbands the Krebs baseball team wore in memory of the miners who died in the 1892 disaster. It wasn't something the families were finished mourning. Matthew wore one on his left arm like the other men as they gathered before the game. Joe "Iron Man" McGinnity led the team as the men rallied around him by their bench.

Over 300 fans had turned out to root for their home team,

and hundreds of people came with the Lehigh team by train to cheer them on. They filled the wooden bleachers set up for the spectators, team banners, and flags ready to wave once the game got underway. Women and little girls wore straw hats to shade their faces, the men and boys had their miner caps.

If Fabio had let Matthew out of playing, Raphael Bianchi wouldn't have. He was the hefty catcher who used a thin glove.

"Well, my friend, ready to knock those Lehigh boys down the shaft?" Raphael bumped Matthew with his shoulder as they stood by their team's bench. "Don't look so worried. You have fans to cheer you on, you know."

Matthew followed his nod to the wooden viewing stands. Cadenza and Raphael's wife waved at him with friendly smiles.

Matthew rubbed his arm. "Not sure I'm up to playing. Shoulder still hitches."

"Don't you worry. The Lehigh boys will be dizzy before this day ends! Look there, Iron Man is about to take the mound. Let's play ball!"

The rest of the Krebs team ran onto the field. Matthew was out of breath when he reached his position at third base. Hopefully, the lauded Iron Man was as good as they said, and Matthew wouldn't have to do much running in the game.

Before the first pitch, Matthew heard a woman call his name.

His real name.

He jerked and looked toward the stands, heart double beating. A traditional Choctaw skirt normally only worn at ceremonies, with its diamond pattern around the worn edges, disappeared behind a tall man standing at the end of the bleachers.

The voice was familiar, and a sense of guilt overwhelmed Matthew. He was playing games instead of looking for Al Percy and the men who killed Matthew's father and brother. The woman was there to remind him of that. Yet in a way as strange as Takba, he was doing that through this game. If she wanted to speak with him, she would wait until it was over.

He turned back for the opening pitch. Three up, three struck out. Relieved, Matthew headed for the team bench, only to have Fabio hand him a bat.

"You're second to bat, grignollo. Give it to them!"

Matthew accepted the bat and stepped to the side of the bench to warm up his swing. No worse than shoveling coal, but what would happen when he connected with the speeding ball?

The Lehigh pitcher took the mound. With the second throw, Matthew observed how the ball dropped low right when it got to the plate.

Strike two!

Strike three!

Matthew's turn at bat.

He stepped to the home plate and steadied himself.

The first pitch flew by. The second.

Whistles sounded from the Krebs bench, and Raphael shouted, "You'll miss every ball you don't swing at, Matt Jameson!"

The Lehigh pitcher spat on the baseball and rubbed it. Matthew waited. When the pitch came, he swung low. He connected with a jolt that went straight to his shoulder joint like he cracked more than the wooden bat with the ball.

"Run, Matt, run!"

He took off for first base and slid in safe. The Krebs fans cheered.

The next batter knocked a good one, and Matthew made it to third base after a fumble by the outfielder. He rested with his hands on his knees to catch his breath as Raphael stepped up to the plate.

"You can do it, Matt! Make the run home next hit!"

Cadenza. She cheered hard for the Krebs team. Matthew didn't know whether it was because of or despite the black crepes on the Krebs team's arms for men like her husband who had died.

Matthew straightened and glanced over his shoulder. The Lehigh third baseman was standing awful close. Matthew recalled what Fabio had said about Torre's illegal tactic of holding a runner's belt.

When Raphael knocked a deep fly ball, Matthew tagged up after the catch then ran for home, leaving his belt hanging loose in the third baseman's hand. The Krebs fans gave Matthew a rousing ovation.

Maybe he wasn't bad at this game after all. He had scored well with every miner family in Krebs who might know Al Percy.

When the game ended, there was no sign of the traditional Choctaw skirt.

CHAPTER 10

$\mathcal{P}$ace in the mine picked up. No more fiestas or baseball games with the deadline for filling the order tightening like a noose around every miner's neck. When Matthew asked Raphael how long it took to mine the needed tonnage, the big Italian laughed in a way that told Matthew they weren't in good shape.

He worked hard, earning extra respect from the miners. He ate lunch with a different group of men each day and casually asked if they knew a miner by the name of Al Percy. None did. After three days of this, Matthew wasn't ready to give up. Someone in Krebs had to know Percy.

At least he would get wages to pay for this trip and not draw from the *Choctaw Tribune* cashflow.

After a long day at the mine on Wednesday, Matthew holed up in his little room, eating the supper Ricco Bianchi's wife had left for him. He hadn't been invited to her table yet.

Balancing the plate of meatless spaghetti on his knee, Matthew reviewed journal entries from the time he'd arrived in Krebs. Not much to speak of, and with the grueling workload that day, he was almost too exhausted to write. But he needed to send Ruth Ann stories for the next edition.

He sketched one out for the baseball game and the reprieve it brought the immigrant miners. He included the final score—Krebs 8, Lehigh 0. Perhaps they should start a section in the *Choctaw Tribune* for sports.

Matthew finished the bland sauce-covered noodles and flipped to the back of the journal where he was working on a letter to his family. Perhaps he should tell them what he was doing. But they would worry if they learned he was in the most hazardous occupation in Indian Territory, maybe in the whole United States.

Matthew kept the letter short and added the baseball article. He should write a story about the potential strike, but he was too tired to keep his thoughts straight and not give himself away in print.

He gently tore the page from the journal. He'd take it to the post office at the noon break and visit with whomever he could in town. There were plenty of baseball fans who would be happy to chat with him.

When the noon whistle blew, Matthew headed away from the coal dust of Mine No. 2. The stiff Mrs. Bianchi had packed him a sandwich, and he finished it as he came to the main street that ran through the Osage Coal Mining Company-owned town. The company was owned by the Katy railroad.

There wasn't much activity on a weekday, much calmer than when he'd arrived amid a fiesta. A handful of miner's wives and their youngsters went about their business, shopping in the general store or paying a visit to the company doctor. Each time Matthew passed an open door, he heard a different language.

The post office was located on the far side of the depot.

Matthew decided to detour through the depot. When a train was due, depots were the best place to learn a useful tidbit for a news story.

His old habit paid off. In the maze of crates stacked head high stood the British mine boss—Tea Kettle Thomas—and the shotgun carrying Sheriff Whitlock who had disrupted the fiesta.

Before they could spot him, Matthew slipped into another passage in the rows of crates. Normally, he would approach the men, introduce himself as Matthew Teller, publisher of the *Choctaw Tribune*, and ask questions.

That wasn't who he was in Krebs. But a conversation between these two important men was worth listening in on. Matthew moved through the maze until he was close enough to hear.

Tea Kettle Thomas looked ready to boil over. "Our best chance is to keep the news suppressed until this contract is finished. "

Sheriff Whitlock folded his arms around the shotgun snugged against his barrel chest. "I'll take care of any troublemakers, including that cursed Hanraty."

Thomas frowned as a train whistle sounded, alerting the depot that the Katy was fast approaching and ready to take on a load of coal. The two men headed out to the platform. Matthew hugged the crates as they passed him unseen.

Keep the news suppressed…

When he was ten, Matthew subscribed to his first Eastern newspaper, straight from Washington, D.C. He wanted to learn how the U.S. government operated daily, how it impacted his people, what he needed to do when he grew up. Then he subscribed to another D.C. newspaper. And a paper from Muskogee Indian Territory. One in McAlester.

He quickly learned no two newspapers were the same. He wrote to them to correct facts in their stories. His letters went unanswered except one. An editor wrote back and said an ordinary citizen wasn't smart enough to understand the news and needed to have it interpreted for them.

Matthew still carried that letter in his Bible. It had driven him to work for the *Dickens Herald* in the newly formed town of Dickens five years before. That paper was no different than the others, but he learned the inner workings of the newspaper business. After three years, he started his own.

Suppress the news.

This was the thing Matthew had set out to fight, to wield the *Choctaw Tribune* as a weapon of truth, a way of letting people read all sides of a story and draw their own conclusions.

An article was forming in Matthew's mind. No matter how tired he was, he had to write this evening and send the story off to Ruth Ann, though it wouldn't be printed for a week.

But writing about the strike and how it affected his people wasn't his reason for being in the coal mining town. He was there to find a man that knew who his father and brother's killers were. If he didn't stay focused, he'd get derailed as he had the past several months.

Matthew went to the post office on the other side of the depot. He dropped off his letter home and managed to bring Percy's name into the brief conversation with the postmaster. No recognition showed from the man who should know everyone in town.

The mine whistle sounded, calling workers back from the noon meal.

Matthew had a lot of work to do.

CHAPTER 11

On Friday, Raphael Bianchi invited Matthew to supper at his house to celebrate the week ending, and survival. Matthew was hesitant at first since he didn't want people asking him questions socially. But Raphael indicated half of Krebs would be there. Maybe someone who knew Al Percy?

Matthew accepted Raphael's invitation. It was better than a cold-spirited evening at Ricco's.

The Bianchi brothers lived at opposite ends on one row of company houses. As Matthew made the walk at dusk, he joined several Italian miners and their families as they paraded to Raphael's. Torre, face still bandaged from burns, leaned heavily on Fabio, but they greeted Matthew cheerfully as they came alongside him. Torre congratulated Matthew on his run to home plate.

Multiple nationalities were gathered inside and outside Raphael's house, passing jugs of Choc beer. Voices from a group rose in chorus:

Show me a Scotchman who loves not the thistle,

Show me an Englishman who loves not the rose.
Show me a true-hearted son of old Erin
Who loves not the land where the Shamrock grows.

Delicious aromas wafted from the kitchen, and Matthew went inside, prepared to fill up. Ricco's wife practiced sparseness at mealtimes, so Matthew wasn't about to pass up the lasagna, crusty bread, and fresh grated cheese Raphael's wife scooped onto his plate.

While searching for a good place to stand and observe people, he spotted the company doctor. This man must know every miner that worked for the Osage Coal & Mining Company, marking him as one of the most important men to speak with. Taking a bite of the crusty garlic bread, Matthew made his way over to Doctor Robinson.

The doctor didn't glance at Matthew as he approached. When Robinson had checked up on Matthew the day after the explosion, he'd said only two words: "He'll live."

Now the doctor kept his eyes down, intent on his plate.

There was just enough room along the wall for Matthew to stand beside him. "I didn't get to thank you for patching me up. Tough business, that explosion."

The doctor responded with a short nod.

Conversation wouldn't be easy. Matthew asked about Torre, how he was healing, and then went into how courageous Fabio had been to pull his father out.

The doctor gave another curt nod.

There was nothing else Matthew could say now except the question he'd asked so many times. He plunged in. "I've wanted to look up a fellow that used to live down where I come from. A friend of mine..." Takba, he reasoned, "...said he worked around the mines here. Thought I'd pass on to him that she's doing well. His name's Al Percy."

Doctor Robinson halted chewing. He looked ready to choke. Matthew held his breath.

But the doctor only grunted, "I keep track of miners by their tonsils, not their names."

Doctor Robinson set his plate on the nearby table with a clatter, strode through the crowd in the kitchen, and out the back door. Matthew stared after him. Did the doctor know Al Percy? Was he helping him hide out? Why?

Matthew set his plate on top of the other and left through the front door where there were fewer people. He had to follow the doctor, see who he spoke with, if he passed messages to anyone. Was Al Percy in the celebrating crowd? If only Matthew knew what he looked like!

Doctor Robinson wasn't on the street in front of the company houses that led back to his office in town a short walk away. Matthew stayed close to the box house, in the shadows, as he went around its corner to see the back area of Raphael's home. Several bonfires lit the area with steaming kettles over two of them.

There was Doctor Robinson, standing by a fire, drinking from a tin mug. He watched the back door that he'd exited from. Watching for Matthew?

Matthew leaned against the side of the house, observing the doctor who didn't seem in a hurry to leave the growing ruckus. The miners gulped Choc beer by the gallon.

If Matthew had a newspaper in Krebs, headlines would be very different from the ones he ran now.

Mine explosion injures four, leaves one dead in Krebs mine

Osage Company Store strips miners of their wages with inflated prices

Mine bosses conspire to conceal truth of coming strike

Illegal spirits flow unchecked in mining communities

Choctaw government held in disdain by miners

The last one concerned Matthew most. If the miners knew he was Choctaw, they'd run him out. The Choctaw government, with its laws and royalties on coal, was considered part of the problem the mine workers faced. Like Raphael said, the Choctaw government would back the mining companies if a strike came.

But tonight, for Matthew's mission, he needed to keep an eye on the doctor, who was on his second mug of Choc beer.

"Why are you hiding here, Matt Jameson?"

Startled, Matthew glanced to his right to see Cadenza coming toward him, a tambourine jingling in one hand. "Are you sick?"

Coming up beside him, she reached to place the back of her free hand against his forehead. He straightened off the wall and out of range.

"Tired from work today, that's all."

He hoped she'd move on to join the festivities at the fires, but she lingered. Cadenza had a way of watching him, like she could see deep inside him. Not something he needed.

The tambourine jingled as she talked. "It's good to laugh when you are tired, Matt Jameson. It makes life…livable."

A rich, reedy sound joined the hubbub as someone stretched out and compressed an accordion. Matthew glanced back to the fires. Doctor Robinson was still there, not as solemn-looking. After a few mugs, was he more inclined to conversation?

Those who'd been sitting around the fires came to their feet when a dance started. Matthew felt a tug on his arm. Cadenza had a hold of it, looking up with a mischievous grin as she pulled him out of the shadows.

"You must dance away that frown."

Matthew dug in, glancing toward the doctor. "I'll sit this one out, Miss Cadenza…"

Yet the doctor seeing him in the dance might help Matthew seem more a part of the community, just another set of tonsils. When Cadenza tugged insistently on his arm again, he relented.

She pulled Matthew into the middle of the dancing, handing the tambourine to another woman who began jingling it alongside the accordion player. Raphael jumped to Matthew's other side, clapping. He was out of rhythm with the music, but no one seemed to care, nor knew what dance they were doing. Then everyone grabbed hands to form a large circle around the musicians.

With Cadenza on one side and Raphael on the other, Matthew was locked in the dance. He lost sight of the doctor, but his spirits lifted for a moment.

Choctaw dancing involved a group of people forming the dance together with a drum and chant, though to a slower beat. The drum was missing tonight, but there was still something invigorating about the accordion, tambourines, a guitar, and movement in the conglomeration of world cultures.

The musicians called out for the host, Raphael, who whooped and danced to the center of the circle, clapping his hands high over his head. The beat sped up, him matching it, laughing. He gasped for air, then pointed out another man to take his place.

Raphael rejoined Matthew in the circle of dancers, hopping and swaying to keep the circle moving, as the other man gave a spirited performance of fancy stomps and squats. The man grinned and shouted as he stomped his way back to join the circle. The people shouted appreciation and chanted for another man to dance in the center.

Matthew tried to stay in sync with the bouncing, but there didn't seem to be a right or wrong way to do the dance.

Then Fabio shouted in Italian across the circle, something about the grignollo. Cheers resounded, and another chant started.

"Matt! Matt! Matt!"

The nervous gallop of Matthew's heart could have served as a drumbeat for the dance. Laughing, Raphael gave him a shove into the center.

Matthew grinned tentatively and shook his head, hands cutting the air in an effort to call off their demand. He looked for a way to escape, but the circle was solid, a dizzying array of colors. He'd almost rather face another explosion than such expectation. Everyone shouting in excitement. Waiting for *him* to dance.

The laughter grew louder. Then Cadenza skipped forward and grabbed his hands.

Matthew followed her lead in a kind of folk dance. They swung around and around, then she released one of his hands to spin under his arm. To his surprise, she fell back, and he had to catch her before realizing that she had ended the dance with dramatic flair, draped back over his arm.

The dancers in the circle broke out in applause. The music stopped.

Matthew lifted Cadenza back onto her feet, and she leaned against him. He carefully took her by the shoulders and moved her back. It was a good thing her fellow, Toby Nicolas, wasn't around.

Raphael pounded Matthew on the back. "A finer dance I've never seen, Matt Jameson!"

Matthew glanced toward the fires. The doctor was gone.

Matthew gave his host and Cadenza a quick nod. "Good evening."

He left the high-spirited people who were pouring another round of Choc beer. He jogged away from the company houses toward the doctor's home above his office in town. No light on there, nor in the downstair's office. The animal shed was empty of buggy and horse.

Doctor Robinson had left, probably to warn Al Percy that

someone was looking for him. Matthew had no idea where that was.

Matthew's only lead to Percy had vanished in the celebration of survival, and a dance that had distracted his focus.

Ricco's solemn dwelling was most inviting now.

CHAPTER 12

Ricco Bianchi's house was dark. The couple seemed to do little other than work and sleep. Matthew started up the steps but halted at the smell of pipe smoke wafting on the breeze.

"Have a good time, Matt Jameson?"

Ricco was seated by the corner of the company house, reclined in a chair. He drew long on his pipe while he stared at the rising moon, a rolled newspaper in his other hand. So far, Matthew hadn't asked the aloof Ricco about Al Percy. Maybe this was a chance since the one with Dr. Robinson had eluded him.

Matthew moved to stand beside the chair, folded his arms, and leaned against the wall. "Mostly."

"I haven't celebrated the end of a week for two years, three months, and twenty-eight days."

Though hardened with grief, the man seemed more relaxed in Matthew's presence than before. Perhaps Matthew had earned his respect with diligent work.

He asked, "The mine disaster of '92?"

Ricco lowered his pipe to rest on his knee. "Many of my

countrymen died that day. My best friend from childhood. My son-in-law. My other brother. My son."

Matthew tightened his lips. Such loss was incredible to comprehend. He still struggled with his own.

Ricco pointed with the rolled newspaper at the bedroom window above him. It was closed tight.

"I married my best friend's wife, Edda, to care for her when he died. My daughter was not happy, though her dear mother passed before we moved to this territory. Edda and I, we don't have much in the way of a relationship. I provide for her. She cooks. We fight. We hurt. She can stand no one in the house, especially young men. Her husband and son were buddies in the mine. They died together."

Matthew looked toward Raphael's house at the other end of the row. The gaiety, the constant need for celebration. It was this community's way of dealing with the tragedies and disappointments that made up their lives.

"I'm sorry for your losses."

Ricco met his eyes. "How is my daughter this evening?"

Heat burned Matthew's neck and face, like burns from the explosion. "Mr. Bianchi, I have no intentions toward—"

Ricco waved the pipe over his head. "I know this. I asked you, how is my daughter?"

Matthew had never seen Ricco with Cadenza, never saw them speak. "She seems happy tonight. She dances and laughs."

Ricco looked to the moon again. "Another question, Matt Jameson—do you tell someone the truth if they do not ask for it?"

Matthew was taken aback. His intention on this journey was to find truth. He couldn't comprehend someone not merely asking for it if they could.

What is truth? Pontius Pilot had asked Truth Himself without wanting an answer.

Before Matthew could form a response, the man went on.

"My daughter blames me for calling off the rescue effort. We didn't tell the families then, but the other miners were killed instantly. We just couldn't stop looking for them. It was after three men got hurt trying that I made them stop. She has hated me since."

"You never recovered the bodies?"

"No."

An unwanted memory flashed through Matthew's mind of two pine caskets, nailed closed. A shudder ran through the core of his being. He hadn't seen his father and brother's bodies.

This wasn't the time to ask about Percy. Matthew's voice would betray him.

Movement on the road coming toward them caught Matthew's attention, and he took a fortifying breath. Ricco stood and dropped the newspaper in his chair, recognition on his face as he watched the rider approach.

The man rode tall and straight, plodding with determination to reach his destination. He halted and slid off the worn saddle. The man was dressed like a miner with a flare of class like a boss. Matthew sensed his importance in the way Ricco firmly shook hands with him.

"Hanraty. You're a long way from home, my friend."

Matthew dropped his folded arms. So this was the famous Peter Hanraty, a household name with every miner in Krebs from what Matthew had gathered in his lunchtime conversations with co-workers. The miners expected Hanraty and his Knights of Labor Union to lead the strike if it came to that.

Hanraty's recessed hairline and solemn expression made the Scottish-born son of humble Irish parents look older than his thirty years. The local ladies liked to gossip, too. Peter Hanraty had immigrated to the U.S. from Scotland in 1882 and worked in the coal mines of Pennsylvania, Ohio, and Illinois. He was black-listed in all those states for his union efforts. He moved to Indian Territory to work in the most dangerous mines in the country—right there in the Choctaw Nation.

This was a valuable man to interview, something Matthew couldn't do directly. He had to settle for whatever he could pick up.

Hanraty nodded at Ricco, but his gaze was on Matthew. "Making rounds with news."

Ricco gestured at Matthew. "Matt Jameson, a newcomer from the south. Jameson, this is Peter Hanraty."

Matthew shook hands with Hanraty. Hanraty gave him a quick nod and turned his attention to Ricco. "You need to call a dawn meeting with the workers. I have news."

Ricco shook his head. "The kind of news you carry will cause harm, my friend. We have a contract to fill for our wages."

"At a twenty-five percent reduction?"

Ricco stiffened. "What do you mean?"

Hanraty gathered the reins of his horse. "News, Ricco. Call the men together. There are decisions to make."

Ricco didn't move. "There are wages to make, too, whatever they may be."

Matthew wanted confirmation before Hanraty left. "There going to be a strike?"

Hanraty eyed him. "The negotiations washed out. We have no choice."

Ricco swore. "There is always a choice. *Tutto fa brodo*. Everything makes soup! We cannot let our families starve. They have suffered enough."

Matthew understood Ricco's reasoning. He'd lost most everything in the mine disaster, and the community was just coming out of the darkness to embrace hope again. A strike might prove demoralizing.

Hanraty turned to Matthew. "You don't seem to have coal soot clogging your veins yet, Jameson. Where do you stand? Do you have safe and profitable working conditions?"

Ricco watched Matthew closely. But Matthew wasn't going to

tell Hanraty how he'd been blasted into a wall his first day in the mine. He wouldn't take any stand in this controversy.

Railroads, mine bosses, strikers, his own people...Matthew was there to find his father and brother's killers.

He lifted his shoulders indifferently. "I'm just here to do a job."

Hanraty smirked and remounted. "A short-sighted goal."

He tugged on the reins of the horse and headed down the row of company houses. At Raphael's celebration, Hanraty would find plenty of men who were fed up with the mine bosses and constant reduction in wages.

Ricco didn't look at Matthew as he brushed by him to go inside the house. He left the door open.

It was early yet, so Matthew picked up the newspaper and took Ricco's seat to stare at the moon, then glanced down at the newspaper in the light of the open door.

The *Choctaw Tribune*.

Before dawn, Matthew lit the lamp in his room and wrote his thoughts from the night before, summarizing what Hanraty said. He couldn't quote him or Ricco without jeopardizing his anonymity, but he could keep the heart of both sides of the story he needed to write about the potential strike.

Finishing quickly, he left the house before Ricco got up. His host wouldn't be at the meeting, but Matthew needed to hear the news. He owed Ruth Ann another article, though he'd tell her to publish it under her name. Odd how she would be his pseudonym now.

But she'd done a good job on the weekly edition he read last night, which he was proud to see included the Enterprise Hotel's first advertisement. He was surprised, though, that it wasn't the larger one he and Blane Johnson discussed. Perhaps there was a change because of the hotel restaurant opening. There was a special coupon for it.

Before he went to the mine, Matthew swung by Doctor Robinson's office. His nurse told him that the doctor made an emergency call in McAlester last night and hadn't returned. Matthew thanked her and walked out, frowning. McAlester had its own doctors. Either Percy was in McAlester, three miles away, or there was someone there who could get in touch with him.

That meant Percy wasn't in Krebs after all. But Matthew had found a trail that might lead to him. Takba had been right about the answer not wanting to be found.

The growing crowd near Mine No. 11 caught Matthew's attention. He could spare a few minutes for that story to send back to the *Choctaw Tribune*. Then it was time to leave Krebs behind.

Three hundred men who worked for the Osage Company in the Krebs mines gathered near the entrance of Mine No. 11, which hadn't been reopened since the massive disaster. Peter Hanraty had just taken a position on a stack of crates when Matthew blended into the crowd that included the miner's families. He found Raphael and joined him.

Hanraty raised his hands, and a respectful hush fell over the crowd. "Fellow laborers, hear me. For weeks, I've negotiated with the owners who operate mines in the Choctaw Nation. Their arguments are the usual, that profits are decreasing and they must cut wages. Again! They are reducing your wages by twenty-five percent."

The crowd erupted with boos and whistles. One woman near Matthew let loose a shriek. Women had trouble enough keeping food on the table when there were no wages. The reduction wouldn't allow them to put anything back for those times between contracts.

Hanraty shouted, "There is no choice. We are shutting down

every operation in the Choctaw Nation until we receive fair wages and safety in the mines!"

Cheers went up, but not all joined the jubilee. Raphael crossed his arms and shook his head. Maybe he and Ricco agreed on some things.

A miner called from the other side of the crowd, "How will we feed our families during the strike?"

Another voice shot back, "How do we feed them on reduced wages?"

Hanraty raised his hands again. "We'll strike as long as it takes. We will win!"

A shotgun blast cut the jubilee short. The people turned to see Sheriff Whitlock aiming his gun at the crowd. Tea-Kettle Thomas stood beside him and held a piece of paper high in the air.

"Hanraty is lying! This is a telegram from McAlester. The negotiations are still going, and there is a reasonable solution being worked out even now. There's no need for a strike."

Someone shouted, "Why would Hanraty lie? He's one of us!"

Whitlock waved the shotgun. "His negotiations failed because he's out for his own gain. Hanraty's trying to stir up the same trouble he did in Pennsylvania. Now that we've got people in the negotiations with sense, everything will get resolved, so just settle down."

Thomas added, "You had your party last night. We are calling for work today to get the contract filled."

The miners grumbled and looked between the hard-set stares of Hanraty and the mine boss.

Suppress the news.

Matthew recalled the moment in the depot, and all those newspapers he read as a boy. He couldn't be still.

He stepped up near Hanraty's crate and spoke for all to hear. "Sheriff Whitlock and Mr. Thomas have their own motivations."

The miners turned toward Matthew. Whitlock swung his direction with the shotgun.

Matthew ignored him. It wasn't the first time someone pointed a gun at him. "I'm not saying one way or another about striking, but you should hear the facts. Send a delegation to McAlester to find the truth before you decide."

Whitlock cocked the hammers on the double-barrel shotgun. "You don't have a stake in this like we do, newcomer, so mind your own business. All the rest of you, get to work!"

Hanraty shouted to the miners, "Jameson is right! Send our own people to McAlester. Just remember, all the mines from Carbon to Lehigh are striking, starting Monday. Krebs will join in..." He looked at Whitlock and Thompson, "...or they will regret it."

Matthew took a deep breath and stepped back into the crowd. He had to get to McAlester and try to find the doctor. If the man warned Percy that someone was looking for him, there was precious little time to find him before he struck out to another part of the territory.

Matthew headed through the crowd toward Ricco's. He would pack his saddlebags, bid all the Bianchis farewell, and be on his way. His work in Krebs was finished.

"Jameson!"

"Yes, he should be on the delegation for sure!"

Matthew bumped into men who slapped him on the back with broad grins.

"And Raphael Bianchi!"

"And Ricco Bianchi!"

One miner spat in the dirt. "Ricco has lost heart."

Matthew tried to twist away from the hands grabbing him, but they latched on and pulled him to the middle of the gathering. He soon stood shoulder to shoulder with three other men: an Italian, a German, and a Frenchman. And there was him, a Choctaw.

"I can't, I—"

"Raphael says you can read and write good English!"

"We need someone with a sharp mind."

"Now go!"

"Go!"

Raphael put an arm around Matthew's neck and yelled in his ear above the ruckus, "Looks like you make plenty of friends now, Matt Jameson! Nothing to it but a stout heart!"

A coal miner delegation? It would provide a good cover for Matt Jameson to search for the doctor. But McAlester was filled with Choctaw citizens who might recognize Matthew Teller and wonder why he was with striking miners.

CHAPTER 13

Matthew hung to the back of the group, them talking away as they tromped down the Saturday-busy road toward McAlester three miles away. He considered telling Raphael that if the news was bad for the mining companies—it would be—they might have trouble getting back to Krebs. Whitlock was too trigger-happy for Matthew's liking. He'd already been in one ambush this month that cost him dearly and profited nothing.

They made good time and soon were in the coal mining boomtown of McAlester, Choctaw Nation, Indian Territory. The town's history was woven into the fabric of Matthew's people. In the 1870s, J.J. McAlester married a Chickasaw woman under Choctaw law. As an intermarried citizen, J.J. McAlester had rights to resources within the Choctaw Nation. He discovered coal seams, staked out claims, and dodged being shot by Choctaw Lighthorsemen. Twenty years later, J.J. McAlester was a prominent and wealthy man in the Nation.

The town held a federal court, the first in the Choctaw Nation, much to the chagrin of the tribal government. Matthew went to the federal court—located in the bottom floor of the three-story Choctaw, Oklahoma, and Gulf Railroad office building—to cover a trial for the *Dickens Herald* before he started the *Choctaw Tribune*. He'd also been to the Tobucksy County Courthouse in town, where Choctaw law and judges handled cases.

Matthew Teller was known in the area. He kept his mining cap pulled low and prayed.

The dirt streets were packed with wagons, buggies, and walkers all in town for Saturday doings. Though the population exploded after the Oklahoma Territory land rush in 1889, the streets were mostly unkept and full of holes. When Matthew was there last, he heard one old-timer call East Pennsylvania Avenue, "Washboard Avenue."

The mining delegation, made up of Raphael and the other two men, halted before entering the busy main road.

"Come." Raphael motioned to the opposite end. "I know a good man who does inventory at the mines. He'll give us a straight story."

They skirted stalled wagons and stayed clear of fast buggies and riders. Down a side street, they arrived at a boarding house where Raphael's friend lived.

It was a short visit. The man confirmed their suspicions: all miners planned to strike that Monday.

On the way back through town, the three immigrant men chattered in a mix of excitement and anger. Matthew put a hand on Raphael's shoulder, slowing him to walk behind the other two men, and said, "Whitlock and Thompson might take drastic measures to keep us from returning with the truth. Whitlock is a desperate man, and desperate means dangerous in this territory."

Raphael boomed a laugh. "Tell me something I don't know! But just to be safe, we'll take another route home. Whitlock couldn't find his own tail in the woods."

Behind them, a voice shouted above the rattle of a passing wagon.

"Matthew Teller! Hey, Teller!"

Matthew kept walking alongside Raphael, steady and slow. "You go on back. I need to take care of something, then I'll be that way."

Raphael gave him a sidelong look. "Wouldn't be a little bambina here got your eye, would it?"

"Matthew Teller!"

Matthew gave a noncommittal smile and patted Raphael's shoulder before turning away between two wagons stopped in front of a store. Thankfully, the Krebs miners kept walking.

He jumped onto the wooden boardwalk and turned to see who was following him. The voice was familiar, friendly, but Matthew couldn't place it in the noise of town.

"Slow down, son, didn't ya hear me call?"

The man hopped onto the boardwalk with ease despite being at least twice Matthew's age. But anyone who judged this man's prowess based on age made a deadly mistake.

"Hello, Marshal Reeves."

Deputy U.S. Marshal Bass Reeves, the legendary black lawman, pushed his hat up his forehead and grinned. "What might you be doing in McAlester, all dressed up like a miner? You joinin' the strike?"

"Something like that."

Matthew needed to be extra careful in this conversation. Marshal Reeves was good at what he did.

Back when Matthew had been shot by Cub Wassom on an isolated road near Finley, Bass Reeves came asking questions. Wassom was tied in with the killing of a white man, too. Matthew held back on telling the marshal all he knew, hoping to do his own work before Reeves cornered his quarry, something he was bound to do with or without Matthew's help. Matthew was unsuccessful, and now the man he had wanted to question about the gang who killed his father and brother, Cub Wassom, was buried six feet under.

Yes, Marshall Reeves was good at what he did.

Bass Reeves gestured to Matthew's work coat and boots. "You're a ways from home. Looking for someone special?"

"Something like that."

Reeves grinned again, looking young despite the flecks of white in his dark sideburns. His six-guns set him apart in a population that didn't wear tied-down pistols. The two Colts rode handle butts forward. While the guns marked him as a lawman, few men he tracked down were privileged to see those guns before he saw them.

"You sure are talkative today, Teller. You after Al Percy, ain't you?"

Matthew flinched. This marshal was too good at what he did. "You, too?"

"Somethin' like that." The marshal casually rocked back on his heels and forward again. "I'm hauling a prisoner from the jail here to Fort Smith. The fool arresting lawman brung him to the wrong court. But I'll be back. Got a subpoena to serve on Al Percy."

Marshal Reeves was well reputed with bringing in hard-to-locate witnesses. And though he was illiterate, he never served a subpoena to the wrong person.

But if he took Al Percy in before Matthew got what he wanted, Matthew would never know what secrets the man held.

"Any leads, Marshal?"

"I got some advice for you, son." Marshal Reeves grew solemn. "You're on a trail that'll only bring heartbreak for you and your family. Best you go on home now."

Matthew clenched his teeth. Marshal Reeves knew a whole lot more about the ambush six years ago than he'd ever let on. "What do you know about my father and brother's killers? Who was in the gang besides Cub Wassom?"

Bass Reeves shook his head. "I'm telling ya, be glad I got Wassom. He was no-good and up to his eyeballs in that killing.

Don't mind anything his crazy old ma told you after the shootout at the Jessop place. Go on with your life. You got a good one going."

So the marshal knew about Takba, Cub Wassom's mother. Why were folks trying so hard not to come out with the straight truth? Why wouldn't Bass Reeves just tell him who the killers were?

Well, Matthew wasn't quitting.

The marshal studied him, then growled out a sigh. "Stubborn ol' Choctaw. You listen here; I'll be back from Fort Smith in a few days. Don't scare him off, hear?"

Reeves dipped his hat in goodbye and strode off the board-walk. He disappeared into the Saturday afternoon crowd.

Matthew stayed still amid the rushing to think. He wished he'd brought his things with him from Krebs, but that would have raised questions from Raphael. Yet he didn't trust leaving them even one night in Ricco's house. The man's wife would throw his gear out the moment it looked like he wasn't coming back.

He would quietly retrieve his things and get a hotel room in McAlester. It might take a few days to track down where Doctor Robinson went, but Reeves had indicated Percy was close.

Matthew headed out of McAlester, though he hesitated when he reached the road to Krebs. Traffic had lightened considerably, making it more dangerous. Raphael's party was supposed to take a different route through the woods. Matthew should do the same. He had left his rifle at Ricco's since it was a short distance to McAlester for four men traveling together in daylight. He hadn't planned on traveling back alone. Krebs seemed a long way off now.

Matthew found a trail cutting through the woods that should take him straight to the company housing. He'd travel quiet and fast.

This worked for about two miles.

Smells of Italian food cooking filled the woods, but a sharp crack and howl ahead stopped Matthew cold. Another yelp sounded, and Matthew sprinted forward on the trail.

Raphael's party hadn't made it back to Krebs.

Three men with rifles and hoods over their heads surrounded the miners. The German and Frenchman were coiled on the dirt path, arms raised, trying to protect themselves from blows. Raphael was on his knees, hands up.

One of the bandits raised his gun to strike him with the stock. Matthew grabbed a fallen branch and charged from hiding with a high-pitched yell. He gained the bandit's attention and whipped the branch across his head, twisting the eyeholes in the hood and blinding the man.

Matthew dropped the branch and went after the next man, who swung his rifle barrel to aim at Matthew's head. Ducking, Matthew popped up and wrenched the Winchester free from the bandit and pushed away from him. The third man was pointing a rifle at him.

Before Matthew could react, Raphael tackled the bandit from behind. The man lost his rifle, scrambled away, and ran wildly for the woods, joining the other two making their escape.

Breathing hard, Matthew listened for signs of the attackers, now unarmed, returning. Silence. They were nothing more than amateur outlaws, unless they had attacked for a different reason.

Raphael helped his companions up while they all spoke at once, in three languages. Raphael waved his hands over his head. "Enough! It is over now."

Matthew kept his gaze on the woods, rifle at the ready, but he handed Raphael a handkerchief for his bleeding nose. "What happened?"

The German and Frenchman started speaking in their native tongues again. Raphael raised a fist as though to backhand them, but stopped and turned to Matthew.

"We could have taken them if these two hadn't lost their heads. Cowards."

Matthew finally lowered the rifle and turned to Raphael with a raised eyebrow. "I thought I saw you on your knees yourself."

Raphael waved off the tease with his big hands. "I'm thinking that *gbenga* wasn't after money. Everyone knows a miner has none! I'm betting they were Whitlock's men, trying to keep back the news just like you said. They want to get the contract filled. That won't happen." Raphael looked toward the woods then back at Matthew. "You finished your business fast, Matt Jameson. Got told off, did you?"

Matthew led the way down the trail toward Krebs, rifle loose at his side.

"Something like that."

CHAPTER 14

When the delegation arrived at the row houses in Krebs, they were surrounded by dozens of miners and their families. Everyone spoke in their native language, asking questions, answering them. Matthew handed the confiscated rifle to Raphael and slipped away from the ruckus.

Ricco was seated alone outside the door of his company house, watching the excitement from a distance. Matthew nodded at him before going inside. Thankfully, Edda Bianchi wasn't around. Matthew gathered his things quickly.

But he hesitated at the back door. Ricco may not have wanted to, but he had given Matthew room and board and shown him a measure of respect. He needed to say thanks.

Matthew went through the front door, saddle hanging over his shoulder, bags over his other arm, rifle in hand.

Ricco glanced up from his pipe. He didn't appear surprised.

Matthew shifted his load. "Thanks for boarding me and pass that on to the missus, please. After the company store takes its chunk from my wages, keep whatever's left to cover what I owe you."

When he got to McAlester, he would sell his saddle rather

than wiring home for money. He didn't need the saddle now, anyway.

Ricco pulled long on his pipe. "Won't be full wages for anyone now."

"I'll be praying for you all."

Matthew headed for the Krebs depot. His gear was too heavy to carry all the way to McAlester, and he was tired.

As he neared the depot, a high-pitched voice called to him.

"Matt! Matt Jameson!"

Cadenza skidded to a halt by him. "I want to go with you, if you're going back to McAlester. I need to see Toby."

"I'm afraid I can't escort you there and back, Miss Cadenza. It's a one-way ticket for me."

She frowned. "You do not need to leave Krebs on account of the strike. We aren't going anywhere."

"I have other work. You'll have to see if your Zio Raphael can take you to McAlester."

The train whistled its approach. Cadenza grinned. Matthew didn't like the mischievous look in her eyes. She turned and ran to the depot.

The train pulled in. Matthew made it inside the depot in time to see Cadenza buy a ticket and go out to the platform.

He bought his ticket, fumbling his saddle in the process. The train wouldn't be stopped for long.

Making his way across the platform, he hopped on board the closest car as the train gave its whistle for departure. The train jerked into motion, and he stumbled, off-balance with the saddle over his shoulder. He steadied himself on the back of a seat. The occupant turned to look up at him.

"Have a seat, Matt Jameson. It looks like I'm going to McAlester with you after all."

Matthew dropped his saddle on the empty bench across from Cadenza and sat beside it. "Why are you so set on McAlester today?"

Cadenza's eyes sparkled. "To see Toby. He will be right in the middle of things."

"Listen, Miss Cadenza, when we get to McAlester, I'm letting your uncle know where you are so he can come for you. You shouldn't run around McAlester alone."

"Well, I'm not, Matt Jameson. I'm with you." She grinned. Matthew frowned.

If Raphael got the idea that Matthew intentionally boarded the train with Cadenza, Matthew would regret turning that rifle over to the man.

Cadenza looked out the window at the wall of evergreen trees flashing by. She began speaking, her voice distant.

"See how the pines bend to the will of the wind? They can not see it, can not cut it with a knife, can not capture it. It swirls around them, through them, lifting their branches, pushing them down, raising them again. Such power from something unseen! There is beauty and terror in it, no?"

Matthew glanced out the window. What was he going to do with Cadenza once in McAlester? He owed it to Raphael, and to Ricco, to look after her. The town would be filled with hotheads from the strike.

But rumors could spread, like the unseen wind she talked about, that he might take advantage of a vulnerable young widow. At least rumors would fall on the reputation of Matt Jameson, not Matthew Teller.

That thought brought no comfort.

Lord, help me.

As soon as they arrived at the McAlester depot, Matthew sent a telegram to Raphael Bianchi, informing him that Cadenza was in McAlester and that he should come for her.

In the crowded streets with evening coming on, Cadenza held

onto his arm. She said Toby was likely at the company row houses, but she was in no hurry if Matthew wanted to take care of things in town first.

He did. He needed to ask around for Doctor Robinson and then at the company houses where Percy may have fled to. But he couldn't do that with Cadenza, could he? Stalling, he headed for the stables, awkwardly carrying his saddle, bags, and rifle with Cadenza on his other arm.

The sale gave him enough to last another week, and he needed train fare home.

The stables were next to the daily newspaper office of the *States-Journal*. Matthew halted by the picture windows and gazed in at the letterpress and shop full of activity that went into publishing a newspaper. He could almost smell the ink and paper and...

Matthew sucked in a sharp breath. Leaned over a tall desk, setting type, was Bill Dodd!

That shouldn't be. Matthew hired Dodd less than a month ago to work at the *Choctaw Tribune*. What was he doing in McAlester?

Matthew moved to the door of the print shop, but Cadenza was still on his arm. He carefully disentangled himself. "Wait here. I have to take care of something in the newspaper, then we'll head for the company houses."

If they could find that Toby Nicolas, he could take over looking after Cadenza, and Matthew could take care of business unencumbered. But this issue couldn't wait.

Cadenza smiled, unaware of Matthew's tension, and went to stand by the corner of the building.

The smell of ink and paper and the clacking of the press Matthew had longed for was more disturbing than familiar. He leaned his rifle inside the door and dropped his saddlebags by it.

A man in a long white apron, every square inch of it ink-stained, greeted him. "May I help you?"

Matthew nodded toward Dodd's back. "Just came to say hello

to someone."

Dodd spun on his high stool, knocking a tray of type pieces to the floor. The tiny bits scattered.

Matthew stepped forward. "Let me help you there."

He scooped up a handful of pieces from the floor and straightened to meet Dodd's shocked gaze. Dodd's chin tucked like a turkey at a chopping block trying to preserve his neck.

"I see you found other employment."

Dodd gulped. He wasn't tough-looking like the miners. Thin, bald, shaken. "I—I, well, your sister knows, I was offered a position here, and it seemed the best decision at the time…"

"When did you abandon the *Choctaw Tribune?*"

Dodd stiffened, his Adam's apple bobbing like that turkey. "Your sister is fine on her own. She had that yapping cousin and—"

"That the reason you left? I was counting on you and Gentry while I was away." Matthew took a step toward the man, clenching the type pieces in his fist.

Dodd came off his stool and pressed back against his cabinet. He raised his voice. "I told you why I left, and that's that!"

Two other workers lifted their heads. The man in the stained apron came over to them. "What seems to be the trouble?"

Matthew shook his head. "No trouble. None at all."

He unclenched his fist, let the type pieces ping on the hardwood floor, and picked up his gear as he left the shop.

Matthew moved out of sight of the picture windows to think. The *Choctaw Tribune* was without a typesetter. Was Caleb Gentry still there, or did he quit, too? Why hadn't Ruth Ann wired?

Because he told her not to.

What kind of trouble was the newspaper in? Matthew should never have left.

But if he found Al Percy tonight, made him talk, got on a train in the morning, he could set everything right at the *Choctaw Tribune* on Monday.

Cadenza.

Matthew's gaze snapped back to the newspaper office, then swept the boardwalk, the street, across the way. She was nowhere in sight. Raphael would have his hide for losing track of the young woman.

A few stores down, Matthew spotted her in a ladies' hat store. He stepped inside, relieved but irritated. Women and their shopping.

"I asked you to wait—"

"Isn't it a wonder?" Cadenza twirled, brushing his face with a stream of ribbons attached to the robust hat she wore.

The store clerk laughed and clapped her hands. "It's perfectly delightful on you, my dear. And it's so inexpensive."

The clerk batted her eyelashes at Matthew. He frowned and used his free hand to take the hat off Cadenza.

"We need to get going. It'll be dark soon."

Cadenza's eyes turned sad. "I just thought how lovely to have something new to wear. Antonio bought me one when...but it's all right..."

She blinked, and a tear slid down her cheek. It was the first time Matthew heard her speak her deceased husband's name.

For a moment, Matthew was tempted to buy her the hat. But what would Raphael, and especially Ricco, think his intentions were if he bought Cadenza frills?

He handed the hat to the surprised clerk. "I'm sorry, but I can't. Your uncle..."

Cadenza latched onto his arm again, smiling. "It's all right, Matt Jameson. I really don't mind."

Matthew apologized to the clerk, who raised her nose in disdain at him.

They went back to the depot and checked for a reply to Matthew's telegram. There was none. He had to take Cadenza with him to the company houses, and hope no one got the wrong idea.

CHAPTER 15

Cadenza guided Matthew to the rows of company houses that lodged McAlester miners for the companies that operated there. The area was much like Krebs, right down to the water wells drilled in the middle of the street, one well per four houses. Cadenza knocked at the door of the house where Toby boarded, but there was no answer.

"Come now, Matt," she said. "There must be a gathering somewhere, perhaps at the Marinos. Toby will be there."

As they passed homes with families lounging in the dusky evening, people called out cheerful greetings to Cadenza but gave Matthew odd looks. In front of a house with four Italian miners loafing around the front door, large mugs gripped in massive hands. They spoke to Cadenza in English, clearly wanting Matthew to understand their words and meaning.

"Good evening, Miss Cadenza."

"Out late and far from home, aren't you?"

"Nice looking fellow there. We should make him welcome."

They set their mugs on the steps of the house and moved forward. Cadenza greeted them warmly, oblivious to the hostile looks directed at Matthew.

"This is Matt Jameson," she said. "He works at the mines with Zio Raphael."

Matthew wiggled away from Cadenza and held his rifle loosely, saddlebags draped over his shoulder. "I've been at the Osage mines, but they're striking there. Is there any work in the mines here?"

The biggest man slowly rolled his sleeves up. "You not joining the strike, eh? Cadenza, bambina, go on in the house. The missus could use your help with supper."

To Matthew's dismay, Cadenza nodded and disappeared into the company house. She closed the door behind her.

The four Italians slowly surrounded Matthew but spoke to one another.

"Didn't take long for the bosses to send out their spies, did it?"

"*Un camaleonte*, a chameleon who changes his principles to his own best interest, maybe?"

"I expected something more sneaky from them."

"Peter Hanraty was right. We won't be able to take a step without stepping on a snake."

Hanraty. Matthew wondered if he could convince the men he'd served on the Krebs delegation just that morning to bring back news of the imminent strike. But they'd just laugh at him.

Matthew nodded toward the house. "I'm here because Miss Cadenza needed an escort. She came to see Toby Nicolas."

The Italians stopped their advance. The biggest man, who sported long black sideburns that met under his broad chin, crossed his arms with their rolled-up sleeves, accentuating his bulging forearms that threatened the shirt seams. "What interest have you in our little Cadenza?"

"I've been boarding with Ricco Bianchi. Figured I owed it to him to look after his daughter. He's a good man." *Hope they think so, too.*

The four abandoned their circle to stand in front of Matthew. He could smell the strong odor of Choc beer on their collective breath as they examined him closer in the falling darkness.

The big man nodded. "You are a fine judge of character, Matt Jameson." He squinted, looking Matthew up and down. "No wonder our Cadenza took to you. You bear a strong resemblance to Toby Nicolas."

The others nodded in agreement.

"Where is he?" Once Matthew turned Cadenza over to him, he'd be free to continue his search.

The men shuffled and glanced over their shoulders toward the house. "Toby is laid up at the doctor's. Almost got caught under a runaway pit car. Saved a man's life doing it, but he got busted good. He asked us not to tell Cadenza should she come around looking for him. Not til some of the damage heals."

"I see." No help there.

Another man in the group stepped closer to him. Matthew braced, but then the man grinned. "Say, didn't you play for Krebs in the game a week past?"

Matthew nodded.

"Aha!" He jabbed the big man with an elbow. "This is the fellow I told you of, who left his belt in the cheater's hand to score the first run of the game. Helped win it, and me, my bet!"

The men laughed, the tension easing out of the moment. Matthew took advantage of it. "Maybe you could help me with some information. I've been trying to look up a fellow. His name's Al Percy."

The name changed the atmosphere. The big man stared at Matthew, hard. "You know Percy?"

This was a different sort of reaction than Doctor Robinson had. "Something like that."

"A close friend of yours?"

Matthew shook his head.

"Then we will stay on pleasant matters, such as they are. Tonight is our last to feast before hunger takes over. Join us!"

Matthew held his frustration in check. What had Percy done to upset these men?

"Thanks, but I have to move on. I'm sure Raphael Bianchi will be here tonight or in the morning for Cadenza."

He turned, only to find himself surrounded by the Italians again. Thankfully, they were grinning instead of clenching their fists.

"What's your hurry, grignollo? You said you wanted work, well, we have some for you. The missus made a whole kettle of Choc beer that needs drinking!"

Matthew shrugged, still trying to move away, but they pushed him along toward the back of the house. One of the men took his gun and another his saddlebags. They tossed them carelessly by the house.

The back area was lit by a fire under the kettle. The big man bellowed a laugh. "Mrs. Marino, come on out here and meet the grignollo. Cadenza, come dance with us!"

Someone picked up an accordion. The back yard flooded with light when the door opened, and three women emerged, Cadenza coming out behind them. They carried mugs and lanterns.

People of all ethnic groups started coming out from the houses around them, singing and swinging their mugs high. The kettle wouldn't last long.

Matthew drew back into the shadows and watched the growing crowd. Tragic times were coming. Hunger. Fear. Violence.

Tonight, they celebrated.

Matthew came against the wall of the house, all of his energy and drive for the day gone. He slid down the wall onto the cold ground.

He leaned his head back and watched and wished he was home. Saturday night. His family, his friends, his community would be at the all-night singing taking place at the First Baptist Church of Dickens. He was a long, long way from there.

But he would stay focused on his task. Nothing was going to stop him from finding the truth—not Marshal Bass Reeves' warning, not a tight-lipped doctor, not striking miners, not sweet little Cadenza.

Do justly. Love mercy…

he sale of Choctaw beer, a drink compounded of barley, hops, tobacco, fishberries, and a small amount of alcohol, is manufactured without stint in many portions of this agency, especially in the mining communities. Many miners insist that it is essential to their health, owing to the bad water usually found in mining camps, and they aver that they use it rather as a tonic or medicine than as a beverage, and this idea, that it is a proper tonic, is fostered and encouraged by some physicians. But it is somewhat remarkable as a fact in the scientific world that the water is always bad in the immediate mining centers, but good in the adjacent neighborhoods. —Indian Agent Dew M. Wisdom

"I'll be there soon." Ruth Ann didn't look up from reading Agent Wisdom's report by light of the lamp on Matthew's desk. She needed to decide whether to include this part about the mining community in Tuesday's daily edition. Saturday morning and afternoon moved far too fast for her to catch up and hope to have a fresh start on the next week. Lance hadn't been able to help much at the newspaper with finishing repairs to the church roof, and school about to start again. And she'd hoped Matthew would be home by now.

It was already past supper, darkness settled in, and still much to do. Ruth Ann couldn't work on Sunday, and Monday's edition wasn't ready for typesetting.

Peter should have understood, but instead, her cousin leaned over the desk and twisted the lamp knob to where she couldn't see the report.

"Peter!" She swatted at him and started to turn the lamp back up, but he stayed her hand.

"Come on, Annie. The singing is half over, and everyone at the church has already eaten. Won't even be leftovers soon."

Ruth Ann raised her eyes to meet Peter's in a way that told him she wasn't in a playful mood. "I told you, go on ahead. I have to finish laying out the articles for Monday."

Peter lifted his hand, and she turned the knob. But instead of leaving, he settled on the edge of the desk, right on top of the report.

"I know, and I'm really proud of how you've managed five daily editions in a row. The Enterprise Hotel says we had more advertisements come in for the restaurant than the *Dickens Herald* this week. But you've got to ease up. You're turning into a monster, here and at home. That is, if you were ever home."

Ruth Ann ignored his comment and flipped through her stack of notes and letters from readers. One caught her eye that she'd put off making a decision on.

A man who signed his name as "Big Injun" wrote to the paper, accusing the ruling Progressive party in the Choctaw Nation of corruption by tolerating alcohol in the territory.

The Government license that they talk so much about does not protect them from the local laws and this is as plain as a Billy Goat on a rock fence. Now what are our officers going to do? They have either got to say that they are taking pie or throw up the sponge! We want this business stopped.

It went well with Agent Wisdom's report, but would Matthew publish this anonymous, colorful opinion? Then again, he'd never faced having to publish content on a daily basis, or directly competing for an advertiser's business. Mr. Johnson passed by the window earlier that week and gave her a respectful nod. But afterward, the latest edition of the *Dickens Herald* featured a front page review of the town's newest and grandest hotel.

Ruth Ann added the anonymous letter to the publishing pile. "I'm doing what I need to do. Now go on. If I don't have some quiet, I'll never get this done."

Peter sighed deep, causing her to look up at him from her seat. His eyes were bloodshot. He worked as hard as she did on the daily editions.

"Annie, you know this isn't what Matthew wants you doing. You'll be an old lady by the time he gets home—"

"Stop." Ruth Ann's tone was sharp, but she didn't want Peter talking about her brother. What if he'd been ambushed like last fall? How much danger was he in? It was too much to think on and keep the newspaper running at the same time.

Ruth Ann felt Peter's hand soft on her shoulder. She relaxed into it and said, "Tell Mama I'll be there later. The singing's going to go all night, you know." She tried to sound light-hearted, but her tone was dull.

The monthly hymn singing at the church brought in families from twenty miles away, then lasted all night and most the day on Sunday. Ruth Ann hadn't missed since the church started doing them at the beginning of the year. She'd just be late, was all. Very late.

Peter shook his head and fished around in his pocket. He produced a key and waved it at her. "I'm locking the door behind me. I'll be back soon with food, if there's any left. I'm not leaving you in this office alone all night."

Once he left, Ruth Ann focused on the stack of stories she'd chosen for the next two editions. Doubt clouded her thoughts.

Her energy and willpower were gone. Trying to match her brother's talent left her knowing how inadequate she was. Why had he entrusted the newspaper to her? What could be more important to him than the *Choctaw Tribune*?

Exhausted, Ruth Ann cried a little over the messy desk.

❧

With the blessed warmth of the spring evening, the crowd at the church spilled out and scattered around the yard area lit with a dozen lanterns. Della moved inside and out while she served food, collected used dishes, spoke with family and friends, and absorbed the happiness in every moment. Her heart might tingle with happiness itself except for the absence of her children. All three of them.

Della poured mugs of cider and gave them to the singers inside the church. Several families were taking turns leading the hymns, and Della knew how parched that left a body's throat.

The Tellers once sang and read the Bible as a family most every night: Jim, her strong, wise, handsome husband; Philip, their rambunctious one; Matthew, level-headed and sure; and little Ruth Ann, the baby girl, coming into her own. None of them were with her tonight.

Della moved to the east side of the church wall, clapping her hands in rhythm with the song.

> *This is all my hope and peace,*
> *Nothing but the blood of Jesus,*
> *This is all my righteousness,*
> *Nothing but the blood of Jesus.*

She looked across the room to see her brother Preston Frazier singing along. Most of his brood was present—grown children with their spouses and grandchildren. It was good to see them all together.

It was also good to have the mixture that made up the town of Dickens and the surrounding area. When they first began the all-night hymn singings, only Choctaws in the congregation came, except for Pastor Rand. Gradually, the rest of the congregation caught on. Now, all races gathered to rejoice in song and praise.

It was good.

After a few more songs, Della went outside in the cool night. A dozen people meandered around the churchyard, talking, praying, laughing.

But someone stood alone under a tree by the wagons. Della moved toward the familiar figure.

Amarillo Jessop didn't flinch when Della approached her in the darkness. The young woman gripped a shawl wrapped tight around her shoulders. "G'evening, Mrs. Teller. Didn't want to disturb the doings."

Della motioned to the lit-up church. "It's open to all."

Amarillo dipped her head. "I know, but it's not like Sunday morning. And I come for another reason. Is that woman, that lady, Mrs. Warren, hereabouts?"

"She went home after the meal. She needs rest after excitement." Della touched the young woman's arm. Amarillo was trembling. "What is wrong?"

"Everything, just everything." Amarillo's voice cracked like spring ice. Her fingers loosened on the shaw. "The Choctaw landowner where we're tenants, he wants us out. The land hasn't turned out a good crop since Daddy died, and the man figures we can't manage on our own. Maybe we can't."

Amarillo's shawl dropped off one shoulder. "It's foolish, but I thought maybe Mrs. Warren meant what she said about us moving in. I wouldn't for myself, but the young'uns need a place to sleep."

Since Susan Warren made her rash though heartfelt offer,

Della had considered the possibilities. There was one problem she always came back to. But it was not her place to say, and she could give Amarillo no advice. "You need to speak with Mrs. Warren. Come, we'll go now."

Amarillo resisted the hand Della cupped around her arm. "I hate to bother her if she's not feeling well."

"When do you need to leave your home?"

Amarillo lowered her eyes. "He wants us gone by morning. He has another family ready to move in and start planting."

"Then now it is."

Della tugged on Amarillo's arm, and the young woman reluctantly followed. But instead of going to the Warren's home, Della directed their steps to the newspaper office to get Ruth Ann. She would best know what to do with Lance Fuller when he heard the news.

Amarillo hung to the back of the group heading to the Warren home at the other end of the road from the newspaper office. Her gut twisted with nerves and fears. How could she even think of begging to live with near-strangers? Worse, with Lance Fuller? Yet she was. Had to. For her siblings.

At the end of the road, the house came into sight. Amarillo's heart beat double-fast. It was a mansion.

She halted, staring at the three-story house, unable to believe this was where Lance Fuller lived. He was so…real, down-to-earth. Kind.

On the walk in the darkness from the shanty to the church, she'd let her mind wander to him, to the moments they spent together working in her garden behind the shanty, of watching him at the plank board table with Neches and Glenrose, gently explaining parts of their lessons they didn't understand. He glanced up once and caught her staring. He smiled. That fine, fine smile. She visualized seeing that smile regularly at the Warren home and imagined perhaps they might plant another kind of garden together someday.

How ridiculous, those thoughts! What a curse that she was forced to that mansion, to show herself as the helpless beggar she was.

Light peered around red velvet curtains in the parlor of the Warren house. Someone was awake. Amarillo caught up to the other two women already on the porch. Della Teller glanced back at her, but Amarillo avoided meeting her gaze.

Ruth Ann Teller rapped on the door in a way that grated Amarillo's teeth. The younger Teller woman wasn't overjoyed at the interruption to her work at the newspaper shop. Amarillo couldn't blame her. Who wanted to spend their Saturday evening trying to place misfits? But Ruth Ann hadn't complained, just picked herself up and led the way.

Shuffling sounded inside the house before the door opened to a bewildered Lance Fuller. His shirt hung loose, hair mussed, a newspaper dangling loosely in his fingers. He dropped the paper at the sight of the entourage on his porch. Ruth Ann spoke first.

"Sorry about the late hour, Lance, but we have something urgent to discuss with your aunt."

Lance Fuller took a step back, opening the door wide, but moving slightly behind it. "Oh. Of course. Come in."

He scrambled to tuck his shirttail in. Ruth Ann muttered something to him as she passed. Amarillo kept her eyes down, but she couldn't help noticing how comfortable the two were with each other.

A flare lit up in her stomach. Jealousy? No. It was fiery pain, a pain of the sudden truth of her fantasies. Lance Fuller was a decent, God-fearing man who deserved a worthy young woman like Ruth Ann Teller. Not the soiled Amarillo Jessop.

From a doorway that led to the kitchen, an older woman

wearing a large apron appeared. A servant. How many did the Warrens have?

"Well, good evenin', Miss Teller. What brings you all out so late?"

"Hello, Mabel. Is Mrs. Warren still up? It's very important we speak with her. With you all, really."

"Make yourselves comfy in the parlor while I fetch her." Mabel headed down the hall toward where Amarillo suspected the bedrooms were. But who knew in a house so large? A wide staircase led to the next floor, and Amarillo shuddered.

Ruth Ann directed the little group toward the parlor. Lance just stood in the hall.

Wall sconces and a pair of cranberry-colored oil lamps lit the room and carpeted floor. The sofa was a matching color of rich cranberry. Cloth buttons. Two mustard-colored armchairs with mahogany wood trim faced the sofa.

Della went to the fireplace and added more wood, bringing the sleepy fire to awake in the cool room. Amarillo planted herself on the sofa and sat rigidly. As soon as she got back home, she needed to get after the young'uns with warnings of what would happen to them if they damaged a thing in the elegant home. If they were allowed in. This was no place to bring children.

She'd see to it they kept to their room or outdoors. This parlor was strictly off-limits for the Jessop clan.

Ruth Ann paced. Lance Fuller finally entered the room, his shirttail in, and he'd found a pair of boots to put on. But he stood awkwardly inside the door and spoke to Ruth Ann.

"How's the singing? I was going to stay, but Aunt Susan was tired." He glanced at Amarillo. She sensed it but didn't return his gaze.

Lance had invited the Jessops to dinner, again, during his last visit, but Amarillo figured his aunt better get more used to them before they came to her home. Too late for that now, though it took considerable restraint for Amarillo not to pick herself up and walk right out of this house. They could never live here! Especially not with Lance Fuller so close.

Ruth Ann absently answered, "I hadn't made it over to the church yet."

Mrs. Warren wasn't long in coming. Her voice preceded her entry.

"Oh my, you say they are all here, in my parlor? Do bring some tea, Mabel, please. Oh yes, hello there, Ruth Ann! And look, the young Jessop girl, Atlanta!"

Mrs. Warren encircled each of them in a bear hug, squeezing the air from Amarillo's lungs as she stood stiffly to receive it. Her family wasn't much on hugs, but this woman seemed to thrive on them.

Della put a hand on Mrs. Warren's shoulder. "You remember Amarillo from the farm. You offered her family a place to live. They need one now."

Still by the door, Lance took a sharp breath. Ruth Ann turned and quietly spoke to him. Fire flared through Amarillo's body, but she banked it.

What claim did she have to him? He belonged with someone like Ruth Ann Teller. Seeing them whispering, Amarillo was quite sure they belonged together.

Then Lance looked at Amarillo, and she couldn't break the gaze. There was that familiar tenderness in his eyes that he had for her siblings, and suddenly, she realized what she had thought was genuine care—love even?—was nothing more than pity. The poor tenant farmers needed his charity, and being the good man he was, he had offered it.

Amarillo shifted so that her shoulder blocked her view of Lance Fuller.

Della explained the situation to Mrs. Warren, who burst out at the end, "Of course, of course! We have plenty of room. Mabel and I will get everything prepared. Yes, right away!"

She spun around, but Della stopped her with a quiet hand on her arm. "We will help. Together, it will be easy."

Mrs. Warren sank onto the sofa and sighed. "At last," she murmured. "At last, there will be children in my house."

Amarillo was already thinking of ways she could leave that house as soon as humanly possible.

CHAPTER 17

In an odd sort of way, it made sense to Ruth Ann that they move the Jessops. The family would be good company for Mrs. Warren, who was comfortably situated financially. The Tellers and Levitts still paid her for the lease they had with former Mayor Warren for the building that housed their businesses, along with other businesses in town.

But it meant moving Lance out of his upstairs bedroom and into the shed by the church to give the Jessops plenty of room. Ruth Ann knew he meant to give Amarillo Jessop plenty of room. It was hardly fair to a young woman to expect her to live under the same roof with an unmarried man, especially when the two were attracted to each other.

Ruth Ann helped air out the two vacant guest rooms in the Warren home. Those three rooms alone were more space than the shanty where the Jessops lived.

But Stephen Austin didn't give it up without a fuss. Lance had to talk him out of the gun he wanted to take after the landowner, succeeding in convincing him the move was for the best. He was able to somewhat handle the growing young man who hadn't set foot in the schoolhouse all spring.

When they finally returned to the Warren home with the single wagonload of all the Jessop possessions in the wee hours of the morning, Mrs. Warren watched in sympathy as her home filled with the children.

Neches, Glenrose, and Belle didn't touch anything except with their eyes, gazing around in awe. Della took them upstairs to their rooms. The girls would share one and the boys the other, leaving the third for Amarillo and the baby.

Ruth Ann didn't linger. Her mother and Mabel were there to help, and Lance was somewhere about. Ruth Ann needed to go to the newspaper office and finish the front page story for tomorrow's edition. Matthew never worked on Sundays, but then, he'd never put out a daily. She had to keep things moving up the hill, or they'd roll back on them. She headed down the dusty street. The town of Dickens slumbered on Sunday. Growing every month, Dickens was almost large enough to justify its two competing newspapers.

Almost.

Ruth Ann was aware of someone coming up beside her. Lance Fuller. He didn't say anything, just walked next to her until they reached the door of the newspaper office.

Ruth Ann turned the key and entered. "I know things are in turmoil, but I really need to work now."

He closed the door with a heavy sigh. "What am I going to do? She's right there in my own house."

At Matthew's desk, Ruth Ann shuffled through her papers, eyes blurry from lack of sleep and the harried move. Hopefully, Lance would realize she could not be a compassionate ear.

"It was one thing to have her siblings in school, to visit their place sometimes, but now..." Lance said.

Ruth Ann settled in the desk chair and picked up a pencil. Lance dropped into the chair by the desk.

"Aunt Susan needs me in her delicate condition—especially with a houseful of strangers."

At least Lance had more on his mind than Amarillo.

Ruth Ann sighed. "There's nothing to be concerned about." She listed the facts, touching the pencil to her fingertips to count them. "One, Mabel is still sleeping in your aunt's room, keeping an eye on her. Two, my mother is astute and visits often. She'll do so even more with the Jessops there. Three, you can take some meals with the Levitts or with us to allow some space between you and Amarillo. Four, this will give you an opportunity to get to know Amarillo Jessop better, instead of brief encounters at church or for school matters." Ruth Ann tapped her thumb. "And five, it's all in the good Lord's hands, so there's nothing to worry over." She smiled in closing. She needed to get to work.

Lance settled back in the chair. "You're right. I've been worked up all night, and then the move and Stephen Austin…" He shook his head. "I am glad I'll get to spend more time tutoring the Jessop children in the evenings, and even work with Stephen Austin, if he'll hold still for it."

Lance went on and on about the opportunities presented by the Jessop's move, how good it was for his aunt to have children in the house, to have a purpose beyond her lingering pain.

Ruth Ann put the pencil to paper while she murmured agreements every once in a while. She couldn't actually write with his chatter going, but she could finish a sketch on material for Tuesday's edition.

Front page stories, advertisements, bulletins, a recap of the pastor's sermon…

"Shoot!"

Lance stopped speaking at her outburst.

She glanced up, embarrassed. "I can't write an article about the Sunday sermon because I missed it."

That meant she'd have to ask Pastor Rand for a summary. Which meant facing him after missing the service. Which was even more embarrassing. Hopefully, Pastor Rand would understand they were "getting the ox out of the ditch," like Jesus said in the gospel of Luke. Hopefully, they wouldn't all fall into the ditch helping the Jessops.

Lance didn't grasp Ruth Ann's distress. "I'm sure Pastor Rand will give you his notes. By the way, can you include another mention about school starting again? I want to encourage parents to make sure their children follow through. Maybe you could sit in on class tomorrow and do a story—"

"I won't have time." Ruth Ann winced at the sharpness in her tone. Lance finally looked at her.

"Of course. I know you're busy." He started to stand, but Ruth Ann held a hand up to stop him.

"I'm sorry, I shouldn't have been harsh. I just, being up all night and the newspaper, and now doing a daily…I don't know what I was thinking." Tears came up, but she breathed slowly to halt them. They lingered at the back of her throat. "I miss Matthew."

Lance leaned back in the chair again and propped one boot across his knee. "Some friend I am, all full of selfish complaints and not helping around here like I promised. Have you heard from Matthew? Where is he now?"

"I'm not sure, nor when he'll be home." Ruth Ann straightened. "But the *Tribune* will be alive and well when he returns."

Lance chuckled. "No doubt in my mind. And I'll write the school article and also the sermon one. I'm not a professional, but I can meet a deadline. I'll have them to you right after classes. Would that help?"

The tears came on up Ruth Ann's throat. "Yakoke. It would."

The bell sounded over the door. Lance quickly untangled his legs and stood. Ruth Ann raised her head to see Amarillo halt inside the door. She looked straight at Ruth Ann as though Lance wasn't there. "Your ma asked me to tell you we're all eating supper at Mrs. Warren's this evening."

Amarillo stepped back out and closed the door. Ruth Ann

watched through the window. Amarillo trotted up the street without looking back.

Lance's mouth hung open as though he'd been about to say something. He closed it and gulped.

Ruth Ann sighed. "I'll see you at supper."

Lance nodded, but he didn't utter a sound as he left the print shop.

She rubbed her temples. She rarely got headaches, but she might have to get accustomed to them. It would be a long week of putting out one edition after the other. Six altogether, in between keeping up home duties, looking after the Jessops, and making sure Peter didn't irritate their lone employee into quitting.

And wondering when Matthew was coming home.

CHAPTER 18

Matthew stretched his arms over his head, pencil hooked between his fingers. In the privacy of a McAlester hotel room Sunday night, he was working on the article to send Ruth Ann about the strike. The article should reach her in time for that week's edition, but he would send her a telegram to let her know it was coming.

He'd done little that day. Even the Lord needed a day of rest after creating the universe. Matthew had gotten good money for his saddle and decided hiding away in the hotel, recovering, writing, was the best way to spend the day and be ready to attack his mission again. And hopefully, Cadenza had gone home.

The night before, he received a wire from Raphael Bianchi after informing them that she was staying with the Italian, Marino, and his wife. Raphael said all was fine. They had many friends among the miners in McAlester.

Matthew was grateful for the privacy of a hotel room where he wouldn't be bothered by a whole community on the other side of the wall. Or so he thought. A knock sounded on the door.

He called, "Who is it?"

"Peter Hanraty."

126

How had Hanraty known he was here? Matthew wished he could locate people so easily.

He stuffed the strike article in his saddlebags hanging on a hook by the plain wood vanity and paused to gather his thoughts. Hanraty was connected with every mine boss, miner, and official in the Choctaw Nation. Matthew wanted to be prepared for whatever Hanraty asked of him, which was likely helping lead the strike. Matthew wasn't going to get further involved with the miners, even if it meant a good story.

He opened the door. "What can I do for you, Mr. Hanraty?"

"Mind if I come in?"

Matthew kept the door between him and the man. "I worked in the mines a brief spell. I don't have a stake in this strike."

Hanraty cocked his head. "Maybe not as a miner. But what about as an Indian?"

Matthew flinched. Hanraty nodded as though his suspicion had been confirmed. "We're up against more than mine bosses. We need an ally within the Choctaw Nation. Can you, in good conscience, support the current working conditions in the mines?"

"What makes you think I have any influence?"

"You've shown yourself as an educated Indian like those running the tribe now. You're smart enough to know you can't stand in the middle during the strike. You have to choose a side."

Matthew didn't want to make an enemy, but there was little left for him to say. "I'm not here to get involved, Hanraty. Once I complete my business, I'm going home."

Hanraty shrugged. "I misjudged you. I thought you were a man who couldn't stand by while injustice happened. Good evening, Matt Jameson."

Matthew let Peter Hanraty leave without argument. He closed the door.

Do justly. Love mercy. Walk humbly with thy God.

~

With the strike officially underway, the town buzzed with gossip and fear. Matthew spent part of Monday morning at the company houses—opposite where the Italians were—but the people he encountered couldn't speak English well. Or didn't want to with a stranger. Even in mining clothes, he stuck out like a sore thumb in this new community.

He went to the McAlester doctor's office to ask about Doctor Robinson's mysterious visit to the town. This doctor claimed he knew nothing of his colleague's visit, and acted as though it would be highly unusual.

Leaving, Matthew caught sight of a newspaper discarded on a pickle barrel standing on the boardwalk outside the general store.

The masthead was as familiar as the back of his hand. He scooped the paper up. He had read the edition Ruth Ann published in his absence, and the next wasn't due out until later in the week. This was neither of the above. The edition was dated the previous Friday.

Matthew sank onto the barrel as he read over the headlines of the thin newspaper. It was high quality, just as people had come to expect from the *Choctaw Tribune*. But two little words below the masthead made his head pound.

Daily Edition.

Daily! How was that possible? For a terrible moment, Matthew wondered if someone had shanghaied his newspaper and set out to run it into the ground. But no. There was Ruth Ann Teller's name on most of the articles. His sister was putting out a daily edition of the *Choctaw Tribune*.

Was that why Dodd had abandoned his post? What was going on back home?

Matthew rubbed his forehead, reading each column at lightning speed. The edition was well done, though three typographical errors made him cringe. There was certainly plenty of news to put out a daily. But they weren't capable of that yet. Or so he had thought.

He needed to get home, prevent things from becoming a disaster that destroyed their hard efforts in building up the *Tribune*.

But he couldn't leave McAlester yet. Bass Reeves would return soon and take Al Percy in for questioning. Matthew must find the witness first. He had to make him talk.

It wouldn't be easy with the strike going, especially since Hanraty knew Matthew wasn't who he claimed to be. Would the man give him away? If it helped with the strike effort, he would.

Matthew made his way back to the mining community. Marino knew Percy.

The dirt roads running between the company houses were clustered with men and families talking. The women handed out plenty of mugs.

Matthew passed one group, the men talking over one another. They spoke in English, the common language among the nationalities represented.

"The mine bosses say a dollar will look the size of a cartwheel before this is over, but that they won't have us back at any price."

"Hanraty says his safety requirements must be regarded with equal importance as our wage."

"We must have a unifying mantra! For those who have died in explosions. Percy will be remembered!"

Matthew halted, shocked, as the men shook their fists in the air and began shouting to other groups.

"Remember Percy!"

"We will not work!"

"Fight on!"

Matthew grabbed the arm of a young boy going by. "What happened? Who was killed?"

At the boy's indignant look, Matthew added, "I came from Krebs, and just heard about an accident here. Who was killed?"

The boy pulled his arm free. His face was young but already aged with the dark lines of years spent underground. "You're the only one who knows nothing. Al Percy and his buddy were working a tunnel when a fire dust explosion rocked a car loose. Two other men were bad hurt. They say Percy was killed as soon as he was hit by the car." The boy joined in shouting the battle cries.

Matthew stood, stunned, as the cheers and threats the miners tossed around continued. The boy's words echoed through his being.

Al Percy was killed…as soon as he was hit…

All of Matthew's work was for nothing. He had nothing to show for the loss of his horse. For the instability at the *Choctaw Tribune*. For the grief of his family.

Nothing.

A hand shook his arm. "Well, are you coming or not?"

Matthew glanced at the boy still beside him, a scowl on his face. Matthew blinked. "Come where?"

"You don't listen to nothing, do you? There's a mine down in Savanna that's not shutting down."

The boy jerked a thumb to point over his shoulder at the people scattering to their houses. Some were already returning with clubs and pickaxes.

The boy smirked. "We're going to make sure those fellers in Savanna know how important this strike is."

Matthew shook his head, and the boy gave a huff before joining the mob.

He might never know about his father and brother's killers. Not unless there was another lead. Bass Reeves? Doctor Robinson? Matthew didn't want to quit. But he had to go home now. He could try again someday.

A man standing on a crate waved his arms and shouted loud

enough to command attention. Apparently, he was respected because the people quieted.

"Listen, all of you! We must exhibit an organized front. Gather provisions for tomorrow, and make a banner. We'll show them exactly how united we are, how we will win! Agreed?"

The people cheered, and the man hopped down from the crate. The crowd dispersed, but hot tempers still flared.

Several men passed Matthew, bumping into him. He was off-balance over the news of Percy's death.

One thing would help ground him. He relented to his reporter instincts and approached the man who had stood on the crate. Matthew reached out and shook his hand. "Matt Jameson from Krebs. How many of the mines aren't joining the strike?"

Up close, Matthew recognized the doubt in the man's eyes as he watched the swaggering miners. "All of them soon enough. But the hotheads never last. We need good, level-headed men to make the strike work."

"I heard about Al Percy." Matthew watched for any reaction. None. "Seems some of the miners will stay in the strike to honor his memory."

The man muttered, "Al Percy became worth something when he died." The man looked Matthew in the eyes for the first time. "I'm Devlin Bishop. I came from the mines in Ohio with too much experience to stand by and watch these workers be sense-lessly hurt every day. Mines in Indian Territory are worse than any in the country, and that's saying something." He looked Matthew up and down. "You said you're from Krebs? What's the feeling over that way?"

Matthew gave a quick answer. "They're joining the strike."

He didn't want the community to become the target of a mob. As far as he knew, they were unified about striking. Except Ricco.

"You seem like an educated man, Jameson," Bishop said. "Keep talking to the men at Krebs. They'll listen to someone like you."

Among so many who had little or no education, Matthew

realized how much he stood out. How often had he been called on as a leader in the past few days?

"But before you head to Krebs, we need everyone down in Savanna. See you in the morning?" Devlin Bishop offered his rough hand.

Matthew shook it, and the man slapped his shoulder before walking away. Matthew stood several moments and finally sighed. He'd just agreed to join a march on operating mines. Breaking that informal agreement wouldn't be the worst thing he'd ever done.

But there was no point in missing the opportunity to gain an up-close account of important news in the Choctaw Nation. It was late in the day, and he could travel home by way of Savanna tomorrow. He would finish the strike article on the train.

Surely the *Choctaw Tribune* could stay on its feet in his absence one more day.

And maybe Matthew would uncover something in that time. Maybe there was someone out there who knew Percy's secrets. And Percy's name was being used as a battle cry for the strike.

Funny how history might remember the man as a hero just because of the timeliness of his death.

*E*arly Tuesday morning, Ruth Ann sat in the lean-to telegraph office and prepared to send a wire to *Matt Jameson* in Krebs. She could hardly believe her brother was using an assumed name, but there had to be an important reason. Still, she remembered the deception Lance Fuller pulled when he first came to Indian Territory. She didn't like falseness, but she trusted Matthew knew what he was doing.

Word came the day before that the miners were striking. Was he covering that story and why he hadn't contacted them? He should send some kind of word!

It was hard to keep the message cryptic yet clear. Ruth Ann finally settled on:

Need to hear from you. RA.

He said to only contact him if there was an emergency, but she needed to know he was all right. Mama stayed up late last night. Each time Ruth Ann checked on her, she was pacing or sitting in the rocker with her Bible.

After sending the message, Ruth Ann squirmed on the telegraph seat, uncomfortable with the quiet in the adjoining print shop, save Mr. Levitt's sanding. She had asked Caleb Gentry to come in early and run a print job they'd acquired the evening before. But Caleb Gentry stuck to his word that he wasn't working extra hours to help them win some "ludicrous race." She wished he didn't know the competition over the hotel was Peter's idea.

She expected the race to be intense this week. What strategy would Christopher Maxwell try next to buckle the *Tribune*? Did he do anything with his time other than plot their demise? He still didn't see that the town was large enough for two newspapers.

Honestly, Matthew never had either. The competition between them was a fierce wind in the sails that Ruth Ann had trouble controlling.

What was Maxwell up to today? Was he focused on another story that would smash the headlines? Had she missed something important?

So far, Maxwell made no attempt to match their daily pace. That worried her. But the *Choctaw Tribune* was still unproven in its new endeavor. The publisher of the rival newspaper might simply be awaiting the shipwreck of the *Tribune* with her at the helm.

With the telegraph sounder silent, Ruth Ann stepped into the print shop. Mr. Levitt had left, probably taking his sanding outside. The early morning was lovely.

Ruth Ann stretched and went to Matthew's desk, which stood close to the back, near the printing press. She would take advantage of the silence and write. But her eyes were gritty and unfocused as she stared at her scribblings for the next story. They didn't make sense. She read them again. And again.

With no one in the shop to observe her unladylike behavior, Ruth Ann rubbed her eyes and yawned wide. She never used to be this tired first thing in the morning.

She tried to visualize the story. Minutes passed. Her head bobbed, and she jerked. She had nearly fallen asleep.

Pencil in hand, she reread the notes, then stared at the printing press. It was too still.

The bell over the door jingled. Her chance at quiet was gone.

Hands in his pockets, Peter whistled his way to the telegraph office. He went in, and the sounder started clacking. He usually said good morning to D at station *Rn* and the other operators. They had conversations and played checkers over the wire when no official telegraphs were going through.

Ruth Ann picked up her pencil again. The lead for this story was coming to her, she could feel it…

"Psst!"

Peter poked his head out the telegraph door. He always whispered when he knew he was breaking her concentration, even though he broke it all the same.

He hissed, "My buddy at the Krebs station said a Matt Jameson was sending messages from McAlester Saturday night. Want your wire forwarded there?"

Ruth Ann nodded slowly. Matthew in McAlester? Why hadn't he let them know?

CHAPTER 20

Every McAlester miner and his family gathered in the center of the community on Tuesday morning. Matthew estimated the number at four hundred people. No children were allowed unless he counted the dirty-faced boys who started working the mines at age twelve. Wagons lined up to help with the nine-mile trek to Savanna and back. Matthew tucked his saddlebags and rifle under a blanket in one of them. He planned to take the train out of Savanna toward home, but he didn't want to be armed on the march.

Two women unfurled a banner to stretch in front of the marchers once they started. Matthew's heart jolted when he read the words: *Remember Percy.*

It reminded him that his search for the man was over, but he couldn't let go. Not yet. He couldn't accept that his search for the killers had ended forever. Bass Reeves knew things. So did the doctor in Krebs. They may know how many of the gang members were still alive. And where they could be found. Matthew had one more day to learn something while he covered the strike story before rushing home to save the newspaper.

As he waited on the outskirts of the crowd, a familiar face

within it caught his eye. Matthew sighed and pressed into the mass of people.

"Cadenza. Miss Cadenza!"

He caught her arm as she accepted a club another woman handed her. The woman scowled but moved on.

Cadenza looked up at Matthew with her intense brown eyes, the club clenched in both hands.

"Well, Matt Jameson, where have you been? There is a fight to be won." She swung the club around to indicate the crowd.

Matthew dodged the swinging club that just missed his jaw. "You should go home. Your uncle wouldn't want you here."

She laughed. "You sound like Toby the way you say that. I went to see him in the hospital and told him about his twin. He is doing well and will dance before long. If we are still dancing after all this."

A loud voice shouted above the rest. Matthew recognized Devlin Bishop's clear resolve as he called, "Are we ready? Are we ready!"

"Remember Percy!"

"Fair wages for all!"

With shaking fists, clubs waving, and the banner leading the way, the marching miners and women headed for Main Street.

Cadenza went to the front where the women led the way. Matthew still felt responsible for her. He owed it to Raphael and Ricco to keep an eye on her.

They marched through downtown McAlester, jamming traffic on the street that ran in front of the Tobucksy County Courthouse. It was a Choctaw court where the laws of the Nation were enforced—if they didn't involve a white non-citizen. The justice system throughout Indian Territory was baffling, another reason so many were pushing for land allotments and statehood.

Matthew took a long look at the courthouse when the march stalled. It was a simple three-room white farmhouse with a steep roof and welcoming porch. The porch was filled now with observers who had stepped outside to watch the marchers. Matthew recognized several of the men on the porch. He ducked behind a tall miner to prevent eye contact.

Along the street, people cheered in support of the miners, and some even joined in the march. Others booed and shook their heads. Since the town depended on coal mining for the local economy, plenty of its people sided with the mine bosses.

The marchers and wagons with them left the fanfare in McAlester behind and began the long walk to Savanna. The women set a vigorous pace.

Before the noon meal, the mines of Savanna came into sight. But miners weren't the only ones working that day.

Braced along the side wall of an engine house, four men stood with Winchester ready. Matthew halted at the sight of them. The McAlester miners bumped into him, pushing him to the side as they passed.

The men ahead with the rifles weren't mine bosses. They weren't sheriffs or deputies or U.S. marshals.

They were Choctaw Lighthorsemen.

CHAPTER 21

Matthew watched the marching miners draw closer to the Savanna mines and its temporary guards.

During the nine-mile march to Savanna, the sky had darkened with the threat of a spring thunderstorm rolling in from the southwest. Sudden storms weren't uncommon this time of year. Sudden storms were never uncommon in the Choctaw Nation.

Matthew fell back in with the marchers before the last of them left him standing alone. Devlin Bishop and three others and approached the Lighthorsemen.

Bishop shouted, "The miners are on strike! Shut this operation down!"

His words were reinforced by the jeers of the marchers.

The Choctaw Lighthorsemen exchanged impassive looks and shrugged. Matthew stayed back where they wouldn't spot him in the crowd. Matthew didn't want to give away his identity. He had the trust of the miners. That put him in a good position to get an impartial story.

Bishop turned and shouted toward the building marked *Office*. "Come out here, Williams! You are going to face us!"

The crowd grew more vocal. Bishop's booming voice could no longer be heard. The women lifted their clubs.

"Remember Percy!"

"Fair wages for all!"

The Choctaw Lighthorsemen looked at one another, worried. It was one thing to face a mob of men. They couldn't shoot women.

And the crowd had gained support, growing to over five hundred by Matthew's calculation. That was ridiculous odds for four men, no matter how well-armed.

Opposite the engine house, the office door banged open. A man strode onto the porch, a dark, fearless expression set on his face.

He shouted, "Beat it, Bishop! You're an intruder in the Choctaw Nation now. All of you! When you quit working, the bosses quit paying your permit fees. All you troublemakers are getting kicked out!"

His last words were tamped down by the shouts. Matthew made a mental note. He hadn't thought about how the bosses were paying the monthly permit fees for their workers. The miners could be expelled from Indian Territory now.

The engine house emitted a whine, a reminder that it was hard at work despite the hundreds of strikers on its doorstep. Beyond it, an elevator cage emerged from a vertical shaft, and several Savanna miners appeared. They tried to ignore the crowd as they went about their work, but that was useless.

Women screamed and rushed past the Lighthorsemen. They scooped up pieces of coal and chunked them at the miners. Those carrying the banner dropped it. *Remember Percy* was trampled.

The Lighthorsemen stepped toward the remaining marchers, uncertain, motioning with their rifles in threat. Their move succeeded by keeping the McAlester men in place, though the miners shook pickaxes at the armed men. Thunder rolled in the distance.

Matthew caught his breath when he saw Cadenza had moved forward with the other women. He started to go after her but knew he could get shot crossing the invisible boundary line holding the striking men back. One shot would set the mob loose.

Matthew prayed. *Chihowa, these are all Your children—miners, bosses, Choctaws... bring Your peace...*

The Savanna miners held up their arms to shield themselves from coal the women still pelted them with. They shouted for help from the Choctaw law enforcement, but the four men with Winchesters were doing well to hold ground where they were.

Williams and Bishop shouted at one another near the office. The men pressed toward the mine shaft, a few daring to leap out then hop back, taunting the Lighthorsemen. They were young. Too young. Matthew remembered Fabio and how quick he was to anger.

He looked at the mob on the brink of losing control. This was not the answer. People would be hurt. Killed.

Matthew sprinted to the office. "Bishop!"

The man advanced one stair at a time toward the mine boss standing up on the porch.

"Bishop!" Matthew got around in front of him and blocked his way. He shouted above the noise, "Call them off, man!"

Bishop didn't look at Matthew, eyes locked on the mine boss.

Matthew pointed at the mob. "You call this level-headed unity?"

Bishop met Matthew's gaze, dark eyes showing he was caught up in the furious energy of the moment.

The clouds began consuming the last of the blue sky.

Matthew hopped onto the top step of the office and looked down at Bishop. "This isn't the way. Call them off."

Bishop finally looked over his shoulder at the women who continued to throw coal at the miners pressed against the shaft entrance. The mob of men had semi-surrounded the Choctaw

Lighthorsemen, who brought their weapons down from pointing upward to aiming at whoever was closest.

Bishop pushed by Matthew to stand in front of Williams. Bishop pointed at Williams with his club. "Out of the way."

Williams crossed his arms and didn't budge. Bishop shoved past him and grabbed the rope attached to the bell near the office door. He yanked on it. The clanging rose above the shouts and screams. The sound gained enough attention for the mob to realize it was coming from their leader.

The miners turned toward the porch one by one. They quieted as Bishop rang the bell again, punctuated by a boom of thunder.

Both sounds reverberated as Bishop shouted, "We came to shut this mining operation down, and we aren't leaving until it is." He directed a plea toward the Savanna miners. "We must stand united. Nothing will change unless we do something. Are you with us?"

The working miners traded looks. More came out of the shaft now, and others cautiously approached from a second mine. There was some murmuring, then they nodded.

Matthew felt the tension leave the five hundred—and himself. He could return home with a story that didn't include casualties.

As quickly as the crowd had turned into a mob, they began to disperse, heading back up the road to McAlester. They were in a hurry now, loading onto the wagons, hoping to stay ahead of the storm. Matthew spotted Cadenza among the women. She would be safe traveling with them back to McAlester.

Bishop started down the steps. Williams barked, "You'll never work again, Bishop. This is your last riot."

Bishop turned and spat at Williams' feet. "If you mean my last strike, I hope to heaven you're right."

Matthew retrieved his gear from the wagon he'd stowed it in, and headed for the Savanna depot. A cold wind snapped around him, warning that winter wasn't ready to surrender to spring just yet.

He looked forward to the train ride where he could write about the encounter while it was fresh in his mind, to salvage what he could of this miserable trip.

He was going home.

CHAPTER 22

Matthew purchased his ticket south with his saddle money, heart heavy that he wasn't riding home on Little Chief. The loss cut deep. The horse had been a gift from his father, and Matthew failed to find his killers. And he doubted how faithfully he had followed the scripture verse that became his mantra for the journey.

He hath shewed thee, O man, what is good; and what doth the LORD require of thee, but to do justly, and to love mercy, and to walk humbly with thy God?

Had Matthew done what was required of him? Was that enough for today? What about tomorrow? When could he begin the search again?

On the platform, Matthew reclined against the side of the depot, blocked from wind gusts that went from cool to cold. He listened to the whistling sounds the wind made, and...

"Matt Jameson!" Cadenza came out the depot door.

He sighed. "I thought you went back with the others?"

"The station master found me before I started off. Toby sent a wire, worried when he heard I went with the marchers. He is coming on the train to take me home, even hurt like he is. I didn't know he cared so."

Matthew tried to smile at the happiness in her eyes. He recalled Raphael saying he didn't know if there was love in Cadenza and Toby's relationship yet, but there was genuine care at least. Perhaps Toby suffered from his own grief, and they were helping one another get through.

That made a difference when someone you loved was ripped away. When news came to Matthew at college of the deaths of his father and brother, he'd gone home as fast as he could to take care of his mother and sister, to comfort them. He'd done it as much for himself as them.

A train whistle sounded from the north. It was Matthew's train, and also the one his look-alike, Toby Nicolas, would be on. That could prove awkward. Maybe if Matthew boarded while passengers were exiting, he could avoid an encounter. He was tired.

Cadenza went to the edge of the platform where the train slowed to a stop. Several passengers disembarked. They eyed each other with suspicion, as though wondering who was on which side of the strike.

Matthew waited by the steps of one of the cars for an opening to climb aboard.

"Matt! Matt!"

Matthew didn't heed Cadenza's call. Enough things were trying to stop him from going home. He didn't want to miss this train.

"Matt!" She latched onto his arm.

"Cadenza, I have to go—"

"Of course, but you must meet Toby first. Toby, over here!"

Matthew turned reluctantly to face his look-alike. The man limped toward them, hand on his ribcage. That was the first thing Matthew noticed as he sized up the man from boots to face.

His face.

In that moment, everything that was true and good and sure in Matthew's existence exploded.

His heart plunged as though the floor had dropped out of a mine elevator, and he was falling down a four hundred foot shaft. His blood turned to ice, and everything blurred. Except the young man's face. The man who was three years, two months, and eight days older than him.

But that was impossible. Absolutely, completely impossible.

The man halted and dropped his hand from protecting his ribs.

"You...you're Matt...*Jameson?*"

He stuttered on the name as though tasting the unfamiliarity.

Matthew dropped his saddlebags from a hand that suddenly felt like liquid. His rifle clattered to the platform. His voice cracked.

"*Philip.*"

Cadenza gripped his arm tighter. "No, Matt, this is Toby Nicolas."

Matthew shook his head, the feel of hot liquid coursing through him. His chest filled, and he couldn't breathe as he stared at the young man's face. *Him.* Toby Nicolas. His dead brother.

Philip recovered first. The look in his rich brown eyes shifted from shock to disgust. He motioned to Cadenza. "What are you doing with her?"

This was real. Philip hadn't died with their father. Their mother hadn't lost a son. Matthew and Ruth Ann hadn't lost a brother. He had been hiding all this time.

Outrage filled Matthew's being. He jerked away from Cadenza and stepped closer to Philip.

"What are *you* doing with her, *Toby?*"

He shouted the last word, but at the same instant, a fist caught his jaw and sent him flying into Cadenza. She screamed.

Matthew righted himself and charged into Philip's gut. They crashed to the wood platform, Matthew on top. Something cracked beneath his knee, and Philip howled, but Matthew pummeled his head with both fists. Philip brought his leg up and dislodged Matthew's position. They rolled, knocking against a stack of shipping crates.

Philip shoved away and stumbled to his feet. He grabbed the front of Matthew's coat, yanked him up. Matthew head-butted him. The action made him see stars, so he took a blind swing. It was blocked. Hard knuckles backhanded Matthew across the temple.

Philip punched him in the gut, but Matthew didn't go down. He shoved his shoulder into his brother's chest, sending him stumbling over luggage someone had dropped near the depot door. Philip fell over a suitcase and rolled onto his face. He didn't move.

Matthew surged forward, but Cadenza planted herself in front of him, screaming in Italian. Matthew started to brush by her, but she slapped him. He stared at her red eyes, tears pouring from them.

This was real, it was all real, from the stinging of his cheek to his brother laying right in front of him.

Matthew carefully stepped around Cadenza and dropped on one knee beside him. He put a shaking hand on Philip's shoulder. "What in the world…"

Philip twisted onto his back, socking Matthew in the eye with his elbow. Matthew wrestled him down.

Someone shouted, and Matthew was hauled up from behind by two men. He struggled, but a Winchester locked around his aching chest, holding him in place.

Matthew spat blood from his mouth. "Stay out of this!"

His spittle landed at the feet of a Choctaw Lighthorseman, one who was using his rifle to bar Philip's follow-up attack.

Matthew shouted, "Where have you been—"

Philip yelled over him, "Jameson, you're a dirty liar! Stay away from Cadenza…and me…or you'll regret it."

Matthew blinked—breathless. Wordless. Philip was a haze.

The Lighthorseman gave Philip a shove in the chest with the rifle stock. "You go on, take your gal and go. We've had enough trouble here about for one day."

Philip took a step back, scrunching his face in pain and holding his ribcage again. Cadenza was instantly on his arm. Matthew parted his lips, desperate to say something. He wanted everyone to understand exactly what he was feeling. The problem was, he didn't know.

As though in a dream where he was stuck in quicksand, Matthew watched Philip escort Cadenza off the platform. Philip said something to the driver of a wagon nearby, and they got on, heading out on the road to McAlester.

The Choctaw Lighthorsemen gave some kind of warning to Matthew then left.

Moment by moment, the platform cleared of human life. The train blew its whistle and pulled away.

Matthew had missed his train home.

CHAPTER 23

*D*ella mounted the steps to the Warren place. These steps were familiar, and so were the events that would take place when she knocked on the door. Mrs. Warren would fling it open and gush how happy she was to see Della, pull her inside and into the parlor while asking Mabel to bring the tea tray.

But that didn't happen this afternoon. Instead, the door cracked open, and a disheveled Mrs. Warren peered out.

"Oh. Mrs. Teller. I wasn't expecting company."

Her eyes were blood red from either lack of sleep or crying. Della motioned to the basket hooked over one arm.

"I brought fresh bread to take to the children at recess. We could go to the school together."

Mrs. Warren's eyes lit up, but only for a moment. Her lips trembled, and moisture filled her eyes.

"I don't think the children will care to see me."

Della put her hand on the door and gave a little push. She had learned there were times to push on a door and times not to.

Mrs. Warren stepped back.

Della entered and closed the door when Mrs. Warren backed away, shaky hands clasped.

"Come." Della guided her to the parlor. The house was devoid of sound. Della wondered where Amarillo and Mabel were. She seated herself and Mrs. Warren on the sofa.

Mrs. Warren sagged against the pillows. She was in her housedress, hair loose around her shoulders in a tangled mess. Normally, Mrs. Warren had herself together by afternoon, though Della had thought she would rise earlier with children around.

Perhaps the children were the newest issue. Having children was unlike any experience in life. Della had contemplated that all night as she'd prayed for her two living ones and grieved the one she'd lost.

Della sat quietly. For once, Mrs. Warren's voice wasn't filling the air.

When she felt she understood enough, Della spoke. "The children have not been what you expected?"

Mrs. Warren jerked upright, meeting Della's eyes and shaking her head.

"Oh, they are no bother at all! They…it's just…" She twisted the bosom of her housecoat. "They hardly say a word to me, tiptoeing around the house, hiding. They don't like me."

Mrs. Warren sobbed. Della embraced her, stroking the woman's matted hair.

When the sobs turned to hiccups and embarrassed giggles, Della eased Mrs. Warren back against the pillows and rose from the sofa. She went into the kitchen. She wasn't familiar with it since that was Mabel's domain, but she found what she needed to make tea.

Della came back into the parlor with a tea tray and set it on the low table in front of the sofa. Mrs. Warren was talkative by then and didn't take a breath while Della poured the tea and sweetened Mrs. Warren's cup with her usual lump of sugar.

She handed Mrs.Warren her cup, not a moment too soon. Mrs. Warren took a breath in order to sip the tea.

Her features relaxed and her eyes closed as she sighed. "Oh, Mrs. Teller, have I ever told you what a simply delightful cup of tea you make?" Her eyes popped open. "Oh, not that Mabel's isn't always. Heavens, please don't tell her I said that. She's such a dear."

Her eyes settled on Della's face, clear for the first time of the visit. "Thank you for coming."

Della took the cup and saucer from her as Mrs. Warren pulled a large white handkerchief from her pocket and wiped her nose. "I just don't know how to love children."

Della set the teacups on the tray. "Give them time. They are frightened, too."

Dropping her hands into her lap, Mrs. Warren's breathing rattled in her throat. "Why are you so good to me? We aren't even related."

Della reached out a hand to cover Mrs. Warren's that twisted the handkerchief. "We are related. Christ makes us sisters."

Mrs. Warren leaned into Della's embrace, resting her head on her shoulder. Della gave her a strong squeeze and said, "You are loving the children. They understand it."

"Thank you for helping *me* understand."

Della and Susan Warren spent the next two hours talking quietly. Della learned Mabel and Amarillo had gone shopping to fill the pantry and cupboards for the expanded family. They likely were having trouble with bridging the menu gap between social classes.

The afternoon moved slowly, with a spring thunderstorm rolling in. Though it sounded fierce, like sobbing could be, it would bathe the land with freshness and renewed hope.

CHAPTER 24

Black clouds spilled a waterfall, a flood from the sky. It seemed to Matthew that people were always in a great hurry when it rained, as if the rain would wash away their illusions of reality. Or maybe it was only Matthew who felt that.

He sat on the steps of the depot platform, hoping for that very thing, hoping for the rain beating on his bare head to wash away the past and reveal a new future.

The depot closed. The rain eased. The station master dropped Matthew's saddlebags and rifle beside him, and said something, maybe asking if he was all right. Matthew waved him off, not committing one way or another. The station master left. Matthew was completely alone.

He rubbed the wet leather of the saddlebags. The sum of his life was in these bags—at least what his life had been. His Bible. Journal. Paper and pencils. Truth.

Matthew had sought truth and found a lie. No. He'd found the truth, all right. The ugly, ugly truth.

But what was the whole truth? What had really happened to his father and brother that day?

Anger propelled Matthew to his feet and helped him hold in a groan from the pain in his bruised body. It was nearly dark, but the road to McAlester was visible.

Matthew slung the saddlebags over his shoulder with a grimace and gripped his Winchester. No one better try to attack him tonight.

The road had turned to a river of mud that sucked on Matthew's boots and proved to be the worst enemy he would face in the trek. The rain didn't let up, but he ignored the chills causing him to shake. He couldn't think of anything other than the questions he would make his brother answer when he found him.

Matthew plowed along at a fair clip and neared McAlester a few hours later. The lights from town were more of a welcome sight than he wanted to acknowledge. From the last clump of woods the road passed through before civilization, a form stepped out of the shadows, stiff and braced for attack. Matthew didn't break his stride and shifted his rifle crossways like a club.

Philip didn't step back, hand on his ribcage. "Do we really want to do all that again?"

Matthew halted so close to his brother the rain hardly fell between them.

"You are a liar." Matthew spat the words, clenching the rifle with all his strength, holding himself in check.

Philip used his free hand to flick away the words. "I know why you're here, but I'm already taking care of it, so just beat it on home."

Matthew had enough of Philip's fake arrogance. He released his hold on the rifle with his right hand and backhanded him. Philip's head whipped to one side, but the blow didn't make him stumble.

Philip slowly brought his head back around, rubbing his jaw. "You don't let go easy, do you? Well, you better listen with both ears like Pokni always said to do."

Pain flared in Matthew, fueling his rage. He balled his fist.

"Don't speak about family. Don't speak at all unless it's to explain why you're alive."

Philip's shoulders slumped, the edgy look on his face washing away. He dropped his hand from rubbing his jaw. Closer, and with no swinging fists, Matthew took note of several days' growth on his brother's face. The Tellers didn't have much in the way of facial hair, but time laid up showed along with Philip's scraggly head of brown hair.

Philip hadn't changed much in six years. He was just shy of thirty now, his smirky grin usually ready on chiseled lips. His jaw was square, like their father, but otherwise, Matthew could be seeing his own reflection in a pond. Not a mirror, just a pond. They didn't look exactly alike, but enough to cause confusion at first glance. Matthew had never thought of himself being as handsome as Philip, but that never bothered him. Matthew's reactions to flirtatious girls in their formative years had been different from his brother. He'd attributed it to their age difference.

Those thoughts were safe territory to dwell in while they stood in the pouring rain and darkness. It distracted Matthew from what he really wanted to think about.

Why didn't you come home? What happened to Daddy?

Philip met his gaze. "I'm still alive to do one good thing. I've been on his trail the past six years, Matt. This is the closest I've come. You don't get out of here, you'll ruin everything."

"Ruin?"

Matthew's chest constricted, and he coughed. It felt like the cold rain had soaked into his lungs. But he took a steady breath and met Philip's eyes. "Do you have any idea what Mama and Annie went through? I should bust you all the way home…"

He clenched the Winchester, raising it chest level, shaking, holding back from striking Philip across the head.

His brother didn't flinch but softened his voice. "Unless you want to cause them more hurt, go home, now. Don't tell them anything."

Philip turned away.

Matthew tossed the rifle and saddlebags aside. He grabbed Philip's arm and yanked him back around. "You think you're stubborn enough to outlast me? You're going to tell me everything, or you'll regret it."

Philip popped his arm free and put his face close to Matthew's, rain streaming down his swollen cheeks like a torrent of tears.

"You want to know so bad? Well, I saw Daddy die! Saw him shot dead. Saw the man who did it. I won't go to the grave until he does, I've sworn to heaven on that. I'm going to trap Dan Holder, and he'll crawl and beg, and then he'll die. But you won't have any part of it, understand? If I have to send you home hogtied, I'll do it. You've never been able to match me, Matt, so don't get in my way."

Matthew heaved a deep breath in his rattling chest and seized Philip's shoulders, shaking him. "Why didn't you come home!"

Philip brought his arms up between Matthew's and broke his grip. He shoved Matthew hard.

Matthew stumbled and dropped to one knee. He caught himself with his right hand. The mud went up to his wrist. He lost his balance, tipping over to sit on the muddy road.

Sighing deeply, he pulled his knees toward his chest and propped his elbows on them. The fire in him was drenched.

A hand rested on his shoulder. Matthew blinked hot eyes. His brother squatted in front of him.

"Look, this is crazy. I know you won't go home, and you know I'm as stubborn as you. We're going to have to work together even if it gets us both killed."

Philip gripped Matthew's chin, leaving no doubt he could fulfill his promise to hogtie him. "But we have to have some rules, like no asking questions. I can't talk about that day." Philip's voice broke, and he blinked several times. "And we can't let people know we're brothers. Keep being Matt Jameson, and I'm Toby Nicolas. We knew each other in Texas. We have a rivalry over a woman. Got it?"

Matthew jerked his chin from Philip's grip. He didn't like how his brother bossed him when they were younger. He didn't like it now. But the best Matthew could do was play along until he uncovered the truth.

"I got it."

Philip examined him over as if really seeing him for the first time. "You look terrible. But from what I've heard, you've done all right for yourself the past few years."

Matthew pushed to his feet, a difficult task with a cough coming from his chest. Philip helped him, though favoring his left side. Matthew wondered how much damage he'd done. "You hurt bad?"

Philip used one hand to work his jaw back and forth. "Well, I'm not hurt good."

Matthew stared at him, six years and a heart full of anguish compressing into one moment. He hooked his arm around his brother's neck, pulling him close and wrapping his other arm around him, holding tight.

Philip stiffened. He didn't return the embrace, but Matthew sensed he wanted to. His brother's shoulders bunched up then relaxed. Matthew closed his eyes, sealing his tears in for now.

The moment passed, and another cough seized Matthew. Philip pushed him away. "Come on, little brother. We have to get you into dry clothes."

He lifted Matthew's saddlebags from the mud and handed them to him, then retrieved the rifle. Matthew stumbled when he tried to step forward. Philip caught Matthew by the arm and growled, "Stubborn Choctaw."

The cough didn't subside. Even in clothes borrowed from Philip and under a warm blanket in a hotel room in McAlester, the cough wracked Matthew's body. With each violent siege, he wondered if the old bullet hole would reappear. He finally drifted into sleep.

Sometime later, a hand shook his shoulder, but when Matthew opened his eyes, it was still dark. The hand pulled on him, getting him into a sitting position. He felt a tin mug near his lips, and he instinctively pressed his lips tight.

Philip chuckled, a sound Matthew thought he'd never hear again this side of heaven. But it was real. His brother was alive and speaking to him.

"Come on, now, open up. It'll be dawn soon, and we have to talk."

Matthew didn't know what was in the cup, but he trusted Philip enough to part his lips. It wasn't Choc beer; the taste was awful but familiar, like the concoction Pokni made when he was sick. Matthew gulped the grainy liquid before another cough rattled him. Philip set the mug aside and lit a lamp by the bed.

Matthew grimaced at the sudden brightness. His body was

sore from the fight and his shoulder hitched the same way it had after the mine explosion, but he didn't have time to be laid up.

Philip leaned back in his chair. "When Doc Robinson came to warn Al Percy that a man named Matt Jameson was looking for him, I had no idea it was my little brother. Who sent you to Krebs? How much do you know?"

"No questions. Remember?"

Philip frowned, then shrugged. "Fair enough. Let's stumble blindly along and see if we get killed."

Matthew swung his feet over the bed and sat on the edge, knees inches from his brother's. "I have a better idea. We each get one question and answer at a time."

He held Philip's gaze, knowing he could best his brother in a staring contest any day.

Whatever he was deciding on, it didn't take Philip long. "Fine. I'll tell you some things, but I go first. Who sent you to Krebs?"

"Takba."

"Who's that?"

Matthew shook his head. "My turn. Why did Doctor Robinson warn Percy about me?"

"Al Percy sells excess laudanum and morphine the doctor has to those who may or may not need it."

No wonder he was a doctor with terrible bedside manners.

Philip didn't miss his turn. "Now, how much do you know about Al?"

Matthew rubbed his forehead. His left temple had a knot. "Percy supposedly knows who killed my father and brother. Guess he can't tell me now. Do you know?"

"I know Al Percy isn't dead."

Matthew dropped his hand but remained silent.

Philip smiled, smug. "Thought that might come as a shock. I helped Al fake his death. You're not the only one hunting him."

"Bass Reeves is, too."

Philip cocked his head. "So. You know about Reeves. Well, I'm the one who set the marshal on Cub Wassom's trail." Philip snapped his fingers. "That's who Takba is—Cub's mother."

Matthew raised his voice. "Marshal Reeves knew you were alive all this time?" He coughed deep, though it wasn't as painful as before.

Matthew remembered Bass Reeves' warning, that he didn't really want to find the truth. The marshal had been talking about this, finding his brother alive. But there was much more to it, more Philip wasn't telling him.

"Uh uh, my turn for a question," Philip said. "I need a new work permit for Al Percy. But I'm running out of time. Will you get it?"

"I'll think about it. Why did you help Percy fake his death?" What Matthew really wanted to ask was how—and why—Philip had faked his own death.

Philip chuckled. "Seems we've been doing the same thing, working the coal mines to get close to Al Percy. Al doesn't know who I really am, and I'm about to trick him into giving up Dan Holder's hideout."

Dan Holder. Matthew checked his mental catalogue of names. Philip mentioned it last night, but Matthew had been too sick and infuriated to realize he finally learned the name of his father's killer.

Matthew stared at the floor, clenching the edge of the bed, his arms trembling. Dan Holder. His father's killer. And he was still alive.

Philip continued. "A few years ago, I met with Reeves in Fort Smith and told him we could work together to track down the Holder gang. I knew where Cub Wassom was, and Reeves knew Al Percy was an informant for the gang, but they had split up. Cub Wassom started his own bunch, and Holder went into hiding. Rumor had it that he wanted to go straight, and Al Percy helped him. That led me here to McAlester, and Reeves told me if I buddied up with Al, we could trick him into giving up Holder."

Philip paused, his gaze drifting. "Trouble is, I double-crossed Reeves."

Matthew resisted smacking his brother. "Why?"

Philip's eyes snapped back to meet Matthew's. "Hey, you're getting more than your fair share of answers. Isn't it time for you to answer something?"

"I'll think about it. Why did you double-cross the marshal?"

Philip leaned back in the chair, grinning. "You're good at this. Did you learn how to ask questions and dodge answering them as a newspaperman? Always getting the facts and details. I've read the *Choctaw Tribune*." His voice softened. "You do right by our people."

Matthew's throat burned with unshed tears. "Why didn't you come home?"

Philip stared at the wall behind Matthew. "I almost did when I heard you got shot. Wanted to go...*home*...so bad. But I knew that would do you all more harm than good. Still, when I read in the *Dickens Herald* that you were dead, I almost..."

Matthew breathed slow, taking in every word. If only the ambush had drawn Philip home. Why had his brother lived a lie all this time?

Philip rubbed the back of his neck, bruises on his face highlighted by the purple hue in the room as the sun began its rise. "All right, enough of this question and answer game. You'll win anyway. Here's my plan: I was supposed to file a permit for Al Percy under a false name so he could stay in the Choctaw Nation, but things sort of blew up, if you know what I mean. I got injured in that explosion we arranged."

"You set off an explosion intentionally?"

"Easy, little brother. No one was in danger of getting hurt except me, and I was willing to take the risk. Al Percy is a nervous man, and the strike came at a bad time. I knew he'd high-tail it out as soon as work ended, but I managed to talk him into my plan to get him away from Reeves, a plan to lead me right to Dan Holder."

Matthew raised his head, aiming a deadly look at his brother. "Lead you, or lead Marshal Reeves? Is that why you double-crossed him, so you could take Dan Holder alone?"

Philip sat forward, all humor leaving his expression replaced by a look of hate so vicious Matthew's spine tingled.

"I want you to listen very carefully, Matt. I've waited six years to put a bullet in Dan Holder's skull. If you don't have the stomach for it, you'd better leave on the next train south. Go home to Mama and Annie."

Matthew shot a hand out and clenched Philip's jaw. Philip jerked and grabbed his wrist but didn't resist.

Matthew seethed. "They have more courage than you. They went on living after Daddy died."

He felt the tightness in Philip's jaw, the stubbornness that ran strong through the Teller family. It kept them together; it was ripping the brothers apart now.

Philip's voice was hoarse. "You think you know so much. You always did."

He broke Matthew's grip and shoved his hand away. "What you don't know, Matthew Teller, will get you killed. Now, I need you to take care of the permit. Time's running out. Will you do it or not?"

Matthew gripped the bed again. "I can't without paperwork."

"I have documents with a false name for Al Percy. They're in your saddlebag."

Matthew rubbed the knot on his temple. *Fake documents. Lying.* How much would this trip cost him? "What else?"

Philip massaged his jaw. "There's the matter of Cadenza. Take her back to Krebs. Tell her I hate her, that I'm dead, whatever. I don't want to be around her anymore. She's too vulnerable."

From the way his brother wouldn't meet his eyes, Matthew

knew what he was talking about. "If I find you've done anything with her…"

"Skip it, Matt. You have plenty of other reasons to hate me. Just do what I say, and meet me in Lehigh Thursday night. And try to keep yourself out of trouble with this strike business, eh?" Philip stood and patted Matthew's head the way he did when they were boys, and Matthew was overthinking their next adventure.

Philip headed for the door, crossing the light of the dawn streaming through the window. The storm had passed.

What is required of thee…do justly, love mercy…

"Chukfi."

One hand on the doorknob, his brother turned at the quiet voice Matthew barely heard himself. He could hardly believe he'd used Philip's infamous nickname. Chukfi—rabbit, the trickster.

He met Philip's unsteady gaze. "I don't hate you."

Philip looked away. He turned the knob and muttered, "It'd be better if you did."

CHAPTER 26

At his hotel room window, Matthew stood in the early morning streaks of light. He wasn't ready to face the next leg in this journey he had thought was over. Al Percy was supposed to be dead, and Matthew heading home. Instead, his resurrected brother wanted him to carry fake documents, get a worker permit, then meet at another coal-mining town amid a violent strike so that his brother could find and shoot their father's killer.

Do justly?

Matthew closed his sore eyes. As much as his heart cried for vengeance, it wasn't what their daddy would have wanted. Matthew had to stop Philip.

Someone tapped softly on the hotel door. Matthew threw on the clean shirt Philip left him, wincing at the pain movement caused as he opened the door.

Cadenza stood there, smile tentative. "Good morning, Matt…" Her eyes widened. "Oh my."

Matthew pulled back, putting the door more between them, but he couldn't hide the repulsive bruises on his face. "I, uh, I'm sorry you were caught in the middle of all that yesterday. He…Toby and I don't always get along. That is, I never knew his last name, and I didn't realize it was someone I'd met before when you talked about him…"

How could he lie his way out of this without lying? And how could he get Cadenza away from this mess without hurting her?

"Let me get my things. I'll meet you in the lobby."

She nodded. "I will wait for you. We must find Toby so you two can apologize to each other for whatever it was you were fighting about."

"I'll be down in a minute."

After closing the door, he checked his saddlebags. The false documents he needed to get Al Percy's permit were in there. Matthew's fingers brushed his Bible, remembering a time he read it morning, noon, night, and all the time in between—the immediate months following his daddy and brother's deaths.

The strike article was also in the saddlebags. He hadn't finished it to mail to Ruth Ann. But the problems of the newspaper were far away. All he could hold in his mind and heart right now was Philip.

Matthew buckled the bags and caught sight of himself in the mirror. His left eye was blackened, and a purple bruise covered a fair bit of his cheek. His lips were swollen, and patches of facial hair made him look like an outlaw on the run. No wonder Cadenza had been startled.

Taking a comb from the vanity, he ran it through his dark brown hair. It had grown out to his collar, longer than he liked to keep it as a newspaper publisher, but it wasn't scraggly.

He found his razor and worked it carefully around the cuts. Rubbing his clean-shaven face, Matthew debated if he looked more European immigrant or Choctaw today. But it had more to do with how he felt than looked.

Today, he didn't feel much but pain.

Matthew gathered his gear and headed out, dreading the conversation with Cadenza.

The young woman was seated on a cream wingback sofa in the hotel lobby, watching people come and go. Delicious smells came from the adjoining hotel dining room, but Matthew didn't have an appetite.

Cadenza stood as he approached. Her smile was genuine.

"Well, you look better. Do you know where Toby is today?"

Matthew's face and heart were too sore to return her smile. He set his saddlebags and rifle by the sofa, aware of people milling around the lobby taking note of them, including the desk clerk.

Sighing, he gestured for Cadenza to sit as he lowered himself. She complied, her eyes trusting. He'd gained a good measure of respect among the miners during his short time with them. When could he tell them he didn't deserve it?

"Miss Cadenza, he…Toby's in trouble."

Her face paled, lips parted to speak.

"Now wait, just listen." Matthew had the sudden urge to strangle his brother for leaving him to break off the relationship with Cadenza.

Well, he wouldn't. There was always another way.

"To be honest, I'm in some trouble, too. And…I could use your help." *Lord, I hope this is the right thing.* "I'm going to tell you something I haven't told anyone else. I hope you don't hate me, but the truth is, I'm a newspaper reporter. I've been getting to know the miners and how things work and writing stories about it all."

Cadenza's lips parted again, her eyes transforming from concern to confusion. Did she feel betrayed? He hurried on.

"I've only written the truth. I want people to make up their own minds about how they should feel when things happen. Please believe me."

Her gaze dropped to somewhere below his chin. She chewed her lower lip, and he waited.

Finally, she met his eyes again and nodded. "I trust you, Matt Jameson. But Toby…is he a reporter, too?"

Matthew resisted a bitter chuckle. "Not exactly. But we are working together on a story. A big one. Meanwhile, I need to keep up with what's happening on the strike. It's important people are informed of all sides, and I could use your help. But it would be best if no one knew why, not even your father or uncle. Are you willing?"

Cadenza studied his face. It was hard not to look away. She could read so much more than he wanted her to know.

She reached out to touch Matthew's bruised cheek. He pulled back. She frowned.

"I'm sorry I slapped you."

Matthew had forgotten about that. He wished she hadn't gotten tangled in him and Philip's messy reunion.

"It'd be best if you didn't mention what happened yesterday to anyone."

It was her turn to chuckle in a bitter tone. "My father has not cared anything for me since…" She laid a protective hand over her midsection, her voice rattling on the words. "…since I lost his grandchild after the No. 11 accident."

Matthew tightened his lips. "I'm very sorry. I didn't know."

She rested her hands in her lap, and her face showed she was back in the present when she looked at him. "Zio Raphael has much on his mind with the strike. Your secrets are safe with me."

Matthew stood. "Thank you. I'm going to escort you back to Krebs before I leave. We'll catch the first train."

She smiled as though trying to lighten the mood. "No need in that. It's a beautiful day for walking after the rain. The wind can push us home."

Matthew thought of the storm within him. *A beautiful day after the rain.* Maybe someday.

"All right, we'll walk." He turned, then paused and looked down at her. "Miss Cadenza?"

"Yes?"

"Your father does care."

He didn't linger for her response. At the front counter, the clerk was reading a copy of the *Indian Citizen*. He quickly ducked behind it when Matthew approached, as though to pretend he hadn't been watching the exchange on the sofa, eavesdropping.

Matthew laid his key on the desk. "I need to settle my account."

"Mhm," the clerk murmured, casually laying aside the newspaper and checking his ledger.

He tapped his temple. "Oh yes. You received a telegram yesterday morning after you left. You...weren't in a condition to receive it last night."

The clerk pulled a slip of paper from a slot in the large wooden cabinet filled with cubbyholes. He must have seen Philip drag Matthew in like they were both drunk.

No doubt Matthew's physical appearance this morning left the curious man with plenty of questions. The black eye and bruises were going to cause a lot of heads to turn.

The clerk handed Matthew the telegram with a flourish as though expecting recognition for his good deed.

Matthew rewarded him with a quick nod, eyes already on the short message.

Need to hear from you. RA.

Ruth Ann. He warned her only to contact him in the event of an emergency. What kind of trouble was she in? Other than having employees quit, and attempting to put out a daily edition of the *Choctaw Tribune*, of course.

"Problem?"

Matthew raised his gaze, irritated with the clerk and his probing. "If it were, it's none of your business. What do I owe?"

The clerk bristled and went to his ledger with a huff. Matthew sighed at his own rudeness. Another mark on Matt Jameson's character. He was beginning to dislike that fellow.

After settling his account, Matthew took another look at the telegraph. What could he tell Ruth Ann? That he'd found Philip alive and well, and that her two brothers were embarking on a hunt to shoot the man who had killed their father?

No. He'd let her assume he was no longer in McAlester and hadn't received the message. Whatever trouble she was in, she'd have to handle it on her own. He had to have faith in her.

Collecting Cadenza and his gear, Matthew set out for the three-mile hike to Krebs. He had to face Raphael and Ricco, and then stop his brother from losing his soul.

What doth the LORD require of thee?

CHAPTER 27

The day after she sent Matthew the wire, and received no reply, Ruth Ann lugged the picnic basket from their house to the Warrens. Beulah suggested that Ruth Ann take a break, find Amarillo, and the two of them carry treats to the school for the Jessop children. And Lance Fuller, of course, by the twinkle in Beulah's eye.

It wasn't a pleasant prospect, though. A few nights ago, Della and Ruth Ann ate dinner at the Warrens, and it was an awkward meal—the silent Jessop children, aloof Amarillo, chatty Mrs. Warren, and tense Lance Fuller. Only Della's presence calmed the atmosphere enough for Ruth Ann to get through.

But Ruth Ann agreed to Beulah's suggestion today. Perhaps it was the burning need to get away from the clacking telegraph sounder, the cranking of the press and the cranky press operator, Caleb Gentry, and the constant strain to put the daily out. Whatever the actual reason, Ruth Ann was going against her promise not to nudge along Lance's relationship with Amarillo.

This distressed her enough to solicit her mother's advice about the situation when she went to the house and packed fresh baked cookies Della said she'd have that day. As always, her mother cleared things up.

"Ask Amarillo if she wants to take the food to the schoolhouse. It will be no surprise to her that Lance Fuller is there."

Ruth Ann headed down the walkway to the Warren home and saw she wouldn't need to knock. Amarillo sat on the porch, rocking, a steaming cup in hand despite the warming spring temperature.

Amarillo gave a polite nod as Ruth Ann came up the steps.

"'Afternoon, Miss Teller. Mrs. Warren is out shopping with Mabel."

Ruth Ann set the basket on the porch. "Actually, I'm here for you. Would you like to take treats to the schoolhouse? My mother baked enough for your siblings and us and all."

Ruth Ann felt silly adding "and all" simply to avoid saying Lance Fuller's name.

Amarillo stopped the rocker. "You don't need me and my brothers and sisters as an excuse to go see the teacher."

Ruth Ann blinked. "What are you talking about?"

"Nothing." Amarillo's steady gaze dropped.

"But…"

In the distance, the school bell clanged. The children pulled the new bell's rope with exuberance when they were dismissed for any reason. This one meant they'd let out for a recess.

Ruth Ann composed herself. "Would you like to go or not?"

Amarillo shook her head and took a sip of tea. The cup was shaking.

Ruth Ann moved closer and placed a hand on her shoulder. "I'm sorry, I didn't mean to sound sharp."

Amarillo didn't reply. Ruth Ann backed away, took up the picnic basket, and headed for the schoolhouse. So much for taking a break from tension.

Whatever was happening within the Warren household, Ruth

Ann didn't have the fortitude to deal with. She had enough on her mind.

Della knew things hadn't gone well with Ruth Ann's visit. Her daughter came home not much later with an empty basket and expression. Della could tell from her daughter's thinning face that she was too preoccupied to bother with eating regularly.

They needed to talk soon. Ruth Ann was worried with Matthew gone, and burdened with the extra work she'd taken on, but the time wasn't right. She had a valuable lesson to learn, and it wasn't time for Della to step in. Yet.

Something else was on Della's heart, something that she felt she should do.

Della removed her apron after finishing the last of the dishes and laid it aside. She retied her hair and set out the back door, taking a worn path through the grass behind the false front store buildings on the south side of Dickens. The path led to the Warren home, the way she often went when visiting. She enjoyed the short walk, a sense of being out in the country, though the heavy traffic through Dickens lay on the other side of the buildings.

At the Warren home, she knocked gently on the door. Moments later, Amarillo opened it, a damp dishtowel over her shoulder and the top buttons of her blouse undone.

The young woman sighed. "Mrs. Warren and Mabel are still out, Mrs. Teller. I'll let them know you called."

She started to close the door, but Della put her hand on it. "I came to see you. May I come in?"

Amarillo raised one eyebrow. She released the door and stepped back. As if suddenly remembering, her fingers flew to the top buttons of her blouse, quickly redoing them. A baby cried from the parlor. "I'm sorry, I wasn't planning on company."

Della followed the young woman into the parlor. Amarillo picked up Charles Goodnight Jessop and paced the room. She bounced him, but he continued to cry.

"I hope your daughter wasn't put out with me for not going to the school."

Della seated herself in the chair with a mending basket next to it and picked up a shirt settled on top, a needle and thread stored in it. She went to work stitching. The baby let out an exceptional wail.

"He will not stop crying until you finish nursing him."

Amarillo halted, then sighed and sat on the sofa. Cradling Goodnight in one arm, she pulled the towel down to cover herself. Moments later, the wails ceased. "You're real observant, Mrs. Teller. I guess you've known all along that he's my son, not my brother."

Della made quick stitches to heal the seam that had torn loose along the shirt sleeve. She smiled, head still down. "Mrs. Warren never had children."

Amarillo chuckled softly. "That's plain enough." She frowned. "I oughtn't to laugh. She's been good to us, too good. Sometimes it's hard to keep the young'uns in hand the way she spoils them."

There was a long pause. Della allowed it. There was no use in rushing the moment. When Amarillo found the right time, she would speak.

It didn't take long. "I've never told anyone here about the baby's daddy. Only Stephen Austin and Takba know."

Della kept her hands steady on the garment. She had her suspicions about what may have happened, and if Amarillo was ready to speak about it, Della would listen.

"I told Pa I didn't like him around, but he said it wouldn't be for long and that I didn't need to worry. That he'd never bother me as long as Pa was alive." Amarillo cocked her head toward the towel covering her baby. "Well, Pa died."

Della nodded. "Your father was an outlaw."

Amarillo closed her eyes. "Pa wasn't always a bad man. You have to know that."

Della lowered the shirt to her lap, hands still. This wasn't the time to do anything but listen. It was time for the young woman to let the hurt out. That was why Della had come.

Amarillo opened her eyes. "We had a good place down in East Texas up 'til ten years ago. Nothing fancy, but we got by. My pa was born and raised on a big ranch that had been his family's since Texas independence. But the war changed everything. Pa lost it all during Reconstruction. But he pulled himself up by the bootstraps, got another place, married my ma, and started raising a mess of young'uns. Like I said, we had a decent place. But with the drought...he lost the cattle herd and figured moving to Indian Territory was the only way. But it plain broke his heart to leave Texas. Ma's too. She died."

Amarillo shifted, and the baby appeared from beneath the towel. She dropped the cloth over her shoulder, laid her son there, and patted his back, her eyes distant. She was unattached to the actions she performed.

"Losing Ma was the last thing Pa could take. He took off for days at a time. At first, he didn't tell us nothing, but I knew, even busy with four siblings while he was gone, I knew. I reckon he reasoned it out with himself. He was just robbing those who had taken advantage after the war, rich old gentlemen who made themselves fat and comfortable on the blood and tears of families who'd lost generations of hard work. But then he got hooked up with...with that man and his gang."

Goodnight burped, and Amarillo cradled him, rocking to put him to sleep. But it looked as mindless as if she were washing clothes.

When a minute passed without Amarillo attempting to say anything, Della asked, "Who was the man?"

Amarillo's eyes flickered away, looking to the fireplace with its dying embers. "I may as well say. It doesn't matter now that

Pa's gone." She paused. "His name's Dan Holder. His gang used to work along the Texas border, then they moved up to the Winding Stair Mountains."

Della clenched the shirt in her lap. The Winding Stair Mountains, the place where her husband and son had died.

"Pa joined the gang, and…Cub Wassom was a part of it. They used to come down and hide out at our shanty until the excitement died down from a hold up. Pa didn't ride with them all the time, only when the crops were in. He said that as soon as the crops did good enough one year, he'd quit that gang. Trouble was, the crops were never good enough, or when they were, he had to pay out heavy to the landowner to catch up. Pa was just trying to make ends meet."

Amarillo locked eyes with Della as though searching for affirmation that her father was justified in his choices. But when she didn't find it, Amarillo broke away and nodded.

"All the good it did. He got killed by a posse, and Cub Wassom came after me. Before that, though, I think my pa was part of…of what happened to your menfolk."

Amarillo went quiet. Della's breathing slowed, nearly halted. She measured every word as she asked, "This gang…Dan Holder's gang. They were the ones who ambushed my husband and son?"

Amarillo's blue eyes, crisp and steady like a mountain stream, turned to Della. "I don't know what all that gang did, Mrs. Teller. Not exactly, anyway."

Her tone was dull as she drew inward. Della needed to draw her back out, help her move a step toward healing from the terrible experiences. But Della had to press for the truth about her Jim and Philip first. She had to. "What *do* you know?"

Amarillo lifted her chin. "I know my pa didn't do the killing. It was Dan Holder that did the shooting."

Della held in a sob. Dan Holder. Was this really the name of the man who had killed her beloved Jim and eldest son, Philip?

Yet knowing the identity of the murderer did nothing to loosen the knot in her bosom that had dwelled there since the news came.

Amarillo sighed, distant. "I shoulda told you a long time ago, but we needed help. Needed it from the start. But your son has to quit looking for revenge and come home, Mrs. Teller. He'll find more than he wants to."

Della spoke slow and quiet, wishing for more time to understand what Amarillo had revealed. "If he is doing anything about this, he will be seeking justice, not revenge."

"Justice ain't always worth what it costs." Amarillo stood, closed off. "I'll tell Mrs. Warren you called."

As Della left, her thoughts turned to her remaining son, and she prayed he used wisdom in whatever truth he sought.

CHAPTER 28

Along the three-mile walk from McAlester to Krebs, Cadenza talked of life when the mines reopened, and the people celebrating every mark on the calendar again. Matthew spent most of the walk trying to come up with a way to explain his bruises and black eye to Raphael and Ricco.

Soon, Matthew and Cadenza strolled through the row of company houses that Raphael lived on. Women hanging wash and men standing in small groups called greetings to them, although on a second look, they began whispering to whoever was nearest. It wasn't difficult to see Matthew had been in quite a tussle.

Raphael was sitting on his porch steps, pipe in hand, in a deep conversation with the visitor standing before him.

Ricco.

Matthew would have to face the brothers together.

Raphael stood at Cadenza's greeting and caught her hands with a grin. "Ah, my little bambina returns!"

"I had a grand time, Zio. There was a dance, and the Marino family let me stay with them. Toby had a terrible accident in the mines, but he is doing well."

Cadenza glanced at Matthew out of the corner of her eye as if to assure him she hadn't forgotten her promise.

She didn't look her father's direction.

Matthew greeted the men with a nod and shifted his rifle to shake Ricco's hand. "Good to see you, sir."

Ricco was equally solemn. "I see not all is peaceful in McAlester."

Raphael patted Cadenza's cheek and looked over her head at Matthew. "Were you on the wrong side of someone's quick temper, son?"

"Something like that." That was easy enough. Matthew shifted his saddlebags on his sore shoulder. "I'm heading toward Wilburton on the next train."

The Katy branch ended there. He would rent a horse and ride to Skullyville, a gateway to the Choctaw Nation, right on the border with Arkansas. Though the Tobucksy County Courthouse in McAlester issued permits, Philip left a note with the false papers warning Matthew to go to Skullyville, where it was less likely someone would recognize him. It would take an extra day, but the precaution was reasonable.

Matthew would sign for Al Percy's work permit in his own name, claiming the man worked for him at the *Choctaw Tribune*. Hopefully, it would work. Hopefully, it wouldn't. It wasn't right, and besides, he didn't know what kind of legal trouble he'd be in. A fine? Certainly, his reputation was in jeopardy, especially if the *Dickens Herald* found out. Their front page headline would read:

Choctaw Tribune Falsifies Legal Document for White Intruder

Cadenza pulled away from her uncle and smiled at Matthew. "Have a safe trip, Matt Jameson. We will see you again soon, si?"

Ricco stared at him. Matthew's vague answer had not satisfied him.

Cadenza glared at her father. "Why do you look at him so? He's done nothing wrong. Neither did I."

She pushed between the brothers and charged up the stairs into Raphael's house. She slammed the door behind her.

Raphael shook his head and muttered something in Italian, but Ricco answered with a sharp retort and walked off. Raphael settled himself on the steps again. He drew on his pipe and watched his brother stride away.

Brothers. Matthew understood the relationship between Ricco and Raphael more than ever.

He slid the saddlebags to his hand and then to the ground beside Raphael's steps. He seated himself beside the man. "Didn't mean to cause trouble."

Raphael shrugged, pipe in the corner of his mouth. "You didn't cause it. Been happening since the mine disaster."

"I don't think either of them understands the truth about what happened."

"Deep down, they use lies to build dams against the floods of pain. Someday, maybe, they will come to themselves, and we will be a family again."

He turned to Matthew. "And you, Matt Jameson? What truth are you trying to understand?"

Matthew cocked an eyebrow. This man saw right through him. Must be where Cadenza got it from. But he wasn't ready to reveal any secrets to Raphael, so he answered with a lift of one shoulder, shooting fresh pain through him.

"What's the matter, son? What happened to you these past few days?"

"A lot," Matthew muttered but knew Raphael needed more explanation to keep him from looking for answers. "I guess you heard about the riot in Savanna. Things got ugly."

"You got caught in the middle, eh?"

"Something like that." Matthew motioned over his shoulder toward the door. "I tried to look after Cadenza, too."

It felt good to be wholly honest about something.

Raphael chuckled, though it wasn't a jovial sound. "She likes to find celebrations and excitement. And Toby Nicolas. He's a good fellow."

Matthew stiffened at the mention of Philip's alias.

Raphael watched him closely. "Did you meet the man?"

"Something like that." Matthew picked up his saddlebags and rifle as he stood. "I have to be going. Maybe I'll see you again."

"Not sticking around to see how the strike comes out, eh?" Raphael stood, one hand in his pocket, pipe puckered between his lips.

"I'm sure I'll read about it in the newspapers." Matthew wanted to chuckle at the irony, but he had no humor left. "I hope things turn out well for everyone."

Raphael pulled the pipe from his lips and spat. "Unlikely, and you know it."

This was the first time Matthew experienced hostility from the friendly man. "I don't have a stake in your fight."

"It's everyone in Indian Territory's fight, most especially us non-citizens. Rumor has it the Choctaw Nation is looking to expel leaders of the union. Without mine bosses paying our permit fees, we're all about to be intruders. Your stake is as good as anyone's."

Matthew shifted his jaw. Truth was a twisted thing sometimes. "I'll make out all right."

He walked away. Raphael Bianchi said nothing to his back.

The swaying of the train car lulled Matthew with the temptation to doze. But he couldn't sleep for thinking about his destination.

The town of Skullyville was aptly named. "Skully" meant "money" in Choctaw, and it was where Choctaws went to collect their annuity payments. It was where Matthew's father and brother had departed with payments to deliver along with their freight six years before. They were both killed by outlaws in the Winding Stair Mountains.

So the story went.

When Matthew rushed home from college, he arrived at Uncle Preston's ranch just as the funeral was about to start. The caskets were closed, and he never saw the bodies. He found out why later, in a conversation with his uncle Preston as they stood by the gravesides.

Matthew had dug his fingernails into the palms of his hands, staring at where his cousins finished filling the graves in the family cemetery on Uncle Preston's ranch. "I wanted to see them one last time, *Vmoshi*."

He stood back, not feeling part of the family again yet. He'd been away too long, had not been there the moment when the greatest tragedy struck the family. In that moment, he made the decision to quit college and look after his mother and sister, to be there for whatever moments they needed him again.

Uncle Preston shook his head. "It wasn't good, *sv baiyi*. It was two days before anyone came on the sight. Panthers had been there. Bones were most all we had. Hats. Your brother's fine boots. I'm sorry, my nephew. So sorry."

Uncle Preston's tears came like a flood. Matthew had only seen him cry one other time—when they buried his own wife after decades of marriage. Matthew hadn't asked anything more of his uncle, then nor since.

Matthew leaned his head against the train window, wishing the rocking of the coach would put him to sleep. He closed his eyes, but peace was far from him. He saw his younger self at college, getting the telegram. The devastation. The pain that drove him to his knees, then back onto his feet, ready to fight for his future and his family.

His mother later scolded him for not returning to college, but that was inconsequential by comparison. He vowed to take care of his mother and sister, and was more driven to write truth than ever.

But what now? If those weren't Philip's bones in the casket, whose were they? Why hadn't his brother come home?

Matthew recalled the last time he'd seen Philip six years ago. He was always after his older brother about not finishing his education. But Philip had the charm to win over his most bitter enemy—if he had one—and he figured that was enough to see him through life. Their last talk before Matthew left for his second year of college was a fight about Philip not going. But Matthew remembered getting on the train and Philip saying something that made him laugh. That was the last time he saw Phillip until the depot at Savanna. He had processed through so many emotions in a split second—shock, sadness, joy. But only emotion held him now.

Matthew hit his fist against the wall under the window of the train car. Those around him looked his way, then went back to what they were doing—reading, chatting, snoozing. They had no idea of the deep pain of betrayal engulfing Matthew's heart. His soul was on fire with a rage that threatened to consume him. He had to control it.

Walk humbly with…

"Wilburton, next stop!"

The conductor walked the aisle of the coach, making the announcement on his way through.

After he got off the train at Wilburton, Matthew would rent a horse and ride west to Skullyville, taking the false papers and…

The train jerked to a halt, and Matthew hesitated before standing. The aisle was full as passengers waited in line to exit. A man glanced his way. "Business in Wilburton or Skullyville?"

Matthew didn't know whether to nod or shake his head no. "Something like that."

What was he doing? Lying, falsifying papers, selling his integrity?

The line moved, the aisle cleared, and Matthew got off the train before the whistle blew, and it pulled out for its turnaround. He started down the depot steps, then halted, staring at Wilburton like it was the first time he'd been there. But it wasn't the first time. This was where he'd unwittingly been drafted into a posse that cost him so much. He didn't know if the boy he'd rescued had survived or if what Raphael said was correct, that the boy was dead. He did know the way to seek justice was with truth, as he'd always strived to do.

No matter how convincing he'd been, Philip's scheme was not the only choice they had. Matthew had almost been deceived by his brother once again. Not this time. There was always another way.

Matthew re-boarded the Katy as soon as it turned itself around. Time to meet Philip in Lehigh whether his brother was ready or not.

This time, it was Matthew who would catch Philip off-guard. It was time to wrench control from him.

It was nearly dark when Matthew disembarked at the Lehigh depot. He had switched lines at McAlester to board the south-bound train to reach the town. The tension in McAlester over the strike was massive. Even in Lehigh, the small number of people on the platform waiting to greet the last train of the day avoided making eye contact with one another. Matthew hoped not to see any of the baseball players, especially the third baseman who'd grabbed onto his belt a lifetime ago.

"Hey, are you Matt Jameson?"

Matthew stiffened and glanced over his shoulder to see the station master waddling toward him. The man squinted in the dim light. Matthew turned to him. "That's me."

"Thought so. Didn't think you were supposed to be here 'til

tomorrow, though. A man left this for you, asked me to see that you got it."

The station master offered Matthew an envelope with *Matt Jameson* scrawled on it. Philip's handwriting.

"Thanks."

He moved to the lantern hung on the wall of the depot and laid his gear under it to free his hands. He tore open the envelope. This should tell him where to find his brother. He read the sloppily scrawled note.

Sorry I lied to you, but I had to get you out of the way. By the time you read this, it'll all be over. Don't tell Mama and Ruth Ann I'm alive.

Matthew crushed the note in his fist. He should have known Philip would betray him again.

CHAPTER 29

Philip aimed his horse's head northeast, into the heart of the Choctaw Nation. After hours of riding, he was tense and ready for everything to come to a head. The devil was on his trail, had been for six years.

The cabin came into sight. Philip pulled on the reins to halt his horse a hundred yards away. Smoke rose from the chimney, light shined through the windows. The man was there.

Philip dismounted on the overgrown trail and tied his horse out of sight. He drew his Winchester from the scabbard.

Moving through the woods, Philip reached a rope corral. There was only one horse sheltered there, but he had to make sure the man was alone.

Staying low and quiet, he crept to the window nearest the chimney. A lamp sat near that window. The glare of light would lessen the chance of the man seeing him. Philip raised enough to take in the sight inside the cabin—the man seated near the fireplace, reading a newspaper. He was alone.

Blood pounded in Philip's temple, but he kept a cool hand on his gun and eased toward the back door where a porch sagged.

He whacked a metal bucket with the butt of his rifle. It clattered across the porch and off the other side.

The light from the lamp went out. Philip pressed against the cabin wall near the back door.

As the door creaked open, the barrel of a Colt .45 came into view, its cylinder glistening in the light from the fireplace. The barrel swiveled Philip's direction, but the man hadn't detected him. It swung back, and a head poked out.

Philip settled his Winchester against the man's temple. "'Evening, Al. Decided to run out on me, did you? And what with me saving your life in the coal mine and all that."

Al Percy froze, his thick lips twitching. He didn't move.

Philip cocked the hammer of his Winchester, savoring the sound echoing in the silence.

Al stuttered. "I didn't...I figured...I didn't think you'd want to go through with joining up with Dan Holder after the accident. But it wasn't my fault you got hurt."

"I'm not blaming you, buddy." Philip pressed the muzzle against the man's temple, and Al squeezed his eyes shut. "But you could have asked if I still wanted to go through with helping you get away from Reeves. Nice and polite, like I'm asking you now if you want to live."

Al licked his lips, eyes still shut.

Philip shoved hard against Al's head before pointing the rifle barrel skyward and uncocking the hammer. "You'll live this time, just so you can owe me your life twice over. Understand?"

Al staggered to the side and opened his eyes, barely turning his head Philip's direction. "Sure. Sure, I didn't mean nothing by it. As far as I'm concerned, we'll go right back to the way things were."

"Not quite." Philip tapped Al's nose with the tip of the barrel. "You owe me your life twice over."

Al Percy swallowed, slowly holstering his Colt .45. "Sure. Whatever you say."

Philip offered him his coldest smile. "Good. Now let's eat. I could smell those beans a quarter of a mile away."

CHAPTER 30

*A*l stared at Toby Nicolas, this fellow entering his cabin peacefully after threatening to kill him. Al wasn't ready to die, but he didn't know if he would make it out of this one.

Toby Nicolas blew out the lamp and seated himself at the table.

"How about those beans?"

Al stumbled over a stool in the dark interior. The only light came from the low fire making the room overly warm. Al wanted to bank it, but he was too scared to do anything other than what Toby Nicolas told him to.

The man was relaxed, confident. What if he suddenly decided he didn't need Al? What if he just swung that rifle around and blasted him dead right over the pot of beans?

Hands shaking, Al brought a full bowl over to the table where he accidentally dropped it the final few inches with a clunk. Juice sloshed over the edge.

"Easy there, Al." Toby didn't move his hands from the rifle across his lap, chair tipped back. "Don't burn yourself."

Al had dealt with many outlaws in his time. Toby Nicolas hadn't seemed the quick killer sort when they buddied together in the McAlester mine, but that was a far cry different from now. Al had been scared stiff of Marshal Bass Reeves finding him in McAlester, and then that Matt Jameson. It was never good when someone was looking for Al Percy. He didn't have time to wait on a busted up man to recover.

Toby Nicolas looked plenty fit now.

With the bandana from his back pocket, Al mopped up the spilled bean juice. "Sure. I mean, no. That is, tomorrow, we better get an early start."

"Are we in a hurry?"

"No, uh, yes. We need to pick up something on the way."

"What would that be?"

The truth bubbled out. "Money. Lots of it." He settled in a chair close to the fire. Hot. Too hot. He stood again.

"Sit down, Al. I want to enjoy my beans."

Al barely glanced up to see Toby's hands still on the rifle. Al lowered back into the chair, running his hands down his pant legs to dry them. "Sure, whatever you say."

"That's a good fellow. Now tell me about all this money we're picking up."

When Toby Nicolas had spotted Al selling morphine to someone wanting the powerful drug, Al thought he was had. But instead of turning him over to the law or mine bosses, Toby just walked away. Al wasn't sure what to make of the fellow, but Toby kept quiet at work all the following week. Soon, they were buddies in the mine, Al trusting him too much.

When it came time to escape McAlester, Toby worked out a way Al could get away clean with faking Al's death and heading for Dan Holder's holdout. Toby said he wanted to join the outlaw gang.

What Toby didn't know, was that Al had sent Lester Cotten, longtime Holder gang member, a letter telling him about a miner named Toby Nicolas who wanted to go to work for their boss. Lester sent him a telegram: *Mine. Thursday. Noon.*

But by that week, with Matt Jameson coming after him and the strike, Al already decided to leave Toby behind and get out alone.

Looked like he had better follow Lester's directions after all.

Toby had finally taken one hand off the rifle to eat the beans. Al wished some of the moisture on his hands were in his mouth as he forced himself to answer. "Money. Yeah, lots of it, golden eagles. Dan Holder keeps it stashed near his hideout and draws from it when he needs to. But he don't know we're coming. We could...we could just get it and head south. I know plenty of good spots to hide near the Red River."

"I bet you do." Toby wasn't looking at him. Then he raised his eyes, a smile in them. "You're talking awful slow, Al."

"I...I, look if you don't want the money..."

"I want to join up with Dan Holder, not double-cross him."

"All right, that's what we'll do. But I still gotta pick up a little bag of it from the hiding place. Always do when I go see him. It's a signal of sorts that everything is all clear. You know how rare double eagles are."

"Yeah. I do." The way he said the words gave Al a glimpse at secrets Toby was hiding.

Al just had to hang onto one of his own—that the hiding place was actually a test for potential gang members. If Toby tried to take the money and leave Al at the bottom of the abandoned mine shaft, Toby Nicolas was the one who would end up dead.

CHAPTER 31

*L*ance stayed late at the school grading papers, then took his time strolling to the house. The Jessop children had gone straight there after classes, but he didn't feel comfortable walking with them, as if they were going home like a family.

The Warren house wasn't really a home for anyone. It was filled with broken people needing a place to live and a way to start life over. He only thought of it as "the house."

It was almost suppertime, but the less time he spent around one Jessop in particular, the better. For some reason since the move, Amarillo was avoiding him. Now that she was in his world and had a chance to see how he lived, maybe she thought he was still a pretender like when he first arrived in Indian Territory. There was no way he could convince her otherwise, except being true to his new faith. Whether or not that was discernible, he couldn't judge.

Lance went through the side door that led into the kitchen. Mabel pounced on him, shaking a doughy spoon in his face before he crossed the threshold.

"Mr. Lance, if you don't quit being late to supper I'll throw your food out to the cats and don't think I won't! Especially on an evening when we got company."

Her hands flapped like little bird wings, waving the spoon in Lance's face. He dodged it. Hope rose. "Company? Are the Tellers here?"

Mrs. Teller and Ruth Ann would help ease the tension when everyone sat down to eat.

Mabel's voice dropped as she glanced toward the swinging door leading from the kitchen to the dining room. "Ain't decent folks like the Tellers."

Lance creased his eyebrows, following Mabel to the stove where the woman stirred a boiling pot. The kitchen smelled scrumptious, but Lance had a feeling he was about to lose his appetite. "Who's here?"

Mabel looked over her shoulder, her eyelids dropping into a knowing glare. "Just be careful what you say around the dinner table. Might end up in print."

She shooed at him with her free hand. "Go on. I got to dish up the soup and see to it the rolls don't burn. I already served the first course."

First course? Why hadn't Lance been told they were having a formal dinner with guests in the middle of the week? But more things than not slipped his aunt Susan's mind.

Lance cautiously went through the kitchen door into the dining room. He lost his appetite.

"Ah, there you are, Fuller. Good to see you."

Lance gave a short nod of acknowledgement to Christopher Maxwell, editor of the *Dickens Herald* and enemy of Lance's best friends, the Tellers. In this house, unfortunately, Maxwell had often been a welcomed guest, but he hadn't come around since Lance's uncle skipped town.

Mrs. Maxwell was seated next to her husband and Lance managed a polite greeting as he headed for his usual spot by his aunt where she sat at the head of the table. The Jessops were absent. In fact, the house was eerily quiet.

But Aunt Susan beamed as though she were entertaining President Cleveland and the First Lady. "Lance, dear, I ran into Dorothy while shopping today and said what a shame it was that we hadn't had them over in so long."

Dorothy Maxwell—petite, finely dressed and as authentic looking as the false fronts on the buildings of Dickens—dipped her head with a stiff smile. "It was yesterday, Susan."

For Lance, Dorothy's smile turned demure, her eyes all over his face, and his stomach rolled. She was far younger than her husband and this wasn't the first time she'd made a pass at him. He'd seen her do the same with Matthew Teller, at church no less, but Matthew never seemed to notice. Lance wondered if Maxwell ever picked up on his wife's behavior, or if he was too busy plotting destruction to catch the looks.

Lance scraped his chair noisily while pulling it out, across from Maxwell. His aunt looked alarmed, so he forced himself to be polite.

"Welcome," Lance said, his steady tone surprising him. "I'm sure you'll enjoy the meal. Mabel is an excellent cook."

Pretending was easy, acting like a gentleman whenever the occasion called for it. Lance was reared that way. Well, rather his old self, Thomas Warren, had been. Now that he'd taken on a new identity, Lance found pretense disgusting.

Mabel swished through the swinging door, carrying two large bowls filled with steaming soup. Lance remained seated when he wanted to rise and help. He'd keep his cultured pretense in place for now.

Treating a servant like a fellow human being had never occurred to him before, but since his conversion, he wanted to show compassion and love to everyone. Well, except the two people who sat across from him. He'd have to pray about that.

The conversation the ladies carried on was stilted but moved them all through the meal.

"Splendid spring weather, isn't it?"

"I am enjoying the sunshine."

"Yes, it is healthy for the skin, they say, though we must mind the danger of freckling."

The meaningless chatter reminded Lance of the dinner parties he'd attended in D.C. The young ladies there, many of whom were trying to gain him as a suitor, bored him to tears with their chatter about things even they didn't care about. Or wouldn't care about if they had any idea of what the world was beyond elegant gowns and the terror of a freckled nose.

Lance did notice Dorothy Maxwell didn't spare him a glance after her initial look. She played the game well, in the most revolting way.

It didn't take long for the dull conversation to send his mind wandering to those absent from the table. He missed the Jessop children's timid politeness, their rare smiles when he praised them in front of their big sister back at the shanty. He longed to see Amarillo. In the evenings at supper was the only chance he had. How foolish to even consider taking meals at a hotel! He missed her terribly just this one evening.

When they reached the main course of roast and carrots, Maxwell finally entered the conversation. He nodded to Lance. "I remember how your father's dinner parties in D.C. could fill an entire edition. Here, though, there's hardly enough news to keep my paper going every week."

Maxwell chuckled humorlessly and buttered a roll, but his eyes didn't leave Lance's face. The newspaper man had purposely insulted the *Choctaw Tribune*, which was putting out a daily.

Lance shrugged, cutting his roast. He ignored the comment about his deceased father, a former U.S. senator. That wasn't a line of conversation he wanted to pursue. "Big news for me is when one of my students reads their first word, or a choir rehearsal goes well. We're planning a spelling bee for May. But I don't suppose that is worthy reading to some people."

Maxwell dabbed his mustache with a napkin, swiping it over his pointed beard that showed signs of graying. "I suppose for some newspapers, anything is worth reporting."

Lance bit down hard on his fork.

Maxwell shook his head, making a genuine effort at pity. "Matthew Teller had so much potential when he worked for me. He could have been senior editor instead of suffering under the strain of trying to keep a newspaper afloat. It'll be a sad day when it fails."

Lance cocked an eyebrow. "You sound certain of that."

Maxwell shrugged like it was as sure as the Almanac predicting rain in April. "Things haven't run right from the beginning, and now with Teller's absence, there's no saving it. Especially if he's doing what the rumors say."

Lance took a bite of roast and didn't respond right away. He didn't want to sound anxious. "Rumors?"

"According to my sources covering the coal miner strike, Matthew Teller is heavily involved in favor of his tribe instead of the good of all."

Lance twirled his fork between thumb and forefinger. He'd seen his father play enough political and social games to recognize Maxwell's. He'd been in them himself and it had ruined him. He was done with games.

"What sort of lies about Matthew Teller do you intend to publish?"

Mrs. Maxwell audibly gasped. Aunt Susan was lost in the conversation. Sending Lance a confused look, she offered a dish to her guests. "More gravy, Dorothy?"

Christopher Maxwell smiled at Lance, making him want to fling a steak knife at him. He had let the arrogant man get under his skin.

Maxwell calmly took a bite of roast, chewed slowly, and swallowed. "Now, Lance, you know that my newspaper only prints what is best for the citizens."

"You are a fine judge for that."

Aunt Susan blustered. "Enough politics, or whatever on earth you two are talking about. There are positively more fascinating things we can discuss. Don't you agree, Dorothy?"

Mrs. Maxwell was glaring at Lance. He stood abruptly. "If you'll excuse me, I have things to attend to."

He sidestepped Mabel who was rounding the table with slices of pecan pie. She gave him a secret wink and he returned it. They might have the Maxwells under their roof, but they didn't have to like it.

Lance went through the long hall and out the back door, hoping for solitude where he could think. The sight in the garden made him catch his breath at the sudden joy in his heart.

Amarillo Jessop knelt in the middle of the large flower garden Aunt Susan had started on her arrival in Indian Territory. Weeds had grown rampant after the mayor abandoned Aunt Susan, but it looked in good shape thanks to the young woman weeding by lantern light.

Maybe Amarillo and Lance could plant a kitchen garden. Aunt Susan would appreciate the fresh vegetables. It could even give her something to do with the children. But Lance didn't try to convince himself that any of those reasons were motivation for the foolish ambition.

Amarillo didn't raise her head to acknowledge him, although it was impossible for her to not realize he'd come out the door. He halted, considering if he should pretend he'd taken a wrong turn and go back inside, or perhaps stroll around the house and head for the shed behind the church.

But he didn't want to leave. He rarely had the opportunity to say anything to Amarillo without her siblings hanging off her or Aunt Susan talking in the background.

Lance shoved his hands in his pockets and meandered toward

Amarillo. There were two dirt paths in the garden, and he chose the one that would lead him to a spot across from her. A patch of blooming pansies between them, Lance came to a stop and nodded her way, though she had yet to raise her head.

"Good evening, Miss Amarillo. Missed you and the children at dinner tonight."

"We took our supper upstairs."

"You are always welcome at the table, even when we have company." He hoped the Jessops would feel a part of the household soon, and not company themselves.

When Amarillo didn't respond, Lance pushed his hands deeper in his pockets. "Been watching the turtles move to higher ground the way Mrs. Teller taught me. Might get rain by Saturday—"

"You want us to leave, just say so." Amarillo tore a weed loose, dirt spraying her skirt, and tossed it in her basket.

Lance's jaw dropped. He shook his head and knelt on the path, still dozens of pansies away from her. "What would make you think I want you all to leave? It's good for Aunt Susan to have children to look after. It gives her purpose."

Amarillo kept weeding.

Lance ran both hands alongside his head, mussing his hair. "I remember the first time I laid eyes on you, Amarillo Jessop. Ruth Ann, Beulah, and I came out to your place and Stephen Austin shot at us. I turned the buggy over and next thing I know, I'm looking at..." He gathered his courage. "At the most fierce, beautiful woman I'd ever seen."

Amarillo stilled.

He chuckled softly. "She was pointing a loaded rifle at me, and I was aiming my pocket pistol at her. And we didn't even know why."

In the faint light of the lantern illuminating one side of her face, Lance tried to discern her expression. She didn't move, didn't flinch, yet he felt the chill between them as sure as a January morn.

He dropped his hands to rest on his knees. "Since you moved in, it seems like you're back to pointing a gun at me, and I don't know why."

Amarillo stood abruptly, shaking the dirt from her clothes and dusting off her hands. She lifted the basket of weeds, took it to the compost pile behind the garden and upped the basket. She gave it a shake then strode to the house.

The tenacious Amarillo Jessop was nothing like the eastern-bred Dorothy Maxwell. Lance wished he was a better man, one worthy of Amarillo. She was honest, unafraid, strong. All the attributes he didn't possess.

Lance watched every move Amarillo made. Though purposeful, with no extra flounces, her movements were graceful, elegant, more so than the sophisticated young ladies he had known in D.C. But he never had to pursue those young women. They always flocked around him, the son of a U.S. senator—charming, popular, wealthy.

None of that did him a lick of good in Indian Territory. First Ruth Ann rejected him when he tried to deceive his way into her affections, and now Amarillo, though he had pure intentions this time. The young women were a different sort in this territory.

That shouldn't be a bad thing. But it broke his heart.

CHAPTER 32

At dawn Thursday morning, two riders set out for the Sans Bois Mountains north of Wilburton. Philip had Al Percy ride in front of him on the narrow game trail. This made the man more nervous, which let Philip relax.

Last night, he learned Dan Holder's hideout was tucked among the cliffs used by a long line of outlaws who favored the area since the war. Holder had built a fort-like cabin to live in safety, though always ready if a posse found him. He'd been in hiding for two years.

Philip hoped Choctaw mixed-blood Lester Cotten wasn't still with Dan Holder's gang. He had no desire to shoot his old friend, even though Lester had played a role in the blackmailing scheme that led to Jim Teller's death.

No. It was Philip's utter foolishness his father paid for that day when the Holder gang descended on their wagon six years ago…

Back when they were younger, Matthew favored their father more than Philip, in physical features and attitude. They shared the same stubborn-set jawline and good looks, but Philip was the only one who appreciated the advantages of that. He'd snuck off more than once in Skullyville while his exhausted father slept in their hotel room on their trips to do freight deliveries and collect annuity payments. His father caught him sneaking out one time. Boy, that was an ugly night.

Jim Teller objected to the girl Philip was seeing because she was white. Well, that was what Philip argued. Jim stood firm in that he didn't care for the young woman's loose morals and reputation.

But it didn't stop Philip from seeing Kathryn Russell again. His childhood friend, Lester Cotten, helped arrange their last secret meeting. That was when Kat gave him the news that committed him to her for marriage.

Philip wanted to bring her home to his uncle Preston's ranch, but she threw a hissy fit and said that if he loved her, he better get them a place near her folks.

He needed a plan, fast. Lester Cotten had one for Philip's next trip to Skullyville.

He told Philip he knew some men who had no trouble getting all the money they wanted and that if Philip would help them with one job, he could set up a life of his own. Lester hadn't come alone with the proposition. A cocky young man, who carried a six-shooter like he used it regularly, came along to convince Philip. He refused at first. But these men knew about him, about Kat, about his family down by the Red River. Cub Wassom made it clear that Philip would cooperate—willingly or not. No one bucked the Dan Holder gang.

Trapped, Philip told them the route he and his father took to reach the homesteads of Choctaw families they were delivering supplies and annuity payments to.

Lester set up everything else. No one would get hurt, other than roughing Philip up to make it look like he tried to fight them off. Lester promised the pain would be worth it.

After doing their business in Skullyville, Jim and Philip set out for their typical run. It was a long haul up the Winding Stair Mountains. An inconspicuous burlap sack full of double eagles and paper money lay under the seat.

Every twitch in the woods lining the road made Philip flinch. His father was alert but calm, slouched in the wagon seat to take the bounces on the rough road. Philip slouched even lower, boots propped on the top end gate, his legs jittery. His boots were too fancy for practical work—hand-tooled leather with a floral motif and etched silver tips—but he had bought them with his own money, despite his parent's protest that he get something durable. He jiggled the boots, nerves eating him until his father gave him a look, dark brown eyes stern.

Philip stilled. He didn't want another lecture on how he needed to stop thinking about a certain gal in Skullyville.

Jim turned his attention back to the road, but the conversation remained on the same topic, just in a different way.

"You'll stay home the next run, help bring in the fall crops with your uncle Preston. We work together, and everyone makes good. It's part of being a family."

Jim wiped the back of his sleeve across his sweaty lips and gestured for the water crock beneath the spring seat.

Philip lifted the crock, never taking his gaze from the woods. His father grunted, and Philip realized he held the crock out of reach. He quickly uncorked it and offered it to his father, but instead of taking it, Jim looked long and deep into Philip's eyes.

"Best get your mind off that gal right now. She's not the one for you, flighty and full of herself. You mess around with her anymore, and I'm telling you, God knows, and He'll tell me."

Jim finally took the crock, handed off the reins to Philip, and drank deeply.

A flare lit up in Philip's stomach, but he banked it. He was in enough trouble as it was.

He traded the reins for the crock and took a swig, trying to not choke on the mixture of water and nervous breathing.

Soon, they would stop by a trail that led to an overlook of the mountain range. His father would hike up there and stay awhile. Jim did it every time, always alone, to talk with God, mostly about his oldest son, no doubt. His father's absence was the opportunity for the robbery Philip was blackmailed into, thanks to his foolishness. And he couldn't have the Holder gang going after his family. He knew they would.

Philip settled his feet near the burlap sack containing not only annuity money but a special bank bag for the chief no one else was supposed to know they had. Lester did.

The road narrowed, the left side dropping away a hundred feet, which meant the trail leading to the overlook was only a few miles away.

A shot rang out. Jim pulled back on the reins to hold the skittering mules. "Whoa!"

Philip gripped the spring seat to keep from being thrown off as the wagon surged close to the edge of the drop on his side.

"Whoa! Whoa now!"

Five riders skidded onto the road ahead, coming out of the woods. It wasn't supposed to be this way!

"Get the rifle!" Jim shouted, but Philip gaped at the riders charging toward them, faces covered with hoods. He recognized one distinct black and white paint. Cub Wassom's pony.

Jim shoved the reins into Philip's hands and fumbled beneath the seat for the rifle. He had it in hand and pumped off a shot before Philip could comprehend what was happening.

The riders scattered, one leaning off the side of his saddle. He'd been hit.

Philip dropped the reins and waved his arms frantically at the men. "No! No shooting!"

Jim's eyes were ablaze as he lifted the rifle and fired again. While the other riders ducked for cover, the man riding a bay horse took steady aim and fired. The bullet found its mark.

Jim Teller jerked and fell back against Philip. The mule team lurched. One of the riders grabbed at the lead's bridle and missed as the animal jerked away, sending the team backward again.

Philip tried to shift his father into his arms, but the left side of the wagon tilted, and Philip slipped. He sought a handhold, but lost his balance and flipped off the seat and over the hundred-foot drop. He screamed, not prepared to face his doom.

But Providence saw fit to land him in a thin bush just strong enough for him to grab onto as he slipped through. He dangled on the edge of the drop.

Philip coughed on the dirt in his dry mouth, grit in his eyes as he blindly clawed for a secure grip. He wanted to live. He had to live! His family, Kat...and he wasn't ready to face the Almighty.

God knows.

That was a terrifying thought.

A rope slapped him across the shoulder. He twisted it around his wrist and gripped with both hands. Someone—Lester?—grunted and pulled on the other end. Philip found purchase on the rough mountainside with his etched silver-tipped boots and scrambled until he was back to the road on his knees, dashing dirt from his eyes.

Thump.

He froze and blinked. A pistol had landed in the dust near him.

A deep, authoritative voice, one Philip had never heard, spoke. "I ain't one for killing an unarmed man if I can help it."

Lester Cotten responded from where he stood over Philip. "He's a friend of mine, Dan. Bad enough you shot his pa. Just let him be."

The stranger had shot Philip's daddy. Why was Philip still alive?

He lunged for the pistol, but a boot kicked his hand. The popping of bones sounded, and he yelled from the pain of his broken fingers. He rolled onto his back in the dirt, gasping.

Lester picked up the gun and stepped out of Philip's reach.

Cradling his fiery hand, Philip's vision cleared enough to take in the scene. A hooded man stood not ten feet away, his Colt .45 holstered, fingers flexed. The wagon was beyond him, two men looting it. The last outlaw, shot by Jim Teller, lay sprawled on the ground, dead.

To Philip's right was Lester with a pistol pointed at the gang leader. Behind Lester, Jim Teller lay in the dirt, crumpled.

"Daddy!"

Still on his knees, Philip knocked past Lester to reach his father. Philip turned Jim over and stared at the blood seeping from the gaping hole over his heart.

Philip heaved in a breath, bile burning the back of his throat. He turned away and threw up. His ears rang, eyes blurred with tears. Somewhere behind him, Lester and the gang leader, Dan Holder, argued.

Spots dotted Philip's vision, pain from his broken fingers clouding his mind. He couldn't think except that everything his daddy ever said was true, and how deep down, all his life, Philip had wanted his father to be proud of him like he was of Matthew. But Philip always fumbled doing what was right.

In a few miles, Jim was supposed to go up to the overlook, the gang would rough Philip up and take the money. He would tell the story, let enough time pass, then run off to confirm the rumors that he was out of his head in love with a girl in Skullyville.

Lester promised the pain would be worth it. But there was never any pain like this. Philip's father was dead.

With a primal roar, he charged into Lester Cotten, grappling for his gun. Lester jabbed his elbow in Philip's face, then grabbed the front of his shirt and jerked him close.

"Look, I'm sorry about your daddy. I told the boys to do things like we'd planned, but Holder figured you'd try to weasel out." He lowered his voice. "What's done is done. I'm trying to keep you alive now."

Lester leaned close to Philip's ear as blood pulsed through his temples. "You can get revenge tomorrow if you live today. You hear what I'm saying?"

Behind Philip, Dan Holder shouted at the other two men, "Jessop, you and Cub finish with loading those saddlebags, now!"

Philip twisted in Lester's grip enough to see the two men mount. Dan Holder stared at Philip, still looking ready to draw his gun and shoot.

Philip cradled his broken hand. Tomorrow. Or a thousand tomorrows. Time didn't matter. He'd see them all dead.

Holder's pinched lips showed in the slit of his hood, considering Lester. Then his eyes locked with Philip's. Blood chilled like a mountain stream was coursing through Philip's veins.

Holder finally turned away, mounted, and nudged his horse close to Philip. He gestured toward Lester, who hadn't holstered his own gun nor released his grip on Philip's shirt.

"You let that cuss go, he'll sic the marshals on you, and I'll see you under before you give the rest of us away, you hear, Indian?"

Lester put the six-shooter to Philip's temple and cocked it. "Go on, get out of here! I'll handle this my own way."

"Just remember what I said."

Holder yanked on the reins, eliciting a protest from his horse. He dug his spurs in and gestured at the other two men. They followed him at a flat-out run.

Pull the trigger, Philip prayed. Then hoped Lester wouldn't. Philip had a lot of action ahead.

Once the gang was out of sight, Lester uncocked and holstered the gun, releasing Philip. "Now, we got to—"

Philip slammed his good fist into Lester's mouth, followed by a kick in the groin. Lester gasped and bent over double. Philip came down hard on the back of Lester's neck with his elbow. Lester tried to catch himself before hitting the ground, exposing Philip's real target. He gripped the handle of the six-shooter and yanked it out of the holster. He stumbled away and blinked rapidly from the pain in his broken fingers.

Switching to his left hand despite the awkwardness, Philip cocked the hammer and aimed the six-shooter at Lester's upturned face. The whites of his eyes showed briefly, begging for mercy, but they quickly turned hard.

"You think killing me will bring your pa back? Go on, then, shoot! You kill me and then see if you can find them without my help. You go on now and shoot!"

Philip's hand shook wildly. He gripped the handle, looking past Lester to Jim Teller, laying on the ground, stone dead. Philip's gaze shifted back to Lester. His finger pressed against the trigger. He hesitated.

Lester hadn't killed his daddy. The other men had. Philip would hunt them all down and make them pay. Lester would help him.

The thoughts made perfect sense to Philip. He lowered the six-shooter and let it hang at his side.

Lester pushed up to his feet. "You crazy Indian."

He took the gun from Philip and holstered it, then whistled up his pony. The horse trotted over, and Lester got his bedroll from behind the saddle. He unrolled the gray woolen blanket and spread it over Jim Teller's body.

Philip didn't move.

Lester shook his shoulder. "Now, listen close. We gotta make folks think you were killed too. Can't let no one know you're alive."

Philip didn't want to hear what Lester had to say, but he did.

"You can't turn the gang in, or they'll say you planned it all, and what would that do to your family? We can get those fellows ourselves."

Philip's arm was going numb. He absently rubbed it. "My mama, she can't take it, both of us not coming back. I got to go home."

Lester shook his shoulder, harder this time. "Nothing you can do about that. Besides, you think you can face your family after getting your pa killed?"

Philip gripped his numb arm. His whole body felt like dead flesh. He wished he could think clearly, think what he had to do.

Instead, he listened to Lester explain how they would trade Philip's clothes with the dead outlaw, shoot the man in the face to make him unrecognizable, and throw him over the ravine. The man had the same hair color as Philip, and by the time the body was found, only Philip's fancy boots could identify him. The scene would convince the sheriff or whoever that Philip and Jim Teller died in a holdup.

It made perfect sense.

Finally able to move, Philip shuffled to the wagon and retrieved a small shovel. But when he turned toward his father, Lester blocked the way.

"Can't bury him, Philip. Got to leave things just like they are."

A moan broke through Philip's dry lips, the taste of bile on them. "Can't leave him to the panthers..."

"Our people used to let the flesh rot off bodies and pick the rest off the bones and save those for mourning. It's not about a grave. Besides, would you rather your family know you set all this up?"

"I didn't plan it...it was that Wassom...."

"Got to do what we got to do, and fast. Can't be hanging around here, someone's apt to ride up the road anytime."

Yes. Someone could come up the road and find Jim Teller on it, and Philip alive. Why was he still alive?

And so he would follow Lester and fake his own death. His mother and brother and sister would never know what he'd done. They'd grieve and go on without knowing how foul their own flesh and blood was. He'd hunt down those men and kill them. Then he'd go back to Kat, take her off to someplace where no one knew them, whether she liked it or not. He'd live the rest of his life being eaten alive by the guilt of what he'd done. Maybe that was why he was still alive, to live with the burning regret.

Lester had lied. It wasn't worth the pain.

Philip's personal hell started that fateful hour. He carried grief and guilt on his shoulders every day.

Hearing about Cub Wassom's death last year brought no relief because Philip hadn't been the one to pull the trigger. Besides, it wasn't Wassom who put a bullet in his daddy.

The memories would never leave Philip, but he could live with them once he blasted Dan Holder to kingdom come.

CHAPTER 33

In a hotel room at Lehigh Thursday morning, Matthew awoke with a cough. He'd thought Philip's concoction rid him of the cold, but getting out immediately afterward weakened him. He rarely got sick, but then, he rarely got into fistfights with a long-dead brother then walked for miles in pouring rain. Matthew's night was sleepless, thinking about where his brother might have gone, what he was doing.

And thinking of how Thursdays were always trimmed with excitement as the weekly edition of the *Choctaw Tribune* went out. None of that today.

Washing and shaving, Matthew felt well enough to deny the head cold would keep him from what he had to do. He gathered his things and checked out of the hotel.

The sky was heavy with dark clouds that spat mist, chilling Matthew, but he resisted the cough building in his chest. He headed to the stables for a horse. The blacksmith might know which way Philip went, if Matthew could get the man to share information.

Matthew avoided the groups of coal miners who cast him wary looks. Some of them might guess he was Choctaw.

But he wasn't concerned about the strike today. He wanted to find his brother, find the killer, find the truth, though that might cost what Matthew had left in body, mind, and spirit.

At the stables, he found the blacksmith bent over, fitting a shoe on a horse.

The man must have sensed Matthew's approach because he spoke without looking up. "If you need a mount, got two mares out in the corral. One's old and slow, but steady as she goes. The other is fast and hearty, but with a mind of her own like any woman. Take your pick, and we'll make a deal."

"I'm most in need of information."

The man shook his head as he lowered the horse's hoof. He took the ill-fitting shoe over to the fire, clamped it between his tongs, and shoved it into the hottest part of the coals. His large leather apron offered protection at the forge. "Information is pretty expensive in these parts."

Matthew thought he was looking for a bribe until the man added, "Sometimes men die for it."

Matthew waited, his throat tickling from the want to cough. He ignored it.

The man pumped the bellows, then held the horseshoe up to examine the red spot formed on one side. "But I don't mind helping an honest fellow now and again. You looking for someone?"

"Toby Nicolas. He was here yesterday."

"You got business with him, do ya?" The man settled the shoe on an anvil and hammered away. The pinging sound filled the blacksmith shop.

Matthew waited until it stopped before answering, "Important business."

"Hmm, well, you seem like an honest enough fellow. Toby Nicolas was in here yesterday and picked out my best mare. Not that the other two aren't good ones. Either can catch up to him, if the rider knew which way to point her head. If he was a man with peaceful intentions." The blacksmith finally raised his eyes to Matthew.

"I'm just looking to talk to him."

The man dipped the horseshoe in a bucket of water. It hissed.

Cooled shoe in hand, the blacksmith ran his hand down the horse's cannon, grasped it, and prodded the horse to shift its weight and raise its foot. He settled the shoe on the hoof and pulled a hammer and nail from his large apron pocket. "Pick you a mount from the corral. Then we'll talk about information."

If getting a horse was the price, Matthew could pay it. He reached the back door of the stables at the same time a man on horseback skidded up to the front door and dismounted. "Hey, Simpson! You get your permit renewed yet?"

The blacksmith finished setting another nail. "Did it last Monday. What's going on?"

Matthew went out the back door and partially closed it, listening. The man dropped his reins and stepped into the dim interior of the stables, waving his arms to illustrate the tale.

"Those crazy Choctaws are expelling intruders. Got federal troops in McAlester now, threatening to round up miners and boot them into Arkansas."

The blacksmith finished hammering the last nail and lowered the horse's hoof. "I reckon the Choctaws can do what they please in their own nation."

The man shrugged. "Reckon so. But everybody better watch their step. They're after the British and Italians especially. You know how many there are up around Krebs. Practically the whole town."

Once they moved on to other news, Matthew stepped to the corral, thinking about the exchange. About his brother. About his Italian friends in Krebs. About the upside-down world he lived in.

An older blue roan plodded over to the fence while the sorrel pranced around. Matthew draped his saddlebags over the top rail and leaned his rifle against the corral. The roan dropped her head in what seemed a gesture of weariness, but she aimed for Matthew's hands and pockets, sniffing. He rubbed the side of her nostril with his knuckles.

"Smart girl. I could use a partner like you."

He could also use a train ticket to Krebs to see the Bianchi family, somehow protect them from being expelled.

But he didn't have time for both. Philip said it would all be over soon.

Had he lied in the note? Did Matthew still have a chance to catch up with him? What about the Bianchis and the strike? How much time did Matthew have?

There he was in the middle of the biggest news since the '93 tribal elections, and he couldn't do a thing about it. No more than he could help the Bianchis.

Could he?

Matthew looked between the mares—the steady roan and fast sorrel. All of life was a choice.

A muffled voice came from inside the stables.

"You heard about the Negro strikebreakers?"

The man had led his horse into one of the stalls near the back door where Matthew stood by the corral.

Matthew eased back against the wall beside the door. The blacksmith said something, and the man continued. "They're carting them straight up from Texas to McAlester. I wouldn't be nowhere near that town for all the tea in China."

Matthew pushed away from the barn and rubbed the blue roan's face again. She bobbed her head, nudging him in the chest. The pressure pushed the lingering cough from him, and suddenly, he couldn't stop. He doubled over and held his chest. Seconds passed before he caught his breath. He was finally able to straighten and rubbed the back of his neck. Eyes burning, an intense sweat broke out on his forehead while he shivered in the mist.

The blacksmith stepped to the back door and asked Matthew, "Make up your mind?"

Matthew held onto the top rail of the corral, steadying himself, contemplating his choices. New friends in Krebs needed his help. Ruth Ann desperately needed him at the newspaper. From the congestion in his chest, he was fast becoming ill. His brother had shoved him away with fists, threats, and lies.

Matthew nodded to the blue roan. "Which way would I take her?"

The blacksmith came on out and stood next to Matthew, giving the roan a pat.

"You seem like a good fellow. I don't want to lie to you." The blacksmith pulled out a small bag that jingled. He tossed it in the air and caught it with the same hand.

"Truth is, that man paid me to send you on a false trail. He headed northeast but said to send you southeast. Something about you running smack into home that way."

The blacksmith glanced at Matthew and shook the bag. "I can't rightly keep this money if you go after him. Take it if you do. Or you can go home."

Matthew reached up a hand to rub the back of the blue roan's ear. Maybe he could find a way to do all the things he had to.

He held his palm out. The blacksmith tossed the bag. Matthew caught it. "I'll see that this gets back to him."

"Safe travels, wherever you're off to. Just don't make it McAlester. Things are about to get ugly there."

Matthew nodded and walked away. He had a train ticket to buy to McAlester, his first of four destinations.

CHAPTER 34

In the pre-dawn darkness Thursday morning, Ruth Ann was running off a flyer about a potato sale at Bates General Store. She had slept only a few hours, in and out of bed making story notes at her vanity, trying not to disturb her mother. She crept out of the house at 5a.m., the earliest she'd ever trekked to the shop. Such emptiness on the streets! But if she couldn't sleep like everyone else, she may as well get work done.

Now her apron was covered with fresh ink stains before dawn. She'd never run the press so much. Ever since she over-inked it and ruined the last of their printing paper in the early days of the *Choctaw Tribune*, Ruth Ann avoided operating the thing.

But they wouldn't have time to run this advertisement once the morning got underway, not if they wanted to put out the daily every day this week. Ruth Ann was determined to stay ahead in the advertisement race with the *Dickens Herald*.

Yet did it make any difference? Did Matthew care? Surely he had seen a copy of the daily as the *Choctaw Tribune* made its way throughout the Nation. They had several subscribers in the coal mining country thanks to Matthew's smart soliciting. Hopefully,

213

he was making more connections, though how could he with using an alias?

The fact that Matthew hadn't sent a wire either stating she was crazy for doing a daily or praising her initiative meant he wasn't able to because he was in a terrible situation. Or maybe he was just busy.

Philip and Daddy had been overdue on their last trip. Lost forever. Dead.

The last thought bolted into Ruth Ann's mind before she could check it. She ruined the next dozen flyers. Her eyes blurred.

The bell over the front door jingled, and Ruth Ann berated herself for not locking the door. She wasn't ready to open the shop for customers and potential problems that needed solving.

Ruth Ann used the backs of her hands to brush her hair away from her wet face. She was immensely relieved to see it was only Lance striding toward her in the first beams of morning light, his face concerned. "I was afraid I'd find you here this early."

Ruth Ann sighed and dropped her arms, not caring how her hair fell over her eyes. "You think this is early?"

She wiped her hands with a rag to clean the ink off. Her hands were always stained these days.

Lance looked at the stack of advertisements she'd already done and what she had left to do. "You have to hire full-time help."

"Are you applying?"

Lance shrugged. "I should. Got nothing better to do in the hours I'm not teaching."

Ruth Ann cocked her head with a teasing smile, grateful for a distraction. "Oh, really?"

Lance's face flushed, and he ducked his head between his shoulders. "I should do more, especially after what Christopher Maxwell said at dinner with us last night."

Ruth Ann straightened, smile gone. "Oh, really?"

She headed for the desk, picked up a tablet, and stared at it. There was a story coming. What was she supposed to do with it? Her mind was blank.

Lance kept talking. "Maxwell is so confident he'll put the *Tribune* out of business with your brother gone, but he won't, not if I can help it. I've been trying to think of some way to trip him up if he tries anything underhanded, like print rumors about Matthew while he's away...Ruth Ann?"

His voice was distant as if he was calling from across a lake. Ruth Ann lowered the tablet, one hand on the desk to steady herself. She stared at the papers scattered on Matthew's desk. What lies might Maxwell print about her brother?

Matthew. He should be here, making the decisions. Standing up to Maxwell. Could she if she had to? Yet none of it mattered—none of this work, this fight for truth, if Matthew were...

"Ruth Ann?" Lance held onto her arm.

"I have to...I have to go to McAlester," she murmured. "Find out what is going on with the strike. We need more front page headlines."

Lance stepped in front of her, looking closely at her face. "You need to rest. I'll go. Beulah can teach classes. I'll find Matthew."

Ruth Ann slowly pulled her arm from his grasp. "I'll leave on the first train north. He has to be...the story is all around McAlester. That's where I'll start."

Lance stayed in front of her, hands out as though he wanted to make everything all right. "Ruth Ann, please, you're wearing yourself to collapse. Matthew wouldn't want this. He loves you more than any newspaper—"

"I have to."

"Let me go, Ruth Ann, please. You're exhausted, and besides, that's a long trip to make alone for a..." Lance halted.

Ruth Ann laughed, feeling silly. Worried silly. "A woman, Mr. Fuller? Perhaps. But I'll be fine." She raised her eyes to meet his, to let him know she was perfectly sane. "You just look after the Jessops, all right?"

Lance sighed, avoiding her teasing gaze. "Has anyone ever told you, you're a stubborn Choctaw?"

Ruth Ann gathered a tablet and pencils. "I hear it runs in the family."

CHAPTER 35

"It's down there." Al pointed to a square hole in the ground, surrounded by a fence and covered loosely with boards.

After riding across the mountains, they were just north of Wilburton. Philip only spared a flickering glance at the abandoned mine shaft. He kept his eyes on the surrounding woods and on Al Percy. The nervous man hadn't looked over his shoulder one time. This was comfortable territory for him, which made Philip uncomfortable. He was close to Dan Holder's hideout at last. He could feel it. Whether or not this was a trap, he wasn't certain.

They dismounted and tied their horses near the dilapidated shaft mine entrance. There wasn't much left of the engine house. It appeared the builders didn't find what they were looking for in this mine.

Al cracked open the door on the engine house and retrieved a battered lantern by a length of rope tied to it. He lit the lantern and nodded toward the shaft opening. "You'll find three gunny sacks alongside the east wall. Get five double eagles from the smallest one. I'll keep watch here."

Philip chuckled to let Al know he wasn't that kind of fool. "Why don't you shinny on down, and I'll keep watch?"

"I...well, it'd be better..."

Philip grabbed Al by the arm and yanked him toward the shaft as though he were going to throw him in. Dust puffed from their scuffed mining boots and floated over the entrance to the fence as Al dug in his heels. The lantern banged against his leg, and he yelped.

Philip kicked away the boards to reveal sheer blackness. He put his mouth by Al's ear as the man breathed heavy. "Some particular reason you don't want to go down there? Snakes? Poison gasses?

Al squeaked. "Nothing like that. Nothing dangerous down there."

"Good. Then you won't mind going first. Don't worry, I'll be right behind you. I've never seen three bags full of double eagles."

The way Al shook made Philip wonder if the man would survive the descent on the rickety wooden ladder that clung to the side of the shaft, disappearing into the darkness.

Al looked like he planned to protest again, but instead, he carefully tied the lantern's rope around his waist. He lowered the lantern over the edge then cautiously began the climb down. One thing about a mine shaft—it wasn't the first time Philip and Al Percy had gone down one together.

The lantern didn't give much light, just enough for Philip to keep an eye on Al, and to spot missing pieces in the ladder. Al didn't warn him they were coming, even when entire sections went missing, and they had to use the wall braces for footing.

For a man with no guts, Al wasn't afraid of mining work. He wasted no time making the two hundred foot descent down the shaft. Wooden platforms along the way offered the chance for rest, but Al didn't take one.

Philip stifled a gasp when the wall in front of him disappeared. A thump echoed below as Al made it to the bottom.

Philip glanced down and realized the last two ladder sections dangled in the air, barely reaching the floor of the mine.

He got his bearings and hopped the last few feet off the ladder, a halo of dust puffing around his feet. He grinned. "No snakes after all, eh?"

Al stretched his arms after the climb, and Philip glanced around at what he could see in the limited light. He wished he had a cap with the headlamp like they used in the mines, but he could make out most of the cavernous room. Cleaned out of all supplies, a low door indicated the only branch of this mine explored before the engineers realized they had dug a hole in the wrong place.

Along the east wall were three gunny sacks, just like Al said. Philip was a little surprised he had told the truth. What was the catch?

Philip headed for the sacks then halted, his heart thudding. The sack on the right looked exactly like the one he and his father had that day…

"Halito, my old friend."

The voice came from the lone branch of the mineshaft. Philip swung around to see a shadowy yet familiar form filling the doorway. The light of the lantern caught a glint on the steel gun barrel pointed at Philip.

Lester Cotten moved into the light. "Don't mean to appear hostile, buddy, but I know you can be quick with a gun…if you were carrying one."

Al stuttered, "You know Toby Nicholas?"

Lester offered him a sad kind of smile, never taking his eyes off Philip. "I know that Toby Nicholas is an alias for Philip Teller."

Al glared at Philip. "You lied to me!"

Philip scoffed. "And you lied when you said there were no snakes down here."

He decided to pay no more attention to Al Percy. The

frontman had done his job—he led Philip to Lester Cotten, who was only one step away from Dan Holder.

Philip flexed the fingers of his right hand, wishing he did have a gun to draw on Lester Cotten.

That day, after the two faked Phillip's death, Lester told Phillip to meet him the following week in Skullyville. Lester never showed.

When Philip went to Kat with the whole miserable story, she wanted nothing to do with him. She acted just like his father warned him, the kind of girl who wouldn't stay committed through bad times. Their relationship continued off and on over the past six years. They were attached because of their little girl.

But Philip had never been able to track down Lester. Now there he was, gun in hand and ready to defend his old leader, Dan Holder.

Philip shifted to eye the bags of money. "Never got around to spending that blood money, did you?"

The line of Lester's lips went flat. "I told you before, I never meant for anyone to get hurt. Your daddy would still be alive if he hadn't drawn that rifle."

Philip laughed, mocking. "Yeah, shooting back at men shooting at you is a real fool thing to do."

His body shook with the energy it took to restrain himself from charging into Lester and strangling him to death. If Lester meant to shoot him, Philip at least wanted a chance to bring a little justice for his father first.

Lester motioned with the gun for Philip to move away from the bags and ordered Al to retrieve them. They were tied together with a length of rope. The coins jingled as Al dragged the heavy load toward the ladder.

Lester beckoned to Al. "Get on up to the first landing."

Al glanced between the two men, then scrambled up the ladder, lantern banging the rungs below him.

Lester didn't move, didn't speak for several moments as he

returned Philip's stare, then said quietly, "I always figured I'd have to kill you someday."

He lowered his pistol slightly. "But not today."

Al was up to the point where the ladder connected with the wall at the first landing less than twenty feet up. Al scooted onto the landing and turned, seated. Lester called to him, "Keep my old friend here covered."

Al withdrew a derringer Philip hadn't known the man carried. Stupid. How could Philip be so stupid?

But hadn't he always been?

Lester holstered his Colt .45 and picked up one end of the rope attached to the bags. He rapidly made the climb and joined Al on the landing. He hoisted the bags up after them.

The lantern still swung in midair, illuminating Lester's grin as he leaned down and began unhooking the top of the last two sections of ladder, sixteen feet worth.

Philip had wondered if he'd meet his demise in a coal mine, but not like this. He calculated the distance between him and the ladder but didn't dwell on the odds. He dashed for the lower ladder section and leaped halfway up it. A bullet whizzed past his ear. He looked up to find Al Percy's derringer feet from his face. He halted, clinging to the rungs.

Lester's tone above Philip was steady. "Be grateful Al's a poor shot. But he never misses from this range. Now off you go."

Philip slowly went down the ladder. Lester finished unhooking it and drew it up, leaving nothing but empty air for sixteen feet.

Lester leaned the ladder section against the wall on the landing then looked back over the edge. "I'll send along a note to your brother. He's been going by the name of Matt Jameson, hasn't he? I'll let him decide if you're worth fishing out."

Philip clenched his fists, glaring up at Lester and Al as he blinked away the grit that dropped when they shifted on the landing.

Lester leaned over to speak to him again, somber this time. "Listen, Chukfi, I've saved your life more than once now. I want you to think about that long and hard while you're waiting. When you see that brother of yours, you just think about him and your family and forget all about what you've wanted to do. It's time you went home."

Philip stared back at him. Lester sighed, pulled up the lantern, and left Philip in total darkness.

cAlester was in a wild uproar. Federal troops were positioned at the train depot, in the maelstrom of people pushing to board the Katy. Cavalry troops delayed things as they checked the identities of everyone getting on and off. Children cried while their mothers tried to hush them, but the mothers cried, too.

Ruth Ann took in the scene from the passenger car with her mouth agape. She twisted in the hard bench of the train car as she watched through the window, shocked.

There were blue uniforms on a train platform in the Choctaw Nation. Federal troops had no business in their territory unless the chief requested them.

Ruth Ann was glad she'd come herself. She should have come here right away to find front page stories for the *Tribune*. Matthew had only sent her a few articles. There was so much more here.

There was no point in trying to get off yet. The aisle was jammed with people working their way to the doors while others struggled to get on.

How could Ruth Ann possibly find Matthew in this mass? Yet

the answer was simple. Her brother would be there, somewhere, right in the worst of things as always.

The whistle blew for boarding. She had to get off. Gathering her tablet, reticule, and courage, she stood and squeezed down the aisle. Her seat was filled by a man who had the collar of his jacket turned up to hide his face. Ruth Ann wondered if he was on the list to be expelled from Indian Territory or afraid he was.

She stumbled on the steps of the train because of the press before and behind her. A strong hand grabbed her arm and helped her stagger unladylike to the platform. She looked up to thank the man, but he barked, "Name and where are you from?"

Ruth Ann bristled when the U.S. cavalry lieutenant didn't release her arm. He was too young for the hard scowl on his face. Troops assigned to Indian Territory had little opportunity for glory, so they made the most of any excitement.

She tried to pull her arm free, but he tightened his grip. She gave him her meanest look, which made no visible impression.

"I'm Ruth Ann Teller, a Choctaw Nation citizen, and if you don't release me immediately, I'll give a scream that will turn your hair gray."

The young lieutenant examined her face too intimately for Ruth Ann's liking, but he finally released her.

"Sorry, ma'am. We have orders to check everyone coming in and out of McAlester. There's a strike going on—"

"Yes, yes, I know." Ruth Ann pushed past him. Another train whistle added to the panic. People surged forward, desperate to board, but the troops held them back, still trying to check each person's identity.

Ruth Ann made it off the crowded platform only to run smack into a roughly dressed man.

"Pardon me." Ruth Ann looked up and gasped. "Matthew! What are you—"

Matthew clamped a hand over her mouth. She squirmed away

and stared up into his battered face. Her jaw dropped, but he looked more surprised to see her.

"What is going on—"

"Keep quiet!" he hissed, giving her a little shake. She just stared at him. Beyond the bruises on his face, she saw something in his dark brown eyes—hurt so deep it scared her.

Matthew's voice was husky like he'd been coughing for days. "What do you think you're doing here, Ruth Ann? You have to leave. Can't have anyone see us—"

"Hey there!" A man who had been loading a wagon grabbed Matthew's shoulder and swung him around. "Don't be bothering decent folks, you coal digger—"

Matthew's arm whipped up and whacked the man's hand from his shoulder. The man, a rancher from his dress, clenched his hands into fists. Ruth Ann stepped between them.

"Oh, no sir, he wasn't bothering me. He..." Ruth Ann put a hand on Matthew's chest in a friendly gesture and felt it rattle with each breath he took. Much like when he'd been shot. "We're old friends. Just surprised to run into each other."

The rancher glared at Matthew before tipping his hat toward Ruth Ann and going back to his wagon.

Hand still on Matthew's chest, Ruth Ann gave a push against his stubborn frame. He didn't budge. She looped her arm through his and managed to lead him away from the uproar of the depot, strolling casually, hoping he would relax. He didn't.

Ruth Ann maneuvered through wagon and foot traffic to a quiet side street before bursting out, "What in heaven's name happened to you?"

"Heaven had nothing to do with it. Now go home. I'll send you a story of what happens today."

Ruth Ann lowered her voice. "Matthew Teller, I am not going anywhere until you tell me what's going on. We've been worried to death, and the newspaper—"

"I know about the daily."

Her heart dropped, and she jerked away to face him. "I have worked myself sick for your newspaper while you've been gallivanting around…"

She halted and wished she could breathe back the words, but they had flown and were no longer her own.

Matthew said nothing, just stared at her, bruised and stubborn. What had he gotten into? He had the look of someone on a mission, yet something else, something she'd never seen in her brother. It was almost as though he were…lost? She couldn't pinpoint it.

Her arms trembled as she kept them to her sides, not wanting to attract attention from those passing by on the boardwalk. She wanted to either hug Matthew or hit him. Instead, she talked fast.

"I've been so worried about you, and the newspaper. The Enterprise Hotel manager, Blane Johnson, came and said Mr. Maxwell offered him a better rate, and then Peter came up with a competition of who could get the most response from ads for the hotel restaurant and then Mr. Dodd quit…"

Ruth Ann trailed off, expecting Matthew to react to her news about the hotel advertising account. But her brother didn't flinch, his eyes brooding, a storm within them. Maybe he'd already known. Or maybe he didn't care about the newspaper anymore.

"Say something, Matt. Say you're disappointed with me, that you shouldn't have left me with so much responsibility, that you regret you couldn't have been there, but the work here is too important. Just say *something*."

Ruth Ann clenched her fists. A year ago, she would have slugged him. But they were too grown for that. And Matthew was too far away from her. He was far away.

He finally spoke. "I have business here in McAlester. You will ruin it if you stay."

Ruth Ann ground her teeth. "You won't tell me anything else?"

Matthew didn't move, and Ruth Ann knew he was still the most stubborn in the family. She wished her mother were there.

Della could make him mind, if she would. This was one of those times Ruth Ann suspected their mother would let her son work out whatever he was doing until he came to the end of it. That was all Ruth Ann could do. At least she knew Matthew was alive, if not well.

She narrowed her eyes. "I'll go home only after I do a few interviews. And I'm going to talk to Mr. Dodd."

She said this last part firmly, though she'd given it no thought until then. But Dodd might have answers to her problems in Dickens.

Matthew nodded. "Fine. Wait here. I know right where he is."

Ruth Ann strained to watch him through the crowded street and caught sight of the store Matthew entered. Only it wasn't a store. It was the *Indian Citizen* newspaper office. He reappeared moments later, Dodd walking in front of him with short, uneven steps.

Ruth Ann darted through the street traffic to follow them to an alley beside the newspaper office. The space was overrun with broken crates and barrels, but that didn't fully obscure the view she had of Dodd cornered by Matthew between the wall and a stack of crates.

She hurried to Matthew's side. "What are you doing?"

Dodd set a panicked gaze on Ruth Ann. "Miss Teller, honest, I just did what I had to do. I—"

Matthew took a step closer to the man, barely leaving a breath between them, looking like he was about to maul the cowering man. "Who made you quit, and why?"

Ruth Ann grabbed her brother's arm. "Be civilized. What would Daddy say?"

Matthew stepped back. Dodd looked ready to crumple.

Ruth Ann wanted to be angry with them both. "Mr. Dodd, if someone threatened you in Dickens...well, I give you my word they won't know the information came from you. Just tell me, was Christopher Maxwell involved in your quitting the *Choctaw Tribune?*"

Dodd stayed pressed against the wall, away from Matthew. "Look, Miss Teller, I really don't know anything. But watch out for Maxwell, he wants to put the *Tribune* out of business."

"We've known that since we started." Matthew's tone was deathly calm.

Ruth Ann tried again. "What is Mr. Maxwell planning?"

Dodd shifted his guarded look from Matthew to Ruth Ann. "He'll go after anyone who tries to work at your newspaper. Most likely do some kind of blackmail." Dodd massaged his throat. "Like he did me."

Odd compassion came over Ruth Ann. "How?"

Matthew's voice was gruff. "It doesn't matter now."

Ruth Ann turned back to their former employee. "Well, thank you for your help, Mr. Dodd. Sorry to have interrupted your day." She felt ridiculous being polite, but she didn't know how else to be.

Matthew stepped to the side, and Dodd nodded to Ruth Ann before breaking into a jog and disappearing around the corner to the *Indian Citizen* office.

Ruth Ann gave an exasperated sigh. "What were you thinking, accosting a man like that—"

"Have said."

She stared at her brother like he'd gone crazy. "What?"

"You said, 'what would Daddy say?' The correct tense is 'have said.' He's gone, Annie. Never coming back."

Ruth Ann stared at her brother through the sudden tears in her eyes. She whispered, "Oh, Matt, why would you say that..."

Matthew headed back to the boardwalk. "You talked to Dodd. Now get on home."

"Matt..." Ruth Ann whimpered as she followed him. She couldn't grasp who this person was with her caring brother's face.

Someone screamed loud enough to be heard over the din in the streets. "Matt!"

Matthew swiveled, a look of dread in his eyes. A young woman, long black hair pulled back in a braid, raced through the foot traffic on the boardwalk. Instead of slowing down, she barreled into Matthew, causing him to stagger back. She smothered her face in his shoulder.

Ruth Ann gaped.

Matthew eased the young woman away from him, but she clung to his jacket.

"Matt, Matt," she sobbed, her trembling head angled down. "They are going to expel my papà from the territory. I'm sorry for everything I've said to him…about him…the mines are all he knows, they are his life. Oh, he didn't do anything!" She buried her face in Matthew's chest.

Ruth Ann stared at her brother and the young woman. Matthew's face flushed. He didn't meet Ruth Ann's gaze.

"This is…um…Cadenza Bianchi. Her father is a miner in Krebs."

She crossed her arms and glared at him, trying not to sputter words she'd regret. His answer was not at all sufficient.

The young woman, Cadenza, pulled back from Matthew and turned to see Ruth Ann. "Oh! I am so sorry, Matt Jameson." She wiped her tears and smiled at Ruth Ann. "I didn't know you had a lady friend."

It was Ruth Ann's turn to flush, and she opened her mouth to correct the notion, but Matthew spoke to Cadenza first. "Let's make this one of our secrets, all right?"

His voice was soft like he was soothing a terrified colt, so soft it wounded Ruth Ann. She wished he had spoken to her like that, like he did before whatever had happened to make him put a wall between them.

What other secrets did these two have?

Cadenza nodded, oblivious to Ruth Ann again. "Please, Matt

Jameson, just save my papà, yes? He'll never work again if they blacklist him."

"I'll do what I can."

Cadenza went up on tiptoe to give him a kiss on the cheek. Then she ran off.

Ruth Ann swallowed everything that was on her tongue. She stiffened with resolve and headed for the street. "*Chi pisa la chike*, Matthew Teller. I hope."

"Hey."

Matthew caught Ruth Ann as she passed and pulled her into his arms. She rested her head against his chest. It rattled with every breath he took.

He stroked her hair and spoke softly. "*Chi hullo li.*" *I love you.*

Ruth Ann breathed in the smell of coal dust and horseflesh on his coat. "I'm going to slug you when you get home."

"I've earned it."

Matthew released her and gazed a long time into her eyes, lips parted to speak, but nothing came out. It was as though he wanted to say something, something so earth-shattering he was scared to speak it. He looked at her like never before, his lips tight, eyes watery, like he'd be willing to give her the world any other time, but for this moment, she asked too much.

Ruth Ann wondered if it had to do with Cadenza, whoever she was. Or the strike. But no. It had to be something beyond her imagination.

"Chi pisa la chike." Matthew left her on the boardwalk, disappearing in the flow of traffic.

Ruth Ann stood still, people passing on either side of her. It felt like all the chaos around was inside her, but it was all right. Or at least, it would be. She trusted Matthew, no matter how he acted. He would set everything right.

Ruth Ann took a deep breath, withdrew her tablet and pencil from her reticule, and headed to the nearest hotel restaurant to observe people she might interview. Matthew had left her on her own in a way that told her he thought she could look after herself and the newspaper. And she would. She had stories to write and a newspaper to publish. A very good newspaper. One her people needed. A newspaper she loved so much it hurt.

The same kind of hurt as loving her brother.

God knows.

CHAPTER 37

Matthew didn't look back when he left Ruth Ann. If he did, his resolve would melt away and he'd tell her that their brother was still alive but lost, and then she'd grieve Philip all over again. The things he'd said to Annie were harsh and sharp, but not as bad as the truth.

Truth. When had he lost sense of what that was? Like Cadenza and her father had done with one another.

Her reaction to her father's impending eviction from the Choctaw Nation surprised Matthew. How many layers of pain were in Cadenza's heart, and which was her father in? If she genuinely wanted Ricco Bianchi in her life, she'd have to unlock the truth about what happened with the mining accident.

God, help them.

Matthew headed for the Tobucksy County Courthouse which was run by the Choctaw government. The irony wasn't lost on him that the very county was named using the Choctaw word for "coal," *tobaksi.*

Matthew knew the sitting judge, and the judge knew him. That wouldn't bode well. Last year, the judge had been angry when Matthew accidentally uncovered an affair he had before becoming a judge. Matthew didn't print the sensational story, but the man was not as appreciative as he could have been. It was time he showed that appreciation.

The wide front porch at the top of three steps was loaded with arguing men. There was no court in session. Most likely the Choctaw men were there about intruders or strikers or lease agreements or demanding to know why federal troops were camped out in McAlester and how long they'd be around.

A few men glanced warily at Matthew as he trudged up the steps. Hopefully, they didn't recognize him in his mining clothes and battered face. He headed straight inside, landing in the middle of the courtroom.

There was no foyer, no hallway, just an abrupt entry to the courtroom with its long bench seats facing the wall to Matthew's right where a single table stood as the judge's bench. A fireplace tucked into the wall behind it was cold, as cold as the feeling in the room. A stern-looking woman eyed him from a small table near the judge's bench. Her hand poised in midair, pencil between her fingers, indicated she was expending great patience to address him.

"May I help you?" Her standard words sounded like she wanted to do anything but help another disgruntled Choctaw or miner, whichever he was.

"Judge Kendrick in?"

"He's busy." *So am I,* her expression said. "You will have to wait outside."

"I see. Thank you."

Matthew stepped back out the door and headed to the side of the porch, keeping out of arm-waving reach of the animated men in heated discussions. He eased off the porch, wincing at the pain in his ribs and shoulder.

There was a well close by, and Matthew took advantage of it. He removed the dusty miner coat and shook it out. With fresh water drawn in the wooden bucket, he used the ladle to splash water over his head and gingerly washed his face. He combed his wet hair with his fingers, feeling chilled and sniffing, but he held the coughing in check.

He folded the coat neatly over his arm and went back to the courthouse. Three men, deep in conversation, brushed by and inside. He slipped in behind them. They blocked the secretary's view as Matthew made a beeline between the observer benches to one of two doors on the far side of the room. One led to a holding area for prisoners. The other was the judge's office.

Matthew gave a quick knock on the judge's door and opened it, stepping inside like he'd been invited. Conversation in the office halted. He nodded at the judge.

"Good afternoon, sir. I have a favor to ask."

Mixed-blood Choctaw Judge Kendrick sat behind his desk, fingers steepled over his stomach pooch as he conversed with the U.S. cavalry officers seated across from him. One was a captain, the other a lieutenant.

The judge collapsed his steepled fingers into a balled fist, frowning. "Matthew Teller of the *Choctaw Tribune*, is it? As you can see, I'm busy."

Matthew shut the door. "I appreciate that, but my business is urgent. It concerns a man about to be blacklisted and expelled from the Choctaw Nation, a miner by the name of Ricco Bianchi. I want you to cross his name from the list and renew his permit."

Judge Kendrick laughed. The cavalry officers exchanged looks and chuckled.

The judge smirked. "You, along with the Italian and British embassies, get the same answer—no. Now, remove yourself from my office, or I'll have the Lighthorse place you under arrest."

"You're forgetting the little favor you owe me."

Judge Kendrick's face turned scarlet. He rose and planted his fists on his desk. "You...you knew nothing about...that is, there was nothing to know..."

His gaze flickered to the cavalry officers, then he glared at

Matthew. This was the opportune moment Matthew had hoped for.

Judge Kendrick slowly lowered himself into his chair, withdrew papers from a drawer, and began scribbling.

The captain sighed loudly. "Judge, we need to finish our business. Now."

Judge Kendrick half rose from his seat to pass one paper off to the captain. He tossed another one at Matthew, which he caught. It was Ricco Bianchi's permit to work as a miner in the Choctaw Nation.

The captain read his paper. "Very well, we'll mark Bianchi off the list. Now, can we please return to important matters?"

Matthew left. Hopefully he wouldn't need any more favors from the judge. He wouldn't catch him by surprise next time.

Matthew picked up his rifle and saddlebags from where he'd stowed them at the hotel. He left McAlester behind for the second destination on his list.

The road to Krebs was crowded compared to when Matthew walked Cadenza down it the day before. People coming from Krebs didn't meet his eyes. Everyone hurried along.

Matthew kept his stride long and was soon in Krebs. He headed for Ricco Bianchi's house.

Devlin Bishop stood in front of a company house, conversing with a group of men. Torre and his son Fabio were among them. Bishop spotted Matthew. The group turned and followed him as he blocked Matthew's path.

"Hello there, Jameson. Come to lead the miners of Krebs in their fight?"

Matthew halted. "I have other business here, then I'm leaving."

"You do that often, don't you, Jameson? Leave, that is. Makes me wonder what your business is. Maybe spying? Trying to get the good men around here expelled from the Choctaw Nation?"

The men made a semi-circle around Matthew. Even Torre and Fabio eyed him with suspicion.

Matthew tried to push past Bishop, but two other men crowded close to their leader, closing off daylight. Like in Savanna, Matthew doubted Bishop's commitment to avoid violence.

The strike leader crossed his arms, eyes ablaze like when he faced down the mine boss. "I thought we could count on you when the chips were down, but no matter what's right, you Indians always side with your own kind."

Matthew flinched. Hanraty had told Bishop about him after all, and now Bishop was telling the world, at least the world in Krebs.

The half-circle of men around Matthew stared at one another and him. Matthew knew the faces of these men from his short time in Krebs, working the Osage Mine No. 2 and beating Lehigh with them in the baseball game. But their faces distorted into strangers filled with disgust. The one that hurt most was young Fabio's, his temper quick to flare. He spat and asked, "That true, grignollo? You are a Choctaw Indian?"

They would never understand Matthew's reasoning, so there was little point in trying to explain. He said nothing.

"What is the commotion about?"

Raphael Bianchi used his booming voice and burly frame to make a way through the circle. He halted between Bishop and Matthew.

"What you fellows doing looking like you want to tar and feather my young friend here?"

Torre stepped forward, scowling, and spoke to Raphael. "It seems this grignollo who calls himself Matt Jameson is a Choctaw Indian, here to spy on us for his people. Why else all his questions and sneaking off?"

Matthew's hand went to his coat pocket, thinking of Ricco's permit. But the men around him grumbled louder.

Raphael met Matthew's gaze. His dark brown eyes showed disbelief, then hurt. "Is that true, my friend? Are you a Choctaw?"

Matthew had to answer his friend who held so much trust in his eyes. "Yes."

The men kicked dust at Matthew and whistled angrily.

When the first wave of dust hit him, Matthew's lungs constricted. He grabbed his chest and coughed into his coat sleeve. His saddlebags slipped off his shoulder and onto his arm. Someone grabbed him, and he let himself be jerked out of the swirling dust and down the road. He blinked as he approached the side of a company house.

That someone with a strong hand swung Matthew around and slammed his back into the wall. The action sprang his rifle and saddlebags from his grasp. The pain was not unlike being hit by the explosion of his first day in the mine, only now, it was a Raphael Bianchi explosion.

"Listen carefully, Matt Jameson, or whatever your name is: you will leave this place and never come back. Capisci?"

Matthew leaned his head against the wall and breathed carefully to avoid another hacking cough, his body shaking more than it should. Raphael had shown Matthew grace by getting him out of the ring, but his sore back wasn't appreciative.

"I never lied to you, Raphael, not in that way." He tried to swallow, moisten his throat, but too much dust coated his mouth. His voice was still raspy when he said, "I only wanted to earn enough trust to do the work I came to do."

"You don't earn trust with lies, Matt Jameson."

Matthew thought of Philip. "This is very true." He pushed away from the wall. Everything was blurry, and Matthew could feel another raging cough coming up his chest, but he held it back. "Goodbye, Raphael Bianchi."

Matthew scooped up his gear, nearly falling over in the

process, and made it to the end of the row houses and down the slope where he collapsed by an old oak tree near the stream. He needed to get his breath and his senses. He should go into the stream; get clean and numb.

"Psst!"

The hiss came from somewhere behind him, but Matthew didn't want to open his eyes yet. He reached into his coat pocket.

Skirts swished as Cadenza approached. He felt her kneel beside him.

"Matt Jameson, I don't know who knows what or why or how, and I'm not being a bit of help to you, but will you please still help my papà? Please?"

Matthew withdrew the permit from his pocket and cracked his eyelids open enough to see Cadenza's tears. He held out the paper.

"Take this to your father," he whispered. His chest couldn't take another wracking cough right then. "No one will bother him."

Cadenza took the piece of paper and gasped. "You're hurt!"

Matthew dropped his hand. "I'm all right…"

She grabbed his arm and examined his sleeve. She raised her frightened gaze to him.

He looked at where he had coughed into the sleeve of his coat. It was streaked with blood.

By the time the southbound Frisco pulled into the Dickens station near evening, Ruth Ann was in a sleepy state. There were no direct train routes from Dickens to McAlester, so her trip included hitching a ride with a family in a wagon which deposited her at the depot in Tuskahoma, the capitol of the Choctaw Nation, and at last, home.

Ruth Ann stretched her neck gingerly and glanced out the window at the depot as the train jerked to a stop. A familiar figure in the shadows of the platform caught Ruth Ann's attention and caused her to raise an eyebrow. Why would Amarillo Jessop be at the depot?

Ruth Ann exited the passenger car into the cool spring air. She skimmed down the steps and saw Amarillo coming toward her. No, she was heading to the other end of the passenger car.

Something wasn't right. Amarillo carried the baby and a small carpetbag.

"Amarillo! Where are you going?"

Amarillo halted and turned stiffly. She looked surprised to see Ruth Ann, at least as surprised as her wooden expression allowed.

"Back to Texas."

Ruth Ann blocked Amarillo's path. "What do you mean? Where are your siblings? Why are you going?"

Amarillo shifted the sleeping Charles Goodnight Jessop. Ruth Ann got a peek of his dark locks so unlike the rest in the Jessop clan.

"You ask a lot of questions, Miss Teller. I'll send money back for the young'uns' board and keep, don't you worry." She tried to go around Ruth Ann.

Ruth Ann sidestepped to stay in front of Amarillo, spreading out her hands, palms out, gesturing for her to stop. "You didn't answer the why. Your brothers and sisters need you, and Mrs. Warren needs you and Lance…"

Ruth Ann winced, but there wasn't much time. The train whistled for boarding. "There are people here who care very much about you. Why would you leave us?"

Amarillo stared straight at her. "There are people here I care about, too, that's why I have to leave."

"What are you talking about?"

The train whistled, signaling final boarding, but Ruth Ann stepped with Amarillo again, causing the young woman to give a frustrated sigh. If she wasn't holding a baby, Ruth Ann would take the sigh as a warning to duck.

"You don't want to tangle with me, Ruth Ann Teller, so get out of my way. He deserves a respectable woman like you, and I don't want any hard feelings to come between us."

Oh, that was it! Ruth Ann laughed as the train whistled for departure. She caught Amarillo's arm when the young woman pushed past her.

"No, no, Amarillo, there's been a misunderstanding. Lance Fuller is in love with *you*, not me. He and I have talked about it, well, not in detail, but enough for me to know he is dead serious."

Amarillo held still, looking at the passenger car as the conductor got on.

Ruth Ann relaxed her grip. "I'm sorry, I shouldn't have blurted that out, but I couldn't just let you leave. You were doing it for Lance and for me, weren't you? You'd have gone off without a word and lived miserably away from everyone you love just to keep from hurting the ones you love so much. You really are something, Amarillo Jessop."

Amarillo blinked, staring at the train, tears in her eyes. Ruth Ann had never seen her cry.

"It's not just that."

The train pulled away.

The baby awoke and whimpered. Ruth Ann held out her hands, and Amarillo passed Goodnight over. "I prayed and thought it was best this way. I can't let someone as fine as him... but maybe...someday..."

Ruth Ann bounced the baby. "I'm glad something good came of my trip, at least my coming back on the right train. My daddy always said, 'God knows.'"

The young mother dropped her gaze to the baby. "His daddy...I think he was a part of what happened to your daddy."

Ruth Ann stilled, shocked. "What are you talking about?"

"Your mama didn't tell you?"

Ruth Ann stared, completely still.

Amarillo raised her eyes. "I wish my pa had killed Cub Wassom first, before all this." She motioned to the baby.

When Ruth Ann thought her stomach couldn't tighten another turn, it did. She tried to detangle her thoughts.

Her gaze snapped back to Amarillo, observing the pain in her eyes. She didn't want to imagine the horrors that caused it.

For now, though, there was life right in her arms.

She reached with her free hand and took Amarillo's. She lifted it and placed Amarillo's hand on the baby's chest and pressed.

"This heartbeat...this life is beauty from ashes. God doesn't want you to despise it, and neither will I. Nor Lance, if I know him at all."

Amarillo curled her fingers then moved them along the round cheeks of her baby, gazing into his face. Goodnight smiled and waved his hands, caught her loose hair in a fist, and yanked. Amarillo smiled and took him to her bosom.

Ruth Ann slipped her arm around Amarillo's waist. "Let's get you two back home."

~

"Oh, my dear, dear Amarillo!" Mrs. Warren exclaimed as Amarillo stepped into the parlor. Ruth Ann Teller stayed in the entryway behind her.

The robust woman rushed at Amarillo, and she turned slightly to shield her baby from the oncoming rush. Mrs. Warren jerked to a halt and covered her mouth with one hand, tears streaming. "When I read your note, I thought I had lost you both forever. Would you ever forgive me for...for not loving you enough? For not being someone you could love?"

All the way back from the depot, Amarillo thought about what she would say to her benefactress who was so determined to love a family that felt so unlovable.

Amarillo met Mrs. Warren's gaze. "You've been nothing but kind to us, ma'am. It's not your fault I got so much baggage I don't know how to carry it."

Mrs. Warren took a step closer and reached out to clasp the hand that Amarillo had supporting her baby. Her precious, precious son.

"Oh, my dear, we are just two broken souls, aren't we?"

Amarillo relished the soft touch of the woman's fleshy hand. She had never known such softness as this woman offered, nor had she realized until now how much hurt was locked behind the enthusiastic mode Mrs. Warren was always in.

Amarillo turned her hand over to clasp Mrs. Warren's, but she couldn't speak. The woman spoke for them. "What if these two broken souls just made up their minds to heal together?"

Amarillo allowed Mrs. Warren to pull her and Goodnight into a gentle embrace.

The front door opened, and she heard the quiet voices of Ruth Ann and Lance Fuller in the front hallway. The door closed again, and Mrs. Warren drew back with a broad smile for her nephew. Amarillo turned to face him.

He was hesitant. No wonder, after the way she treated him the past week. She didn't know if he would want anything to do with her once he learned the truth about Goodnight and his father, but if there was any way, she would take it.

Amarillo looked between Lance and Mrs. Warren. She gave the older woman's hand a squeeze. "Would you both sit there on the sofa, please? There's something I have to tell you."

CHAPTER 39

atthew trudged through the dark woods, shadows bounding across the rocky path along the way to Wilburton, his third destination. According to the blacksmith in Lehigh, Philip had headed northeast. Dan Holder's hideout must be in the mountains north of Wilburton. That was where Matthew was headed. At least, he hoped. His brain burned with a fever that rendered him senseless every time a cough overtook him. Traveling by foot to Wilburton instead of waiting for the train the next morning wasn't a good idea, but it was the only one he had.

The streaks of blood on his sleeve continued. He needed help.

Krebs was far behind, along with the tearful Cadenza, who begged him to stay at her uncle's home. He was far from the care of his mother, farther from the care of Pokni, the healer in their family.

Something moved in the brush behind Matthew, and he turned, trying to bring his rifle up, but it was too heavy. Through hazy vision and the darkness, he made out a multitude of shadows darting in the woods. One crept his direction. A panther?

244

Matthew took a step back. The shadow became nothing more than a pine tree. The fever was causing his eyes to terrorize his mind. He kept moving.

Moonlight shined beneath an old oak, and Matthew sank into the circle of light, letting his gear slide away from him, legs stretched out.

He leaned his head against the tree and spotted an opening in the budding branches filled with stars.

"Chihowa."

Matthew swallowed what moisture was in his parched throat and tried again. "God. Thank You for being with me, even when my heart wasn't always right. But I don't know what to do now."

He hath shewed thee, O man, what is good; and what doth the LORD require of thee, but to do justly, and to love mercy, and to walk humbly with thy God?

A cough rose in his chest, but Matthew held it down, trying to understand the verse echoing in his heart. The shadows started moving again. He began to sing softly, barely a whisper.

Perfect submission, all is at rest
I in my Savior am happy and blessed
Watching and waiting, looking above
Filled with His goodness, lost in His love.

Matthew couldn't suppress the next cough. It rattled him to the top of his head. He trembled. The moonlight reflected off fresh blood on his sleeve.

Shadows danced before him. The fever? But this time, they morphed and became one, slinking toward him in the darkness outside the moonlight. Matthew wasn't alone with God out in these woods.

He fumbled with the rifle, but his weak hands wouldn't grip it. He drew his legs up, wanting to stand, to fight off the black panther slinking toward him. But he couldn't stand, couldn't fight.

Another round of wracking coughs made his eyes water. When he wiped them clear, the darkness was on him. Matthew braced himself.

The presence of a warm body. Dark hair falling over him, long and silky. Skirts swished in the stillness. The familiar presence was a memory buried deep in his mind. But he couldn't bring it fully to form.

The old woman struck a match, the brilliant light blinding Matthew. An aroma swirled around him, familiar, like his grandmother. When he had asked what the scent was, she just smiled.

Secrets. Too many secrets. When would he get answers?

Matthew closed his eyes. This woman's presence was enough to bear. "Takba. Why did you send me to Krebs?"

When she didn't answer, Matthew opened his eyes to see the Choctaw woman, Takba, mixing something in a bowl. She unbuttoned his shirt and slathered the cold mixture on his chest.

He shivered, then the rattling eased. Matthew took a careful breath and asked, "How did you find me?"

Takba looked into his eyes. Matthew winced. Her gaze was piercing, the kind that would stay with him for nights to come.

She drew a cloth-wrapped bundle from her bag and unfolded it. Cornbread and *nipi shila*—salt pork. She handed it to him. Matthew nibbled on the cornbread, then devoured it. He hadn't realized how hungry he was.

Takba finally spoke in Choctaw. "You must go further north. Hurry. Others will find him soon."

Matthew swallowed the last of the cornbread with a gulp from the canteen she offered. "My brother, Philip? Do you know where he is?"

Takba's eyes darkened. "You must find Dan Holder, the one who led my son on a bad path. The lawmen have not stopped him. You must."

Matthew ripped into the salt pork. He finished it, giving himself time to think before asking, "Is that why you sent me to Krebs, to find and kill Dan Holder to bring rightness to your son's life? What about Philip, did you know he was in McAlester?"

Takba withdrew a tied bundle of herbs from the bag that lay on the ground next to where she knelt. She lit one end and waved it over Matthew in slow, measured motions. Smudging for purification. He breathed in the healing aroma of the herbs.

"I knew he lived."

The reporter side of Matthew was frustrated with the lack of direct answers to his questions. The man inside him said it was enough. He had to continue the journey.

Matthew pushed to his feet with the aid of his rifle. He was weak, but Takba's care refreshed him. He could make it.

She stood. "You must promise. The white man's law will not bring him to justice."

Matthew didn't know how to respond to this woman who had witnessed Marshal Bass Reeves shoot and kill her son in the Jessop cabin. She had seen the kind of man Cub Wassom was.

Was Matthew dishonoring her by not promising to do what she had wanted him to do from the beginning? But God would send him down the right path. He had already sent a healer. "Yakoke."

Takba stood still, piercing Matthew with her eyes. Then she hefted her bag, turned, and became a shadow once again.

CHAPTER 40

At dawn, Matthew found his way to the Katy spur and rode the short train into Wilburton. Takba had confirmed his suspicion that Holder's hideout was north of there, in the same mountains where outlaws like the Abernathy gang hid.

Shoulder pain had started again after the cold, damp night, but whatever treatment Takba used brought his fever down. Maybe it was gone. His cough mostly was, and the food revived him. He needed to keep his strength up all the way through his last destination.

The platform at Wilburton was empty, save for two elder Indian men seated on the steps.

Matthew descended the steps in between them. "Pardon me."

The men, wrinkled as old potatoes, looked up. One lifted his eyebrows.

"If you come to join the posse, you'll need a horse."

Matthew winced, thinking of losing Little Chief in the last posse he'd ridden with. He'd do what he could to avoid another. He shifted his saddlebags as he faced the two men. "What posse?"

The old men exchanged smirks and the one who held a whittling knife and stick whistled low. He muttered to his companion in Choctaw, "He's greener than a spring pasture!"

They chuckled and elbowed one another. It reminded Matthew of the jokes the Italians shared in their language. Except in this language, he understood every word. Matthew replied in Choctaw, "Green or not, I would still like to know what is happening."

The two men stared at him and started chuckling again. The one put aside his knife on the step, stood and shook hands with Matthew.

"Halito. I'm Sanders, and this is Lawechobe. You look like you chasing someone, or someone chasing you."

"Something like that. Who's the posse after?"

Lawechobe eased to his feet. "They's a rumor that two old members of the Dan Holder gang are ridin' up to hide out at his fort. No one knew where it was, but a little boy chasing his dog saw them and followed 'em to it. He hightailed it to tell the sheriff. The posse aims to flush them out once and for all."

Matthew kept emotion from his face, but his insides churned. Was he too late to get Holder? That question demanded a deeper one: Was that the reason he had made this journey, to bring the killer to justice himself?

Matthew wasn't prepared to answer that, so he turned his thoughts to the fact that Al Percy and Philip might be at the hideout. His brother might get caught in the posse's crossfire…

"When did the posse head out?"

"Early this morning. You going to join up with them?"

Matthew shrugged, but he already knew he would. Wherever Al Percy or Dan Holder was, he'd find his brother.

"I joined a posse from here that went after the Abernathy gang." He recalled what Raphael Bianchi said to him in the woods when they first met—a lifetime ago. "A young man was shot, I heard he died later."

Sanders shook his head. "Young Russell? He pulled through all right. Should've seen the balling out his ma gave the sheriff, though, for putting her son in the posse. He would have rather faced a thousand outlaws than her!"

Sanders and Lawechobe chuckled, and Matthew joined them, tension releasing. The boy was alive. That was one positive mark Matthew could put down for this trip.

Lawechobe added, "The sheriff broke up the Abernathy gang last week. Captured their leader and shipped him off to Fort Smith."

"*Chokma*. Good to hear that."

"You'd hear more if you took the time to read this paper."

Lawechobe reached inside his coat pocket and pulled out a rolled-up newspaper and offered it to Matthew.

Matthew took the well-worn, well-read newspaper. It was the Choctaw language version of the *Choctaw Tribune*, the latest of Ruth Ann's daily editions. It caused warmth to spread through his chest, comforting, reassuring that he did some good things in his life.

The headlines featured stories about the mining strike, though with just general information. He hadn't sent Ruth Ann anything useful in days, and she'd already burned through all the content. She likely hadn't had time to write about her experiences in McAlester yet.

What she was doing with a daily was ridiculous, but what right did he have to complain when she was pouring her heart and soul into it, and he'd done nothing but snap at her? He needed to get back to Dickens and straighten everything out...

Matthew rolled the newspaper and handed it back to Lawechobe. Painful as it was to see his sister and the newspaper—his life's calling—suffer, he couldn't abandon this journey he was on, not when he was this close to the truth, to justice, to Philip. What price was he willing to pay to redeem his brother?

"Haven't had much time for reading."

"Eh, you young'uns are all the same, got no time for the

important things." Lawechobe opened the paper again with a shake and pointed at the first byline. "This little gal here, Ruth Ann Teller, she's something else, putting out a daily paper. Why, I never paid this newspaper no mind before, but it's really giving me a new outlook on our nation. Like, thinking about all them Europeans coming to work in the coal mines. I never knew nothing about them, 'cept what trouble they cause. But I read things in here like them playing baseball, and how their little ones go to school and church, and how gutsy them men are working in the mines…it makes a fellow think."

Matthew stared at the two Choctaw men, nodding at one another in agreement. The daily. Little Annie's crazy daily.

No time to ponder it now. "So, where is this so-called outlaw fort?"

Lawechobe shrugged. "It's so-called because the thing is built like one, according to the boy. But the sheriff has something special."

Lawechobe grinned knowingly at Sanders. Matthew asked, "What's that?"

"Well, now, I reckon you'll just have to ride up there to find out. Take the road straight up the mountain. Better get a horse though, Mister…what you say your name is?"

There was no point in using an alias any longer. "Matthew Teller from Dickens, near the Red River on the Frisco line."

Sanders whistled and poked Lawechobe with his elbow. He pointed at the paper.

"Say, don't you write for this paper sometimes? You any relation to that Ruth Ann Teller?"

Matthew suppressed a smile. "Something like that. Where can I get a horse to catch up with the posse?"

CHAPTER 41

atthew slowed the Choctaw filly to give her a breather after climbing the mountain trail awhile. He noted a shaft mine entrance near the rough road, the earth yawning in a cry of abandonment. This wasn't because of the strike. No one had been there in months, maybe years. Weeds sprouted from the dirt to stake claims around the black hole.

Matthew pushed a few miles further, up the ever steepening rocky terrain of the Sans Bois Mountains. The clacking of the filly's hooves echoed in the woods on either side of the road. A horse whinnied from somewhere above and to his right. He halted and spotted a beaten trail between two large oaks that led up an incline of nearly sheer rock. It fit the description of the trail Lawechobe gave that led to Dan Holder's hideout.

The filly pranced, and Matthew stroked her neck. She was as jittery as Lawechobe had said with a wink. He was letting Matthew borrow her for the experience she would get of being up in the mountains.

When the filly settled and pricked up her ears, Matthew turned her toward the path between the oaks. He urged her up the trail despite the thick overgrowth and spilling of rocks. He grabbed a handful of the filly's brown and white mane as she charged up, wincing at shoulder pain still annoying him. He leaned forward, using his whole body to encourage her in the climb, her lungs beneath Matthew heaving to draw in air. She slipped once, but he kept her head up, and she regained her footing.

They topped the rise, shaking but steady. Good thing Matthew had taken time to eat breakfast in Wilburton. He needed all the strength he could muster.

He turned his attention to the woods ahead, nudging the pony forward. They entered an opening in the woods that held picket lines where a dozen unsaddled horses were tied. The horses twitched their ears at the new arrival, but were calm despite shouting not far away.

Matthew dismounted and tied the filly to one of the lines. He withdrew his rifle from the scabbard, gave the filly's neck a calming stroke, and headed toward the commotion. The posse.

He spotted clumps of men ahead in the woods. Beyond them lay a clearing, and in the middle of it was Dan Holder's "fort."

Matthew entered among the men in the woods where they collided with one another, darting back and forth, checking for activity at the outlaw hideout. He slipped in among the sentries to get a good look at the home of the man who had killed his father.

The area around the fort was free of trees and brush, affording no cover for the posse to get close. A chopping block and axe were off to one side, left as though someone had been in the middle of work. A shed sat further away and downhill, not close enough to provide protection for attackers in a gunfight.

The solid two-story log cabin fort boasted no windows on the two sides in Matthew's view. A heavy door on the front appeared to be the only way in or out. Squinting, he detected a glassless narrow window on the second floor of the square and harsh cabin. An impenetrable fort.

Was Philip inside?

Tree branches rustled beside Matthew, and one of the men from the posse joined him.

"Don't wander out, he's already picked off two." The man spat a stream of tobacco. "You just come up from Wilburton?"

Matthew nodded. "Heard you could use some help."

The man grinned, a thin dribble of the tobacco leaking from the corner of his lip. "Sure, but don't think you'll get to light the fuse. You can help in the turkey shoot after."

The man headed back. Matthew followed. "You're going to try burning them out?"

"Can't catch the fort on fire from this distance, but we brought up something special that's going to put a hole in that thing big enough to drive a stagecoach through!"

Matthew spotted the something "special" placed at the edge of the woods in a head-on position with the fort.

A small cannon.

Matthew blinked. How much damage would it do? Philip...

"Just shoot the blasted thing!" One of the men shouted. "We've moved it enough. Fire away, we've been waiting all morning!"

A man with a badge, who Matthew recognized as the Gaines county sheriff, waved his arms over his head.

"Quiet down, all of you! We only got a dozen shots, and I want everyone in position before we start. Thatcher, I told you to take four men around back. If the ball blasts all the way through, it'll open a way of escape. Go on, now! Leroy, check the charge, we don't want to blow up the cannon."

Everyone continued to argue. Matthew looked toward the fort. He had to find out if Philip was in there before...

The sheriff threw his hat down. "Cover your ears, boys!"

He struck a match with his thumb and lit the short cannon fuse.

The men close to the cannon shouted and ran to take cover, though most of the posse had enough sense to hold their Winchesters ready and aimed at the fort. As the fuse burned down, Matthew visually measured the distance to the fort and size of the cannon. He suspected what would happen.

The little cannon made a pop, and the ball shot out with a puff of smoke. The ball sailed in an arc before thunking into the ground near the chopping block.

The posse came out of hiding. The sheriff stared at the cannonball buried in the dirt.

A laugh sounded across the distance from the second-floor window. "You got me scared good, boys, bringing out the big guns!"

A chill swept through Matthew. Was that the sound of Dan Holder's laughter?

Surely Philip couldn't be inside. Holder would be dead by now.

The posse launched into blaming each other for the placement of the cannon, the amount of powder used, even the length of the fuse. They hurried to reload the cannon. The sheriff repositioned it, closer and angled higher. With no pomp and circumstance, he lit the fuse. The men scattered and took cover or aimed at the front in anticipation of the Holder gang flooding out when the cannonball knocked a wall down.

The cannon popped again. This time the ball hit its mark on the wall, bounced off and landed on the ground, smoking.

More laughter from the window.

The sheriff stared across the open space at the smoldering ball. "Guess them walls are two logs thick. Might need to get more shot from town."

Matthew shook his head. This posse was no more capable of getting Dan Holder than Matthew was by himself. In fact, he would probably do better alone.

It was only a matter of time before the posse ran out of

cannonballs and willpower to flush the gang out. When they returned to Wilburton, he would have a chance. Maybe it was the moment Philip waited for, too, if he was inside.

Matthew moved to the edge of the woods and studied the fort, searching for vulnerability, for the best way one man alone could…

He sensed a presence. Someone was sneaking up behind him. Matthew whipped around to find a small man creeping close, one hand outstretched, the other in his coat, a garment too heavy for the warm day.

The man blanched and sputtered, "Don't move or say a word if you want to know what happened to your brother."

Matthew stared at the snip of paper the man clenched in his outstretched hand. He must have meant to drop it near Matthew, not actually face him. He had his collar flipped up as though that would shadow his features enough to disguise himself. But Matthew knew. This weaselly man was who he searched for—Al Percy, in the flesh, face to face. The one who had the answer to what happened to his father and brother.

Percy's other hand twitched in his coat pocket, the outline of a small pistol there. He glanced to where the posse was reloading the cannon for another futile attempt, then snapped his gaze to Matthew, dropped the note, and backed away. "You mind what it says and forget you ever saw me. You hear? I want nothing to do with any of you."

He took several quick steps back and tripped on a tree root. His arms swung wildly until he regained his balance, then he stumbled for the picket line. He mounted and rode away.

Matthew didn't move until the man was out of sight. He didn't want to touch the note settled in the leftover fall leaves, didn't want to read what it said.

"…*if you want to know what happened to your brother.*"

Matthew squatted by the note. His shoulder caught, making

him hesitate another moment. Then he reached for the crumpled paper and opened it to read the unfamiliar handwriting.

You'll find Chukfi at the bottom of the mine shaft near the fort. Every body deserves a grave eventually.

Matthew jerked, tearing the note in two. He leaped up and ran for his brother's life.

CHAPTER 42

Matthew rode hard down the trail and to the abandoned mine shaft he had passed. The yawning earth took on new significance as he tied up the filly and rushed to the mine entrance. Wrapped by a wooden fence and toe boards, a ladder clung to one wall of the black hole, secured to the shaft by a wire. A lantern sat by the edge with a rope tied to it.

Entering through the narrow fence opening, Matthew dropped to his knees by the black hole, staring down. Was he looking at his brother's grave all over again?

He didn't call down the shaft. He wouldn't be able to make the climb if there was no answer.

Matthew tied the rope crossways on his chest and shoulder so that the lantern would dangle below him as he climbed. He lit it and swung over the lip of the shaft. He gripped the sides of the ladder with his bare hands and began the climb down. His muscles warned against too much exertion, and his shoulder hitched then popped.

The mine he'd worked in Krebs was a slope one that gradually went deeper into the heart of his people's land. But this was like climbing down a hundred-foot throat. Matthew shivered. The Krebs mine disaster in '92 had been a shaft mine with a vertical tunnel like this rather than a slope. The explosion cut off the elevator shaft, trapping hundreds of men below.

The ladder creaked with Matthew's weight and movement. He kept track of the depth by counting ladder joints. The massively long ladder was connected in eight-foot sections. Fifty feet down in the darkness, Matthew passed a platform that miners used for resting. Or breaking a fall.

He couldn't rest. Not until he reached the bottom.

Another fifty feet. Matthew's right foot met air. He quickly pulled it up to the previous rung and looked down. The dangling lantern illuminated a break in the ladder.

A thought flashed through his mind. What if this was a trap?

His forearm muscles strained with the hesitation. Then he stretched his foot to the closest brace. Dust puffed beneath and drifted down the shaft, but the brace held.

Matthew saw man against the power of nature in those boards. Hewn wood holding back tons of rock and dirt that had laid undisturbed for thousands of years. Shafts could take men—men who had been burned, blown up, underfed, who were strangers in a land far from home, willing to take the most dangerous job in the country to have work, who had families to think of and provide for—down to an early grave.

One brace at a time, Matthew descended by the shaft boards until the ladder sections restarted. At nearly two hundred feet, he glanced down to see the lantern had settled on another landing, inviting a reprieve. Matthew took it, stepping off the ladder, out of breath and wondering how much further down it was. The ladder had ended again, but there was a section on the landing. Broken?

A familiar voice greeted Matthew from below. "You're crazy as a loon."

Still facing the wall, Matthew laughed with relief, tension released from his body. "You're alive."

"At least you're not socking me for that this time."

"I still might." Matthew turned toward the edge of the small wooden platform. He lowered the lantern over the edge by its full length of rope to reveal a cavernous room with no way to reach the bottom. But on the floor of the mine sat his brother, cross-legged and craning his neck to look up.

"Halito, *Luksi*," Philip said. "You crawl all the way here from Skullyville?"

Matthew felt a smile tease his lips. No one called him a turtle anymore. Really, only Philip ever had, saying Matthew was slow in making decisions, in getting things done—thinking too much instead of taking action. Maybe that was why Matthew developed the habit in his teens to think less and act more. That had gotten him in trouble more than once. He should rethink his policy on that.

Matthew sighed. He was thinking too much even now.

He examined his brother's features in the shadows cast by light of the lantern. Philip wore a bright smile, but it wasn't his usual grin. It was tinged with something Matthew hadn't seen there before, something beyond the stubbornness, the anguish, the self-loathing of when they'd reunited. Terror? Relief? Joy? They all seemed present.

"How did you get stuck down there?"

Philip shrugged. "You know what they say—fool me once, shame on you. Fool me twice, and, well, here I am."

"How long have you been down there?"

Philip didn't try to stand, seeming to relish sitting in the circle of light from above. "Just long enough to get a little crazy talking to myself." His voice went soft. "But I knew you'd come."

Matthew eased down to sit on the platform, legs over the side. He blinked away the moisture in his eyes, heart thumping in his throat as he looked down on his broken brother. "Tell me, please. Please tell me, Chukfi, what happened that day."

Philip returned the stare only for a moment, then bowed his head. "You'll hate me."

"Just tell me the truth."

Philip rubbed the back of his neck. He raised his head slightly. His lips trembled and parted.

"I keep thinking on that scripture in Proverbs Mama had me memorize, about how a brother offended is harder to win than a strong city, and contentions being like the bars of a castle." He sighed. "Funny what being in a pit for a night and day will do to you. Like Jonah and the whale. Since I was going insane talking to myself, I really had to…I had to talk to God." He paused. "Think He heard me?"

"What do you think?"

Philip nodded. "Yeah. He did. And I think…I think He forgave me. But Matt, I'll never forgive myself. There are some things even Jesus can't save you from."

Matthew clenched his hands, trying not to think about his father, of all the anguish their family had gone through. "What happened to Daddy? Just tell me, Chukfi."

Something like a growl and a wail came out of Philip. He gripped his knees. "All right! I'll give you the truth, you want it so bad." His chest heaved, and his voice lowered again. "The whole miserable truth, so help me God."

Matthew strained to catch every word of his brother's confession. Word by word, the story came out—of a girl named Kat in Skullyville and youthful love. Of fairytale dreams, of a friend named Lester Cotten who had clever ideas. Of threats of retribution against family, of wicked men, of death on a lonely road in the Winding Stair Mountains. Of deception to hide the foolishness and guilt and fear. Of the drive to revenge.

Matthew unclenched and re-clenched his fists, anger encircling his heart, banging to get in and rage to the death. Philip's loose morals and careless choice in friends had led to their father's death.

Perhaps the outlaws would have learned of the freight route another way, of the extra bank bag, of the ideal ambush opportunity, but in the end, it was his own brother who had given them all they needed trying to avoid the consequences of his actions.

On the flip side of the coin, Matthew had always obeyed his parents, worked hard through his teens, gone to college, then was willing to sacrifice his future to take care of his family after his father died.

God had greatly blessed Matthew in the following years, yet he couldn't help but think of what could have been if his father were still alive. If only Philip had come to his family with the truth, they could have protected one another! Was it really that hard to choose what was right?

He hath shewed thee, O man, what is good; and what doth the LORD require of thee, but to do justly, and to love mercy, and to walk humbly with thy God?

Matthew tried to open his hands to surrender the bitterness and pain. He wasn't ready. The pain and fiery anger were too much for Matthew to think through now.

Below, Philip kept his eyes on the wall as though not having the courage to see his brother's reaction to the long tale. He whispered, "Kat never loved me, we were just a couple of fools. But she has my little girl. I gotta go back someday. My little girl." He choked, spittle from a sob glistening in the lantern light. "I just want to go home."

Matthew swallowed hard. When he first saw his brother alive on that depot platform, he'd wanted to break him, wanted the whole truth in an instant. There, in the abandoned shaft, his brother was broken, truth spilling out of him like water from a shattered clay pot. Matthew had no idea how the broken pieces could all fit back together.

God knows.

Matthew closed his eyes, feeling the deepness of dark around him, yet seeing a tiny glow of light somewhere in the distance of his heart. The glow of his father's spirit had never departed from Matthew, the wisdom and courage and love and faith left behind.

"Go on," Philip choked out. "Go on and say how much you hate me and get on out of here. We both know I'm not worth saving. This way, no one will ever know."

Matthew took a deep breath, eyes still closed. "Don't be a fool." He exhaled. "I'd never leave you."

"No? I got Daddy killed. Left the family. And I still plan on blasting Dan Holder if I get out of here. You really think I'm worth anything?"

Matthew opened his eyes. "God knows."

Philip jumped to his feet, staggering, and spat in the dirt. "Don't throw that at me! I'm hurting plenty, all right? You don't have to remind me of Daddy every second."

Matthew stared down at him. "That's not what I—"

"Get that ladder hooked up and let me climb out of here. I got business to take care of."

The tears Matthew thought would pour out snapped back in sharp retreat. "Like adding grief on grief?"

"Either drop that ladder or leave and let me die. Either suits me."

Matthew glared at his brother, then pushed to stand. He winced and stumbled back toward the wall. His legs had gone numb from dangling. Tingling shot up and down them, and he felt lightheaded. He should have eaten lunch. Could he make the climb out?

Ignoring the spots in his vision, he took the heavy double section of ladder and carefully lowered it over the edge. Philip helped steady and guide it to the floor. Matthew attached it to the joint and leaned against the wall, resting, while Philip clambered up. He hopped onto the platform, drew up the lantern, and reached to untie it from Matthew.

Matthew batted him away, teeth clenched. "I'm taking the lead from now on, you understand?"

Philip snorted. "You don't look any better than when I left you."

"You mean when you lied about needing to get the fake permit?"

"You surprised I lied to you?"

"Yes."

Philip sucked his lower lip between his teeth, chewed it a second, then gestured toward the ladder. "Lead the way, little brother."

For the next several minutes, Matthew yanked and pulled and dragged himself up the shaft. He tried to keep his mind off the pain and fatigue by recalling how, when he and Philip were boys, they competed on who could climb a tree the highest. The champion alternated by the tree until little Annie spoiled the fun by finding them and threatening to warn Daddy how high the boys were climbing again.

"Good thing Annie isn't here to tell on us."

Below, Philip laughed like Matthew remembered his laugh—high, carefree. Convincing. "She would."

Matthew's muscles trembled, informing him they'd give out before he reached the top. He came up next to another platform at the spot where the ladder ended, and they'd have to climb the bracing aways. He crawled onto the platform and rested his head on his forearm. Halfway up the mine shaft, and he was spent.

Philip climbed on next to him and sat with his back leaned against the wall, moaning. "We're getting old."

There was silence for a time while they rested, then Philip began to ramble.

"It always came easy for you, but not me. It's like when the starting gun goes off, and suddenly, you don't want to race. Everyone has helped you get ready to live life right, but suddenly, you got no desire to do it. You have to, but you just don't. That's what it feels like. You always leave me behind at the starting line."

Matthew mumbled, "What are you talking about?"

"I don't know. What you do. Making the right choices, running the race. Integrity, I guess."

"Yeah, sure. Comes easy for me." Matthew raised his head to shake it, trying not to laugh. "No problems, no temptations."

Philip's eyes shimmered. "Really, Matt. Daddy was proud of you. I always wished..."

Matthew pushed up to his hands and knees. Philip was jealous? Why didn't he just do those right things, and then...

Matthew stopped thinking. Jerking to his feet, he started climbing the bracing.

Philip scrambled to follow. "Matt! Not so fast, you'll fall."

Matthew sunk the toe of his boot into the silt between two boards, seeking a high hold. Philip coughed.

"Easy on sending that stuff down. It can clog a man's lungs, you know."

Matthew tried to push himself up with that foothold. His legs and arms quivered, and he gritted his teeth as moisture gathered in his eyes.

"Easy, brother. Easy." Philip's voice was calm. "We'll make it."

Matthew took a deep breath and tugged his boot from the dirt. Choosing a more manageable foothold, he climbed on. He didn't look up. He didn't look down. He only looked for the next place to put his right hand, left foot, left hand, right foot. The next place. There, that was a good spot to grab. Another to plant his boot. Up, up, up at a luksi pace, a turtle. But up he went.

The wooden ladder appeared once more. He latched onto it, muscles straining, his shoulder threatening to freeze up.

On he climbed. Fifty feet up. No stopping at the last platform. Another twenty feet. He lost count of the ladder joints.

"You're almost there, Matt."

He finally looked up the shaft. Somewhere above should have

been light to show the rest of the way. But there was no light. The sun had not waited. It set without them. But the wooden structure around the shaft was visible, just out of reach.

Matthew groaned. He felt like his back was facing straight down, like if he let go, he'd simply land on his back—two hundred feet below. If only this dark pit would vomit him the last few feet like the whale spitting the prophet Jonah out of its belly.

Matthew called on every muscle in his body to pull himself up the final three rungs until his hand met air. He gasped and frantically searched for the flat surface of the edge, stirring dust that got in his eyes.

"Take it easy, Matt. Move to your left to the gate opening. You can do it."

Matthew shifted and hugged the ladder. He felt around until he located flat ground. He crawled out of the mine shaft, over the rough boards and outside the fence. Rolling onto his back, he breathed heavy.

His brother collapsed beside him with a chuckle. Matthew chuckled, too, but it died quickly.

Philip said softly, "I lost you down there, didn't I? For good this time."

Matthew closed his eyes. "Let me think about it."

They lay there a while, their breathing matched as though they'd run the same race and crossed the finish line together.

Matthew sat up and rested his arms on his knees, looking toward the dark throat they had climbed out of. "Truth. Integrity. Those are things worth dying for, to me, anyway."

Still laying, Philip rested his dirty sleeve over his eyes. "It's harder to live those things. For me, anyway."

"You're running from them, Phil. It's time to stop."

"At least you can go back to everything. The family, your newspaper." Philip sat up. "You were willing to sacrifice it all, weren't you?"

"Something like that."

"Would you have done it if you'd known that you might lose your newspaper over all this? I've heard rumors."

Matthew pushed himself to stand only to collapse again. "As soon as we get on our feet, we can take care of everything."

Philip chuckled, reached for him, and together, they pushed themselves up. "For a reasonably intelligent fellow, you do a lot of dumb things. Stubborn Choctaw."

Matthew looked Philip square in the eyes. "We can make sure the *Choctaw Tribune* keeps putting out truth to people across the country with that reward money for Dan Holder."

Philip dropped the supporting hand on Matthew's back, face solemn and serious.

"He's wanted dead or alive, you know."

"I know."

Philip sniffed and wiped a sleeve under his nose. "Well, let's get to it, you crazy loon."

CHAPTER 43

The boom of the cannon welcomed the dawn. Matthew and Philip had arrived in the posse's camp late in the night, riding double on the filly. They picked a spot in a cluster of pines and ate from Matthew's food stash, then watched the sunrise and the knot of men gathered around the Gaines county sheriff and the cannon.

Matthew shook his head after the cannonball bounced off the wall of the cabin fort. The cannon had been moved forward and was braced by heavy logs behind the wheels. This was the posse's latest failed idea.

Patience was all Matthew and Philip needed. Soon, the posse would give up and go home. Then the real battle could begin. The question was, whether they would take the outlaws alive, if possible, or if Philip was determined to finish what he'd set out to do.

But the posse didn't give up that morning nor afternoon. They argued and spat and tried theories that they had mocked previously. They used too much powder and cracked the barrel of the cannon; used less powder, and the ball fell short of the chopping block; raised the barrel, and the ball struck below the second story window; lowered it and struck the bottom half of the door. It didn't rattle. With one ball left, even the sheriff gave up on the cannon, but he and the posse didn't leave.

Throughout the day, Matthew and Philip watched and rested, recovering from the arduous climb out of the mine shaft. Matthew found himself staring at Philip often, and his brother knew it. How could it be possible that his brother had made a series of decisions that led to their father's death, shattered their mother's heart, devastated their sister, and wrecked Matthew's reality?

Yet in all the sorrow, there was beauty from ashes. His family was closer than ever and loved one another fiercely, and Matthew owned a successful newspaper. But still...the ashes hadn't needed to be.

There are some things even Jesus can't save you from. Philip's words haunted him.

What did the path to forgiveness and redemption look like in a truly broken world? How could Matthew get Philip started down it? Could he?

Yet...there had to be an answer, one that didn't require shredding hearts all over again.

Was killing Dan Holder part of the resolution? That was what Takba—and Philip—believed.

By late afternoon, the posse men were red-eyed and staggering from fatigue but still determined for a fight. One man, who had brought a bow and quiver of arrows, suggested they shoot arrows of fire at the cabin and burn it down. Someone else insisted they could use a cart as a battering ram to break down the door. Several were for rushing the fort with guns blazing.

In the end, the posse decided to try all the foolhardy ideas at the same time.

Matthew and Philip stayed back.

The men used the cart that had hauled the useless cannon and loaded it with wood and hay. The man with the arrows wrapped the tips with torn bandanas and soaked them in kerosene. The others made sure all the guns were loaded.

The sheriff stood by the cannon and coordinated the attack. "You four men use the Winchesters to fire at the window and don't let up. You, send some arrows through the hole to catch the fort on fire from the inside. We'll run the cart across the yard and into the door. If it doesn't go down with the first blow, we hit it again while the rifles keep us covered. If we have to, we'll light the cart and leave it to burn the door down. We've got them this time, boys!"

Philip glanced at Matthew where they stood further back, sheltered between two pines, and smirked. They would have their chance. Soon.

Gaze on the cabin fort, Matthew asked, "Who all is in there?"

Philip answered quietly, "Dan Holder, for sure. Likely his woman."

Matthew sensed his brother was holding back. "Who else?"

"Who knows?"

The sheriff took his position with the other men behind the cart, ready to roll it from cover at the edge of the woods. Rifle tucked under one arm, the sheriff raised his other and signaled the riflemen. They shouldered their Winchesters and fired at the same time.

Matthew frowned. They should alternate their shots so the firing would be continuous. Now, they all jacked their levers in unison while the cart rolled into the open.

"Ouch!" The bowman slapped at fire on his sleeve. The arrow burned uselessly on the ground.

Gunfire poured from the narrow window of the fort and into the woods. The riflemen dodged for cover and began returning fire sporadically, their shots not well aimed.

With the riflemen scattered, the outlaw gunfire turned to the cart. Bullets whizzed off the side as the cart lumbered precariously. The five men pushing it stayed hidden behind the back end and couldn't see where they were going. The cart headed for solid wall instead of the door.

Someone shouted from the woods to correct the course, but it was too late. The cart bumped into the wall. The sheriff peeked around, then motioned for his men to back the cart up several feet and turn it enough to reach the door. Rifle fire continued from the window.

An arrow finally launched and promptly clattered on the chopping block. The arrow burned out in seconds.

Shots from the posse ceased suddenly as they all reloaded at the same time, leaving the sheriff and his men behind the cart with no protection. They were quick to realize this when a barrage of bullets tore around the cart. They tried to return fire, but it was impossible from their angle without exposing themselves.

Matthew glanced at Philip. They had agreed to stay out of the doomed attack. But the sheriff and his men were helpless.

Matthew braced against the pine tree, raising his rifle. He aimed at the narrow window, fired, and jacked the lever. Rifle fire sounded beside him. In rhythm, the Teller brothers kept a steady stream of bullets splintering the window frame. The barrage aimed at the sheriff ceased and turned their direction. Bullets struck the branches above him, but Matthew kept his focus and his rhythm. So did Philip.

By the time the brothers emptied their guns, the other four riflemen had begun firing again. This time, only two of the men fired while the other two waited a few minutes, then began firing while the first set reloaded.

Matthew wiped moisture from his forehead. He wasn't feverish, but the hot lead was making everyone sweat and wonder when they might get hit. "There are at least two men inside, both dead shots."

"And a third reloading," Philip added.

Matthew shifted to face him. "Who all did you say was in there?"

Philip shrugged and reloaded his rifle. Matthew leaned toward him in a way that said he wasn't joking. Philip glanced up, feigning fear with wide eyes.

"All right, don't drop me down a mine shaft." He turned solemn. "Holder's in there for sure, and probably the woman that's been living with him. That's likely who's doing the reloading."

"And the other crack shot?"

Philip gazed down at his rifle. "Lester. It's Lester Cotten."

Matthew shifted his jaw. Philip might feel he owed that man something for saving his life during the robbery, but to Matthew, Cotten was as guilty as Holder. His conniving ultimately got Jim Teller killed. Then Cotten helped Philip fake his death and leave the remaining Teller family in turmoil and grief.

Philip narrowed his eyes at the cabin fort. "I wish Lester had run. I hate having to kill him too."

Matthew reloaded his rifle and turned his attention to the fort. The men finally rolled the cart into the patchy dirt area in front and bumped into the door. The men rested against the cart. They had pushed it uphill while dodging bullets. But at least they were in a somewhat protected position directly below the window. The angle was too sharp unless the shooter leaned out and fired.

The sheriff motioned for the men back the cart up and then, together, they shoved it into the door. The only thing that shook was the cart.

Again and again. Matthew leaned against the pine tree and observed the fruitless efforts. The men stopped with the cart against the door, exhausted.

With a whoosh, the door flew open, and rapid-fire exploded from the black opening. Bullets struck flesh. The men behind the cart yelled and hit the ground.

Matthew reacted by pumping off shots into the dark doorway. Philip joined in. Half the other riflemen were reloading, and the others were focused on the window.

Over the sound of ringing in his ears from gunfire, Matthew heard a maniacal laugh. The door slammed shut. He kept firing at it—one, two, three shots. Then he directed his aim at the window.

The uninjured of the posse men at the cart helped the wounded as they scrambled across the open area to the woods. With six rifles firing on the window, the men made it to safety.

A flaming arrow arched over the open space and landed in the cart loaded with wood and hay. The cart was soon engulfed, burning at the door of the fort.

The posse men watched the flames dance and smoke drift past the window. The hole was partially covered with a blanket to block out the smoke.

Three wounded men were tended while everyone else watched the fire reach its peak. The cart collapsed on its side. It burned for a half an hour before it fizzled to a smoky heap. The door itself showed only smoke damage.

The Gaines County sheriff went to the cannon sitting neglected from its last attempt, positioned as close to the edge of the woods as they could have gotten it without exposing themselves. Two men helped the sheriff roll the cannon toward the clearing where the horses were. The rest of the posse gathered the guns and supported the wounded. They headed out on their horses, cursing each other. The last man disappeared from sight, heading back to Wilburton.

Philip glanced at Matthew and nodded. Matthew tightened his lips and returned it.

~

Spring was marching into Indian Territory, but the nights were still cold. Matthew snugged his coat close, though the layers of coal dust gathered in it wouldn't let him breathe the fresh night air. He leaned against the pine he'd fired from earlier, watching the cabin fort while Philip slept. The Teller brothers hadn't made a fire, and stowed their horses further down the trail. There was nothing to give away the fact that two brothers waited for Dan Holder to peer out the fort door.

But what exactly were they waiting for? What would Matthew do when Dan Holder finally showed his face? Philip wanted to kill Holder. Was Matthew there to stop or aid him?

A cool breeze shifted the air, carrying the burnt smell of the cart with it. Matthew rubbed his stinging eyes. He could no longer keep back the echoes of Philip's words of confession.

How could Matthew live with that knowledge? How could he keep it from his family? Should he?

Pain twisted his gut, but Matthew quieted the echoes again. Eyes on the fort, he whispered, "God, You know. Help me know. At least help me know what to do here."

Philip was partly responsible for their father's death. But it was Dan Holder who pulled the trigger. Matthew could see it—his handsome father, smiling, shaking Matthew's hand right before he boarded the train for college—then the roadside, gunshots, pain...

The image faded as the door of the fort slowly opened. A form darkened the doorway, indistinguishable behind the burned cart.

Matthew had kept his Winchester in the crook of his arm while on watch. Now he shouldered it and took aim at the shadow. He settled his finger over the trigger, took a breath, cocked the hammer.

Another image flashed in his mind. *Jake Banny.*

Matthew had felt what it was to hold someone's life in his hand. To end someone's life.

This was Matthew's decision, the time to decide. Revenge, or to do justly. The choices blurred with his father's smile, the warmth of his hand like sunshine, the joy in his eyes...

Love mercy.

Matthew lowered the barrel, breathed, uncocked the hammer. He'd made the decision long ago.

The figure moved, and a skirt came into view from behind the cart. Matthew did a long blink, relieved.

A woman stepped into the moonlight, then darted down to the shed. She retrieved a bucket and went to a spring on the other side of the shed. Seconds later, she ran back to the cabin fort, water sloshing from the bucket. She went through the door and slammed it shut.

Matthew let his rifle sag at his side.

"You remember that old story about Chief Pushmataha and the powder keg?"

Matthew didn't flinch at the sound of Philip's quiet voice behind him. He'd wondered if Philip was watching him watch the shadow. Did his example help his brother on the road to truth and justice?

Philip continued. "A man once called Chief Pushmataha a coward. The chief calmly went to a keg of gun powder, sat on it, and lit a match. He invited the man to come sit on the keg with him. No one called him a coward after that."

"Meaning?"

"It's my turn on the powder keg, prove my courage."

"You want to throw the race of integrity."

Philip shrugged. "I'm already marred. The path home for me is too overgrown with briars and thorns to walk it."

Matthew looked at his brother. "I'm still in the lead here. And right now, Holder thinks everyone left. They'll come out in the morning."

"And then?"

"Then." Matthew turned away, finishing the thought to himself, *we try to take them alive. No revenge killing.* He walked toward the clearing, saying low over his shoulder, "One of us needs to sleep, and since you're up, you have watch."

Was he right to trust Philip to do the right thing? The day and night in the belly of the mine had changed the look in his eyes from sheer confidence and an underlying rage to uncertainty and even fear. It felt right to give him a chance to make a decision for himself now.

Still, Matthew hoped the door didn't open again until morning.

~

Matthew lay awake, staring at the moonbeams shooting through the pine branches that offered him shelter. He prayed, sang softly to himself. But soon, the lyrics jumbled with the conversation he'd had with Philip the night before Matthew left for his second year of college.

They'd argued about Philip not going. Matthew accused him of not caring about bettering himself, of doing his part to serve their people when he had the means and opportunity to do so. Philip shot back that Matthew was so intent on life that life would whizz by him without looking back. He'd called Matthew self-righteous. Matthew said Philip was pig-headed.

They hadn't spoken the next morning. But when all the family went to the train depot to send Matthew off with cheers, Philip had made him laugh.

Laying on the cold ground with the moonbeams flittering above, Matthew tried to recall what made him chuckle as he took a window seat on the train and waved goodbye, but he couldn't remember what it was, because it wasn't the words or mannerisms of Philip that brought laughter. It was simply him, simply Philip. His jovial spirit brought happiness to those he knew.

Why had that ended so tragically for them all?

Matthew prayed and finally slept.

CHAPTER 44

*D*eep in the traditions of Matthew's people lay the turkey gobble challenge, a kind of fair warning to the enemy that they intended to kill them.

It was the shrill sound of a turkey gobble that awoke Matthew the next morning.

He grabbed his rifle and scrambled for cover in the low pine branches. He waited for his groggy senses to catch up. When he got his bearings, he realized the call hadn't come from the fort. It came from nearby.

He headed for the edge of the woods and halted at Philip's side. His brother gave the turkey gobble challenge again, face grave.

Matthew slowly shook his head. "It's not our way, not Daddy's."

"You know, I did a lot of thinking down in that shaft. And I thought I might be able to walk away from this. But I can't, Matt. It's time to make sure, for certain and always, that Dan Holder never shoots anyone's daddy ever again. But I'm giving the warning. Lester knows."

"We can try to bring them both to justice without killing."

Philip rolled his eyes. "In Indian Territory? Holder likely wouldn't even be tried for Daddy's murder because we're Indians. He may hang for something else, but it won't be the same. This is the way, Matt. You got one last chance to go home. Take it."

Philip turned and sprinted through the woods toward the side of the fort. Matthew stared after him, then at the fort again. It looked lonely in the light of the rising sun. A tomb, not a home.

Near the front door, burned cart still sagging there, Philip slipped along the wall out of range of the window. But if someone opened the door, there was nowhere to take cover.

Matthew braced against a pine, hands frozen on his Winchester with a clear shot at the door.

The door was slowly opening.

He shouldered the rifle, but the door stopped moving. It hung half-open as though someone had slipped through and forgotten to close it. The door swayed in the breeze on the hill.

Philip must have heard the hinges creak. He halted. Matthew moved into Philip's line of sight and waved fiercely, but Philip ignored the warning and, hunched over, continued toward the door.

Movement in the narrow window caught Matthew's attention. A rifle barrel edged out at a downward angle. The shot wouldn't hit Philip, but if it distracted him, someone could step out the door and shoot him from ten feet away.

Matthew fired two quick shots at the window then ran across the open yard toward the other side of the front door. Philip looked ready to cuss him, but Matthew didn't have time to see anything else.

A man appeared in the doorway of the fort behind the cart, gun pointed Matthew's direction. Matthew dove to the ground as shots skimmed over his head. He hit hard but kept the grip on his rifle and rolled to his feet. In the blur, he saw Philip dash for the door. But Matthew's immediate threat was the rifle barrel poked through the window.

He fired upward and ran like he was headed for home plate, and the ball was flying to beat him to it. He skidded to a halt but still slammed into the wall of the fort, jolting his senses. Catching his breath, he looked toward the door. It was still open.

Matthew edged toward the doorway and heard voices. His eyes adjusted, and he could see inside the dim interior of the cabin. Philip stood with his back to a loft. He spoke over his shoulder to the man standing on the platform with rifle in hand, aimed at Philip, eyes flickering with indecision.

Philip spoke calmly. "Lester, put that gun down unless you plan to shoot me in the back. The turkey gobble wasn't for you. I never wanted to kill you. Well, except when you pulled up that ladder in the mine."

They were in a standoff, Philip with his rifle pointed toward someplace out of Matthew's sight—likely at Dan Holder—and Lester in the loft with gun trained on Philip. Crouched low, Matthew inched toward the door and halted. He took aim at Lester, who hadn't spotted him yet.

Philip raised his rifle from a general direction to a specific target as he said, "I've been mighty patient to get to this moment, Holder."

He cocked the hammer. The woman inside screamed. Philip swore. "Get away, woman! I'll put a bullet through you to him if I have to!"

Lester shouldered his rifle. Matthew fired, the bullet hitting its mark in Lester's exposed left arm. The man yelled as the impact threw him off balance. He stumbled forward and stepped off the loft platform, falling, and hit hard. He lay still. Matthew jumped through the doorway and spun to land next to Philip. He faced what he'd been searching for since leaving home.

His father's killer.

Heat pumped through Matthew's brain, turning his sight red. So this was how Philip saw the world.

Before him was Dan Holder—one of the most notorious outlaws in the territory. A man who killed when he didn't have to, who stole more than money—hearts, love, futures. The man who had taken so much from the Teller family. From Matthew.

...what doth the LORD require of thee...

Matthew blinked and adjusted his sweaty grip on the rifle.

Before him was Dan Holder—balding, bleeding from the arm, eyes dull, skin thin and sagging from years of bad living. He stood weaponless, his uninjured arm around the woman who clung to his shirt, weeping hysterically. Holder was a pathetic creature who had thrown away all he'd ever stolen and then some.

Dan Holder peeled the slim woman away from him and shoved her to the side. He spoke to Philip. "Go on, do what you come to do."

Philip raised his rifle, finger on the trigger.

Either side could have raw courage. But life—and death—took more than that.

Matthew put the stock of his rifle on Philip's barrel. He pushed down firmly.

Philip fought it, his hands shaking. He said through gritted teeth, "Stop trying to save him."

"I'm trying to save you."

The gun went off, the bullet striking the floor in front of Dan Holder's boots. The sound reverberated in Matthew's heart, reminding him of all the violence he'd lived through in recent years. The shootout at the Barnes' mansion. Drunks on a road at Daniel Springs. Shot by Cub Wassom. Killing Jake Banny. Mine explosions. Fighting with his brother. This moment.

Doing justly, loving mercy, walking humbly with his God.

This was what was required of Matthew. He'd never lose sight of it again.

Philip jerked away and took a step back, rifle pointed down, seething, but he said nothing.

Matthew gestured at Holder with his rifle. "You have a trial to stand. Justice will be served."

CHAPTER 45

Getting back to Wilburton proved challenging. Lester Cotten regained consciousness but was woozy from his bleeding head and arm. That left Matthew and Philip with two wounded men and a woman to transport. But they finally made it that evening.

The sheriff wasn't happy about losing credit for the capture, and that the brothers would receive the reward money. Matthew hoped his name was left out of newspaper reports. Matt Jameson and Toby Nicolas should get the credit anyway.

The rest of Wilburton welcomed them as heroes. The two old Choctaw men, Sanders and Lawechobe, waved hats and cheered. But Matthew's mind was on his silent brother.

While Holder and Cotten received medical attention in their jail cell, Matthew headed for the hotel and rented a room. Philip followed.

Matthew collapsed on one of two beds, boots still on. Now that he was still, the icky after-cold effects of his sickness reminded him he'd better sleep awhile to keep it from roaring back.

The other bed creaked under the weight of Philip, who broke the silence between them. "You couldn't have taken him alone."

"I know."

"I would have killed him."

Matthew sighed. "I know."

Silence. Then Philip said, "I'm glad you were there."

Matthew rested his arm over his eyes. "I know."

The next morning, Dan Holder and Lester Cotten were taken to Fort Smith while Matthew and Philip headed to McAlester. There was someone Matthew hoped to find there.

He got a room in the hotel that housed the federal courthouse and found Marshal Bass Reeves. Matthew started right in with questions, knowing the old marshal had more answers than he shared before.

Marshal Reeves obliged, telling Matthew the whole story of what happened in the Jessop home shootout.

When they were at the Jessop shanty, Cub Wassom regaled his new partners Bass Reeves and Frank with tales of exploits of the notorious Dan Holder. He talked about how Al Percy was tied up with the gang. Percy knew all the hideouts and shuffled dirty money for people like Sam Mishaya, who paid Cub and Frank to shoot Will Hocks and Matthew. Cub had scoffed at how Lester Cotten bailed on them, not wanting anything to do with killing another Teller man. Cub criticized Dan Holder for not killing Philip Teller years before.

Marshal Bass Reeves, pretending to have joined their gang, watched the outlaws closely in the cabin. He also watched the mother, Takba. She went about preparing them a meal, one that Reeves didn't take a bite of. Who knew but she might poison even her own son after hearing more of the atrocities he'd committed. The girl, Amarillo Jessop, was in the lean-to room, tending a baby.

The day ended in a shootout where Reeves put an end to Cub Wassom in a fair fight the marshal hadn't pressed for. From there, he wanted to track down Al Percy and the rest of Dan Holder's gang but was delayed by assignments from Judge Isaac Parker. That brought the story to where Matthew came in, sent by Takba to find the man she blamed for corrupting her son. She had learned Al Percy worked for the Osage mines in Krebs and McAlester.

Dan Holder would be tried by Judge Isaac Parker in Fort Smith for a variety of crimes blamed on him, hopefully including the killing of Jim Teller.

Lester Cotten's situation was more complicated. Since he was Choctaw, the tribal courts would want him, but the federal might claim him first for crimes he was accused of committing against whites.

Marshal Reeves admitted he'd suspected Philip Teller was in on the robbery, but since it didn't involve a crime against whites and Philip was willing to help catch the rest of the gang, he let it be.

Matthew took all this in while standing in the hotel lobby with Philip and Bass Reeves, going over the complications of law and order—or lack thereof—in Indian Territory.

Marshal Reeves shook his head. "Well, they'll get their come-uppance one way or another."

"What about what I told you that Doctor Robinson is doing?" Matthew asked.

"Well, I'll tell Judge Parker, but I don't reckon he can do anything. I don't know that there's any kind of laws about it in the territory. It'll likely depend on the public protesting that sort of thing." Reeves looked at Matthew with a wink. "Newspapers are mighty handy for things like that."

Matthew nodded. "It'll be one of the first stories I publish when I get back."

The marshal scratched his chin. "There's just one last little piece to all this, though it's really none of my business." He glanced at Philip.

Matthew looked between them. "What do you mean?"

"He means..." Philip sunk his hands deep in his pockets and stared at the high ceiling. "I'm guilty of that robbery along with Holder and Lester, and it's time I turned myself in to the Lighthorse."

Matthew stood very still. Of all the scenes he had contemplated facing when he reached home, telling his family that Philip was alive but in jail wasn't one of them.

Matthew turned to Bass Reeves. "Is that true?"

The marshal shrugged. "Like I said, it's not my worry, him being Choctaw involved in a crime against your own. Up to you boys how you handle it."

Marshal Reeves tipped his hat and left among the bustle of people entering and leaving the hotel.

Philip sighed and shook Matthew's hand heartily. "Well, it's been nice knowing you."

He started to let go, but Matthew gripped his hand hard and yanked him back.

"You don't get off that easy. What about Mama? And Annie? Uncle Preston and Pokni and—"

Philip jerked his hand from Matthew's grip. "I have to do what's right for once and turn myself in. You got to do what you can to keep the family from ever finding out I'm alive and giving them more grief. That'll be enough."

"Enough!" Matthew exploded, balling up his fist.

A couple passing by gave him a curious look. Matthew took a calming breath. He was tired of fighting Philip on every point. "Fine, take the coward's way, like you've been doing." Matthew turned away.

A hand gripped his shoulder and pulled him back around. Philip got in his face. "That's right, I'm a coward. I can't face my family after what I did. I'll never see them again." Philip's eyes swelled, his lower jaw shifting back and forth.

Matthew cupped a hand behind his brother's head and pulled his face down onto his shoulder. He whispered, "If I can forgive Holder and Cotten, I can forgive you. And I can love you. You're my brother. Nothing in life or death can ever change that."

Philip rubbed his eyes against Matthew's shoulder and sniffed before pulling himself up straight. He chuckled, avoiding Matthew's gaze. "You should have been the older brother."

He tried to cuff Matthew, then swiped his eyes clear and shrugged. "If I can't be an example, at least I can be a warning. But I got to do this alone, Matt. And maybe someday…maybe all this can be set right." Philip headed for the door. He looked back one last time.

"Chi pisa la chike," Matthew whispered, forcing himself to stay in place.

CHAPTER 46

$\mathcal{M}$atthew stood in the hotel lobby awhile after Philip left, letting the flow of traffic move around him. He finally headed for the grand staircase where he could spend the day in his room, gathering his thoughts and making a plan to return home.

A commotion started behind him, near the front door. He halted.

Someone shouted, "Strikebreakers are here, and the miners formed a barricade! Better send any troops that are loitering in the court!"

People hurried to watch the bedlam from the picture windows, but most rushed outside into the excitement. Matthew was one of them.

In the distance, a train whistle blew long, again and again. It sounded desperate.

From where they billeted in hotels and a warehouse, federal troops poured down the main street of McAlester. They were armed and grim. A wall of Indian police pushed through the crowd on horseback.

The streets were jammed with wagons and buggies that all

tried to leave at once. From his vantage point on the top steps of the hotel, Matthew spotted the reason for panic.

Hundreds of coal miners clogged the thoroughfare, waving clubs and pressing toward the train depot.

Matthew sprinted down the stairs of the hotel, skirted the main street, and took a route around to the far side of the depot. He made it just as the train inched to a stop. Even behind the depot, the mass was so thick Matthew had a hard time getting to the platform. But he squeezed through and scrambled atop a load of crates. He crouched there, observing the federal troops forcing a knot of angry miners away from the platform. A line of Choctaw Lighthorse was closest to the train, forming a wall between the passenger cars and the crowd.

But this was no ordinary train up from the south. The windows of the passenger cars were draped with blankets, blocking the view to the inside. Matthew focused on the windows. One of the blankets moved enough for a dark face to peer out before the blanket dropped back in place.

The mine bosses had brought workers in to break the strike.

Women took the front lines, facing off with the federal troops who tried to establish order. It was worse than Savanna.

From behind the line of troops, Matthew spotted the captain and lieutenant he'd seen in Judge Kendrick's office a few days before. They conversed with the conductor and engineer. Before long, the train gave a pitiful whistle and began to pull away from the depot. Matthew raised to stand on the crates, mindful of his head since he was under the awning of the depot. On the tracks, a horde of women blocked the train from going further up the line to the mines.

The Indian police managed to clear the tracks. The train filled with strikebreakers broke free from the McAlester mob and huffed away. They would likely stop somewhere out of town and take the workers on by wagon to the mines.

And end the strike.

The crowd roared, but the train acted like it didn't hear a word.

Matthew stayed atop the crates until the crowd thinned. He watched, listened, and felt the pain, fear, and discouragement. Miners had been blacklisted or even expelled from Indian Territory for taking part in the strike. Some in the Choctaw Nation would give a hearty "good riddance!" while others grumbled about intruders continuing to strip the natural resources of the nation. These disagreements would lead to more violence for his people. When he returned home, he'd write about it. But for now, for Matthew, this journey was over.

Almost.

Matthew cut through McAlester and headed down the road to Krebs. He needed to check on his friends, whether they wanted to see him or not.

The road was ladened with people shouting to one another, spreading the word of the new workers. Many of the miners would lose their company housing to make room, and of course, their jobs.

Matthew went straight to Raphael Bianchi's home, ignoring the clusters of men and women who stood talking animatedly. He thought he heard a taunt or two tossed his way, though there was no organized effort to resist the strikebreakers that they must know were coming. Without a strong leader in the community, Krebs had taken a sideline in the game playing out in their lives.

He found the whole Bianchi family gathered at Raphael's house. They made their own group to discuss the events. But at the sight of Matthew, Ricco's wife spun away and marched back toward her home.

Cadenza ran to greet Matthew. She skidded to a stop just when Matthew thought she was going to hug him. He'd braced himself, but she just smiled. "The strike isn't ending the way we hoped, Matt Jameson, but our little secret is over, and maybe you and Toby can be friends, si?"

Matthew looked over her head to Raphael and Ricco. Matthew had come to the coal mining area seeking truth. He needed to leave it behind with the Bianchi family. "Cadenza, about Toby—"

Her face turned ashen. "Is he dead?"

"No, he's all right. I'll take you to him. It's something he needs to tell you himself, tell all of you. So do I."

He approached Raphael and Ricco, their arms folded with identical stares. They must have been close before tragedy tore them apart. Like Matthew and his brother.

"My real name is Matthew Teller, publisher of the *Choctaw Tribune*. I needed to find someone without them knowing who I was. I did, and this part of my journey is over. I'm sorry for the trouble I caused you."

Raphael sighed, his stiffness released. "I suspected you weren't who you said you were, but I trusted that you were a good man, and I was right. We know what you did for Ricco. *Tra il dire e il fare c'è di mezzo il mare*, between saying and doing is the ocean, yes? Torre and his son Fabio were expelled, along with so many of our countrymen. But we thank you for your help and are sorry for the way we treated you last you were here when..." His gaze dropped.

Matthew finished the thought. "When you learned I was Choctaw? And now with the strike going to ruin, how do you feel about me?"

Ricco uncrossed his arms and answered instead. "Right or wrong, every man has to stand responsible for his own deeds, not those of his nationality."

Matthew wished he had his tablet. "Can I quote you on that?"

Ricco smiled for the first time since Matthew had known him. "I knew you were writing stories when I read about the ball game. I say to myself, 'That is our Matt Jameson writing about us.' But you write well, so I didn't complain."

Raphael boomed a laugh. "You are going back to your newspaper work now, eh? No more coal dust to be had for you?"

Ricco motioned to the community around them. "I've lived in your nation four years but knew nothing about it, about your people, of what you have been through, and why you must be so protective of your land and heritage. I have learned much from your newspaper each day."

Matthew swallowed the intensity of the emotions that struck him. He was always so focused on his mission with the *Choctaw Tribune*, yet it still hit him when people were impacted by it. Ruth Ann did them all proud. "And I have learned much of your people by living among them. I will write the story about the mining communities, the whole truth. People can decide for themselves, same as you with my people's story."

Ricco glanced down the street, at the clusters of Italians speaking in their language. "I know what it is to feel your country slipping away, to know there is an end to your way of life. It is coming to an end for your people, isn't it? Your sovereignty? What will you do then?"

Matthew thought of the Dawes Commission, the infighting among his people, the coming of progress into his world. What stood foremost in his mind, though, was the *Choctaw Tribune*. It had brought understanding for Ricco, and maybe it would make a difference in this whole mess that Matthew's people faced.

As long as there was the Choctaw Nation, the newspaper would be in it—Lord willing.

There's nothing more powerful than the press short of God Almighty, he often said.

He shrugged and gave Raphael a side grin. "Nothing to it but a stout heart."

Raphael laughed, but Cadenza, who silently took in the

exchange as she watched her father, then closed her eyes. "Oh Papà, I am so sorry about the baby…"

Ricco blanched. He took his daughter into his arms. "No, no, mi bambina, it was too much, all too much for you, for me, for us all. You did not cause the loss of the baby. I am the one who distressed you so when I called off the search…"

She raised her tear-streaked face to stare at him. "No, no. I knew he was gone. My heart knew. It already knew."

Ricco pressed his lips on her hair. "Mi bambina."

Matthew hated to intrude on the tender moment, but there was one last truth to resolve. "We all need to have a talk before I leave. We have to go to McAlester."

Ricco nodded. "Let's be on our way, then." He and Cadenza parted, though she held her father's arm.

Ricco's wife marched back to them with a cloth-covered bundle clenched in both hands. She paused at Cadenza. For a tense moment, Matthew worried they might start yelling at one another in Italian. But there was a sort of understanding that passed between them, and they nodded at each other.

Mrs. Bianchi shoved the bundle at Matthew. "Bread. For your journey home."

Matthew accepted the cloth bundle from the stern-faced woman, taking it as her smile. He smiled back.

The streets in McAlester weren't back to normal. Tense people milled about, not sure what to do. With careful navigating, Matthew led Raphael, Ricco, and Cadenza to the Tobucksy County Courthouse.

Inside, Matthew asked to see Judge Kendrick and was told the man was busy. So Matthew did what he'd done before. After asking the Bianchis to wait outside, he crossed the room and went straight into the judge's office, the secretary protesting loudly.

Judge Kendrick sat behind his desk, reading a letter. He looked up when Matthew entered.

He growled. "No."

Matthew raised his eyebrows. "Halito, Judge Kendrick. I'm looking for someone. He was headed this way earlier."

Judge Kendrick waved Matthew away then halted. He suddenly looked pleased about something. That could only mean trouble.

The judge directed his voice toward a closed door off his office. "Jensen, bring Philip Teller in here."

A moment later, the door opened and Philip came through, followed closely by a Choctaw Lighthorseman. Philip didn't seem surprised to see Matthew, but he said nothing.

Judge Kendrick motioned to Jensen. "Wait in the other room." When he left, the judge leaned back in his chair and interlaced his fingers behind his head.

"Well, here we have one brother returned from stirring up trouble with miners, and the other back from the dead. To commemorate this very special day, I would like to offer pardon to Philip Teller for crimes he committed against citizens of the Choctaw Nation."

Philip looked sharply at the judge. Matthew crossed his arms. Something was wrong. He had a sick feeling he knew what it was.

"In exchange for what?" he asked.

The judge sat up again, eyes wide in mock surprise. "Matthew Teller, what makes you think there's a cost? Well, it must be your keen senses as a newspaper reporter. Speaking of which, I have a few tiny suggestions for your next several editions." He paused for emphasis. "You maintain discretion as to my personal life, and also regularly and favorably feature myself, my colleagues, and the work we do for the good of our people."

Matthew tightened his crossed arms. To be able to take his brother home with nothing hanging over his head, Matthew would sacrifice a great deal. Even the integrity of the *Choctaw Tribune?*

"Don't even think about it, little brother," Philip said.

Matthew met his brother's hard stare, then broke eye contact and looked back at the judge, who was smiling.

Philip spoke low. "Don't compromise. There's no finish line once you start down that road."

Matthew knew the right answer. He just needed it to be all right somehow. "You won't be running this race alone."

Philip's eyes reddened. "I don't want Mama to know…"

"She will want the truth. And speaking of truth, there are some folks you need to talk to. We'll be back, judge."

Ignoring the infuriated Judge Kendrick, Matthew beckoned for Philip to follow him. They cut through the empty observation seats and exited onto the wide covered porch of the court.

When they cleared the doorway, Cadenza grinned and threw her arms around Philip's neck and held tight, laughing. Raphael and Ricco watched, but they seemed comfortable with Philip. They seemed to trust and respect Toby Nicolas.

Philip let his arms hang at his sides. He stared at the sky, and Matthew wondered how he could help his brother sort through every regret of the past several years, maybe a lifetime. Matthew would be there, to sit and listen and unfold it layer by layer. Philip had given himself over to God in the mine shaft, and fully surrendered when they captured Dan Holder. Now they would go together in prayer and work toward Philip becoming the man the Creator meant him to be.

It took a few seconds, but Cadenza realized Philip wasn't returning her embrace and pulled back to look up into his face, confused.

Matthew stepped closer, knowing her father and uncle could hear what he said as they stood behind her. "Miss Cadenza, I told you who I really was, but not who Toby is. This...this is my brother, Philip Teller."

The Bianchis brothers exchanged surprised looks. But there was an understanding that passed between them, as though acknowledging they should have realized it all along.

Cadenza clutched Philip's arms, slowly shaking her head.

"How could I not have known? But you lied to me, Toby...Philip?"

He sighed heavily. "I'm sorry, Cadenza. I could never care for you like a real man should. There's trouble tailing me that shouldn't have ever crossed your path. It's best we just say goodbye for good."

"I don't want to."

Matthew cleared his throat. "We don't have a word for goodbye in the Choctaw language. We say chi p̲isa la chike, I will see you again someday."

Philip gave him a cross look, but Matthew figured his brother owed Cadenza something for her loyalty. They could work it out later.

Cadenza smiled and brushed Philip's cheek. "All right, Toby Nicolas or Philip Teller or whoever you are. I will see you again someday."

She stepped back to join her father, who gave Philip a stern look. "You see to it."

Philip smiled reluctantly. "I will. You deserve the whole story...someday."

Raphael looked at Ricco, then nodded to Matthew. "Yakoke. Isn't that how you say thank you in your language?"

Matthew nodded.

Ricco, one arm around Cadenza, locked his gaze on Matthew. "Yakoke."

He led Raphael and Cadenza down the porch steps. Cadenza gave a steady wave. Matthew returned it.

When they disappeared, Philip pointed with his lips toward

the door. "The judge will let me loose until my trial, so don't look for me here the next time you're in town."

"Come home with me."

Philip's eyes brightened at the word *home*, then dimmed despite the grin he put on. "Nah. I'm going over to Skullyville, someone I need to see there. She needs to know her daddy loves her."

Matthew recalled what Philip had said about having a daughter, and his heart stirred with sudden realization. He was an uncle. His mother—a grandmother.

Wearing a sturdy grin, Philip added, "After that, I'll sit on a powder keg somewhere until the trial."

"We'll get you the best lawyer we can afford with the reward money."

"I'm counting on that. And Matt?" Philip hesitated, then said, "Tell Mama I love her."

Matthew nodded, his face tense with unshed tears. "Chi pisa la chike, my brother."

The Lighthorseman, Jensen, opened the courthouse door then, and Philip nodded at Matthew. "Ome."

Jensen took Philip inside the courthouse and the door closed, its click sounding final to Matthew. But this wasn't the end. It was only the beginning of the next journey.

He'd have time to think on it during the ride home—his fourth and final destination.

Immense relief washed over Matthew.

Chukka ia li. I'm going home.

CHAPTER 47

There was a sense of rain in the atmosphere, the scent of it drifting through the open print shop door, reminding Ruth Ann that spring was a time of new beauty. And today, the shop looked like a festival ground. Though it was only Monday, they had something to celebrate.

On Saturday, Blane Johnson came to the print shop and announced that after their trial period, the *Choctaw Tribune* had more than double the number of advertisements claimed at the restaurant than the *Dickens Herald*. He was happy to negotiate for permanent advertisement in the *Tribune*. In the end, Ruth Ann managed to secure a satisfactory daily advertisement for the hotel, which made the account much higher than the original amount Matthew had arranged. Johnson even offered his hand to shake first.

Ruth Ann saw no reason for her not to throw a private party on a Monday. Nothing was ordinary in this shop. To be so surrounded by love and harmony was a joy her soul could hardly contain.

She and Beulah spent the early evening decorating with the first spring flowers to fully bloom out back. The Jessop children made paper chains from discarded newspapers with Stephen Austin overseeing and making sure they did everything right. Even Caleb Gentry was there, polishing the press. He said he stayed late because they'd have food, but Ruth Ann had watched his dedication to the *Tribune* grow the past few weeks. He took pride in their besting the *Dickens Herald* and didn't mind saying so.

At sunset, Lance and Peter arrived with a load of food sent from the Warren home where Mrs. Warren, Amarillo, Mabel, and Della were preparing a feast. The train whistle sounded in the distance, and Ruth Ann wondered at how many trains went through each day compared to only a year ago. To some, it meant progress. To her, it was news. To her people, it meant a variety of things, and no one agreed on them, which was why they published the *Choctaw Tribune*. Every day.

Glenrose Jessop draped a paper chain around the printing press after Caleb Gentry finished polishing it. "This feels like the all-night gospel singing at church," she said.

At that, Beulah began clapping her hands and singing.

> *I came from Alabama,*
> *With a banjo on my knee,*
> *I'm going to Louisiana,*
> *My true love for to see*

The children watched her wide-eyed when she started dancing. Mr. Levitt picked up the song as well. Beulah grabbed Ruth Ann's hand, and she, in turn, took Peter's. "Come, let's teach the children to dance!"

Ruth Ann laughed and tried to match Beulah's hopping and bouncing while Peter drew a blushing Glenrose in, who brought her brother Neches along, who dragged Caleb Gentry in.

Lance started to join the dance forming in the open floor space of the shop but then went a different direction. Ruth Ann glanced out the large picture windows showing the dusk of the setting sun. The rest of the women were coming, each carrying a loaded dish.

Lance opened the door, greeting each as they came in. Ruth Ann was certain he saved his most amiable smile for Amarillo, who ducked passed him with a shy smile, carrying a ceramic dish in one hand and totting baby Goodnight in the other. Whatever they discussed after Ruth Ann left the Warren home Friday night must have ended well. Lance and Amarillo had sat on the same pew at church Sunday morning.

Mrs. Warren wore the brightest smile of all, her hair slipping from its bun as she held little Belle's hand. The youngest of the Jessops siblings hid her face in Mrs. Warren's skirt. She peeked up at the woman for reassurance, and Ruth Ann understood where Mrs. Warren's happiness emanated from.

As soon as the dishes were set aside, Beulah drafted the new arrivals into the dance circle, laughing as she guided the group in swaying and hopping in one direction. Glenrose captured the baby from Amarillo, nodding for her to join the circle while she danced with her nephew.

Ruth Ann tried to catch her breath. Arms linked with Mrs. Warren on one side and Stephen Austin on the other, Ruth Ann joined in singing, *Oh! Susanna.*

It rained all night the day I left,
The weather it was dry,
The sun so hot I froze to death;
Susanna, don't you cry

Ruth Ann was facing the front of the shop. The singing drowned out the sound of the bell over the door. But what she saw made her squeal, bringing the dance to a halt. It wasn't a cry of fright, but joy.

Rumpled yet in one piece, Matthew walked through the print shop door.

Ruth Ann broke through the circle and caught him in the biggest hug a sister could manage. "You're home! You're home!"

Matthew laughed—his deep, familiar laugh, and Ruth Ann wanted to cry with relief. The damage to his face she'd seen in McAlester was healing, though he was still bruised, and a cut on his lip was scabbed over. But his eyes…they were calm, at peace, not the boiling disturbance of a storm in them. What exactly had he been doing in McAlester? What did he suffer? And what about that girl who flung herself at him? So many questions, but Ruth Ann held them in check. For now.

She stepped aside to allow her mother a turn engulfing Matthew. Then everyone else shook his hand or patted his back. Ruth Ann's attention to detail caught his wince each time someone touched him. She wondered what other injuries he had. He looked like he needed a hearty meal and three days of sleep.

Things quieted enough for Matthew to look around. "I'm gone a few weeks, and you all turn this place into a barn dance."

Beulah folded her arms. "And you are back for two minutes, and you cannot say how pleased you are with the magnificent job your sister has done for this newspaper! She is quite the businesswoman."

Matthew chuckled and pulled Ruth Ann under one arm while her cheeks warmed. He said lightly, "Haven't you been told a woman's place is in the kitchen?"

Ruth Ann resisted elbowing him in the side. He tightened his arm around her shoulder and spoke for all to hear. "You know, when I first saw the daily, I thought you were one crazy Choctaw woman. But then I got to see what a difference it made in some serious situations. I couldn't have done it better; in fact, I wasn't. You did it, Annie, and I think it's clear where your place is—right where God wants you at the *Choctaw Tribune*."

The room broke out in applause, and Ruth Ann sniffed. "Here

you are, just back, and already making speeches. I'll bet you left poor Little Chief at the barn without feed, you were so anxious to get over here. Peter can tend him; he's gotten very adept at doing my chores."

Peter punched Matthew's shoulder, and Ruth Ann felt a shudder go through her brother. "No need." His voice caught. "Everything's fine. I…" He glanced down at Ruth Ann and then their mother. "I have something to tell you, soon. But…"

"I'm sure you have a lot of stories, but first one from us!" Lance Fuller grinned and fanned a handful of the daily editions at Matthew. "Your sister's brilliant plan to start the daily increased subscribers by seventeen percent, new advertisers by twelve percent, and Johnson plans to advertise the Enterprise Hotel exclusively in the *Tribune!*"

Beulah eyed Lance. "While you also are gushing with flowery speeches, perhaps there is something else you would like to say." She nodded toward Amarillo.

Amarillo's face flushed, and she looked quickly at the many boots on the floor around her. Ruth Ann raised her eyebrows and looked pointedly at Lance. God knew it was time to intervene in the moment.

Lance rolled the newspapers together and twisted them.

"I, that is, Miss Amarillo, I know we haven't known one another all that long, but, well…" He halted.

Beulah rolled her eyes. "You had better do it right now, Lance Fuller, before I do it for you."

Lance loosened his tie. "What I'm trying to say, Miss Amarillo, is that I've prayed, a lot, and I feel it's time…well…will you allow me to court you?"

Amarillo lifted her eyes a touch, then all the way to his. "All right."

Lance coughed on his own breath and nodded. "All right." He chuckled. "All right!"

He grabbed Amarillo by the hands and swung her around and

around while she laughed, and her siblings clapped. Ruth Ann had never heard Amarillo laugh.

Charles Goodnight chose that moment to start wailing in Glenrose's arms. Lance grinned as he took the baby. "That is, if it's all right with you, Goodnight."

Beulah started the circle dance and singing again while they swayed and hopped around Amarillo and Lance, trapping the couple in the middle. Goodnight snuggled contently in his arms.

Ruth Ann stayed to the side with her mother and brother. Della slipped her arm around Matthew's waist while Ruth Ann grinned at the puzzled look on his face. He shook his head. "Guess I missed a few things while I was gone."

Ruth Ann giggled. "Something like that."

Matthew kissed the top of her head. "Have I said how proud I am of you?"

Warmth spread through Ruth Ann's being. "You just did."

While the celebration continued, Matthew slipped out back, into the darkness where the clouds covered the moon, to his favorite writing spot among the overturned crates behind the print shop. He wasn't there to write, though. He was there to think. Which was the first thing he always did before writing. And he had much to write. So many stories. Immigrant coal miners and their families. Doctor Robinson and his highly questionable medical practices. The end of the Dan Holder and Abernathy gangs and the pending trials in Fort Smith.

Ruth Ann had pleaded, in a joking way, that Matthew take the newspaper back to its original weekly edition, claiming there weren't enough front page stories for a daily. He disagreed, saying she'd made a smart move, one that would propel the *Choctaw Tribune* to places it had never been before.

Thinking about getting to work with the *Choctaw Tribune* was the most comfortable place to start. Very soon, Matthew would have to find Takba and tell her what happened inside the outlaw fort. He would have to tell his mother and sister that Little Chief was dead. That Philip was alive, and that he had been a part of the robbery. That Della had a granddaughter, and Ruth Ann, a niece.

Soon.

But for now, Matthew didn't write. He sang softly to himself.

> *Perfect submission, all is at rest,*
> *I in my Savior am happy and blest,*
> *Watching and waiting, looking above,*
> *Filled with His goodness, lost in His love.*

> *This is my story, this is my song,*
> *Praising my Savior all the day long.*

Soon. He would think. He would write. He would take a trip up to the Barnes' place and get another horse.

Now, though, Matthew was content to be home.

The sky opened, and a gentle rain fell. Matthew let it wash him. The verse from Micah flowed through his being.

Nana hosh achukma ka, hattak a, pisachi tuk oke; Chihowa yvt nanta asilhha, amba nana kvt ai vlhpesa yvmohmikma nukhaklo ya i hullo micha hopoyuksa hosh Chihowa iba nowa hinla cho?

To the heavens, he whispered, "He has shown you, Matthew Teller, what is good; and what does the Lord require of you, but to do justly, and to love mercy, and to walk humbly with your God?"

Matthew closed his eyes and breathed deep. "Amen."

AUTHOR'S NOTE

As with most of my historical fiction works, the incidences portrayed draw a great deal from actual happenings of the time period. That said, I want to mention a couple of specific items within this book:

The description of Choctaw stickball players wearing bandanas originated from a historical photo I viewed at the Choctaw Nation Health Clinic in Idabel, Oklahoma, of a stickball game during the turn-of-the-century.

Some of my research on coal mining in the Choctaw Nation came from the booklet titled "When Coal Was King: Coal Mining Industry in the Choctaw Nation" published by the Eastern Oklahoma Historical Society in 1975. I filtered the information through the lens of Choctaw history and culture.

GLOSSARY OF CHOCTAW WORDS

~

Chihowa: God

Chi hullo li: I love you

Chi pisa la chike: I will be seeing you / I will see you again

Chukka ia li: I'm going home

Chukfi: Rabbit

Halito: A friendly greeting

Luksi: Turtle

Ome: Expressing a ready assent, agreement or acknowledgment

Pokni: Grandmother

Sv baiyi: My nephew

Vmoshi: My uncle, my mother's brother

Walakshi: Dumplings

Yakoke: Thank you

THE EXECUTIONS *(CHOCTAW TRIBUNE SERIES, BOOK 1)*

Who would show up for their own execution?

It's 1892, Indian Territory. A war is brewing in the Choctaw Nation as two political parties fight out issues of old and new ways. Caught in the middle is eighteen-year-old Ruth Ann, a Choctaw who doesn't want to see her family harmed.

In a small but booming pre-statehood town, her brother owns a controversial newspaper, the *Choctaw Tribune*. Ruth Ann wants to help spread the word about critical issues but there is danger for a female reporter on all fronts—socially, politically, even physically.

But what is truly worth dying for? This quest leads Ruth Ann and her brother Matthew, the stubborn editor of the fledgling *Choctaw Tribune*, to old Choctaw ways at the farm of a condemned murderer. It also brings them to head on clashes with leading townsmen who want their reports silenced no matter what.

More killings are ahead. Who will survive to know the truth? Will truth survive?

The Executions is available on multiple retailer sites.

TRAITORS (CHOCTAW TRIBUNE SERIES, BOOK 2)

"Someone's going to be king in this territory.
No reason it can't be me. It sure won't be you."

Betrayed.

Someone is tearing at the fabric of the Choctaw Nation while political turmoil, assassinations, and feuds threaten the very sovereignty of the tribe. It stands under the U.S. government's scrutiny.

When heated words turn to hot lead, Ruth Ann Teller—a mixed-blood Choctaw—fears losing her brother who won't settle for anything but the truth. Matthew is determined to use his newspaper, the *Choctaw Tribune*, to uncover the scheme behind Mayor Thaddeus Warren's claim to the townsite of Dickens. Matthew is willing to risk his newspaper—and his life—to uncover a traitor among their Choctaw people.

But when Ruth Ann tries to help, she causes more harm than good— especially after the mayor brings in Lance Fuller, a schoolteacher from New York. How does this charming yet aloof young man fit into the mayor's scheme?

When attacks against the newspaper strike and bullets fly, a trip to the Chicago World's Fair of 1893 is the answer they need to save the Choctaw Tribune. The trip holds a key to Matthew's investigation.

But Ruth Ann must find the courage to face a journey to the White City —without her brother.

Traitors (*Choctaw Tribune* Series, Book 2) is available on multiple retailer sites.

The day I betrayed Isaac, I vowed never again to speak my native language in front of white men.

When America enters the Great War in 1917, Bertram Robert Dunn and his Choctaw buddies from Armstrong Academy join the army to protect their homes, their families, and their country. Hoping to find redemption for a horrible lie that betrayed his best friend, B.B. heads into the trenches of France—but what he discovers is a duty only his native tongue can fulfill.

War correspondent Matthew Teller is ready to quit until an encounter with a fellow Choctaw sets him on a path to write the untold story of American Indian doughboys. But entrenched stereotypes and prejudices tear at his burning desire to spread truth.

With the Allies building toward the greatest offensive drive of the war, the American Expeditionary Forces face a superior enemy who intercepts their messages and knows their every move. Can the solution come from a people their own government stripped of culture and language?

Anumpa Warrior: Choctaw Code Talkers of World War I **is available on multiple retailer sites.**

Touch My Tears: For this collection of short stories, Choctaw authors from five U.S. states came together to present a part of their ancestors' journey, a way to honor those who walked the trail for their future. These stories not only capture a history and a culture, but the spirit, faith, and resilience of the Choctaw people.

Tushpa's Story: Young Tushpa, his family, and their small band embark on a trail of life and death. More death than life lay ahead.

A continuation of the anthology *Touch My Tears: Tales from the Trail of Tears*, this story follows an original manuscript written by Tushpa's son, James Culberson.

Touch My Tears and *Tushpa's Story* are available on multiple retailer sites.

YAKOKE

I want to thank you, faithful reader, for your extraordinary patience with this third installment in the *Choctaw Tribune* series. You all have been marvelous during the extended time I worked through hard edits and final research for *Shaft of Truth*. Your love for the characters and this storyworld kept the fire glowing in me, and I can't wait until we meet again in the next book!

I had three unbelievably kind and thorough developmental editors for this project. All three of these women are diehard fans of this series, but they don't let me get away with anything when it comes to critique! Talented writer/editor and dear friend Catherine Frappier analyzed an early manuscript version in a way that made it clear where I was off the path or on the path in the story I wanted to tell. My dear writer-sister, Mollie Reeder, paid exquisite attention to the characters and their internal motivations, keeping me from portraying certain conditions in ways I had not intended. I'm a fan of all her wondrous storyworlds! Choctaw artist and all-around amazing soul Lynda Kay Sawyer (my mama!) was often a daily sounding board as I worked through final edits. Her dedication to detail made sure you readers only got the very best out of me.

Jen Wingard, who is also a tribal member—thank you for your feedback and encouragement as a reader and fellow writer. I love your enthusiasm for this series and its characters!

Thank you to Dr. Ian Thompson, director of the Choctaw Nation Historic Preservation Department, for checking on the Choctaw cultural aspects along with locations, correct county names, and other details I may have otherwise missed. I would also like to extend a special thank you to Megan Baker for her deep insight from the perspective of a Choctaw and a researcher of the coal mining industry during the time period featured in this novel.

A hearty yakoke goes to a couple of sweet ladies at the School of Choctaw Language: Teri Billy, assistant director, for editing the glossary, and Dora Wickson, translation specialist, who took great care in translating a verse from the Holy Bible (Micah 6:8, KJV).

Yakoke to Ryan Spring at the Choctaw Nation Historic Preservation Department for giving me a research lead to the little yellow book ("When Coal Was King: Coal Mining Industry in the Choctaw Nation"), and also connecting me with Megan.

My brother Doug Davis was such a help when I asked him weird questions about ladders and general guy stuff, drawing from his 25+ years as a commercial construction superintendent. Also an avid history researcher, his love for our Choctaw heritage, especially our family's, inspires me. I'm always tapping his knowledge base for my stories.

I appreciate historian Michael Cathey giving me the opportunity to speak at a special opening of the original Choctaw Tobusky County Courthouse in McAlester. He and others are working to restore the frame building to its original condition—just like it was during Matthew Teller's time period.

I appreciate the folks at the Lutie Coal Miners Museum near Wilburton, Oklahoma, for their work in preserving this history. Special thanks to Joyce Pryor for literally giving me the key to the museum, allowing me the experience of unlocking the door and stepping back in time.

Above all, thank you to Chihowa, the God of the Bible, Who fills the creative well that I draw from and Who gives me the strength to write each word. 2018 and 2019 were intense for me as a writer, and in recovery from my novel, *Anumpa Warrior: Choctaw Code Talkers of World War I*. God recovered my joy for creating this year, and I pray that I always love mercy, do justly, and walk humbly with Him.

ABOUT THE AUTHOR

SARAH ELISABETH SAWYER is a story archeologist. She digs up shards of past lives, hopes, and truths, and pieces them together for readers today. The Smithsonian's National Museum of the American Indian honored her as a literary artist through their Artist Leadership Program for her work in preserving Choctaw Trail of Tears stories. A tribal member of the Choctaw Nation of Oklahoma, she writes historical fiction from her hometown in Texas, partnering with her mother, Lynda Kay Sawyer, in continued research for future works. Learn more at SarahElisabethWrites.com, Facebook.com/SarahElisabethSawyer